Sisters of Mercy

Also by Caroline Overington

Fiction
Ghost Child
I Came to Say Goodbye
Matilda is Missing

Non-fiction
Only in New York
Kickback

Sisters of Mercy

CAROLINE OVERINGTON

BANTAM
SYDNEY AUCKLAND TORONTO NEW YORK LONDON

This is a work of fiction. Names, characters, places and incidents either are the product of the author's imagination or are used fictitiously. Any resemblance to actual persons, living or dead, events, or locales is entirely coincidental.

A Bantam book
Published by Random House Australia Pty Ltd
Level 3, 100 Pacific Highway, North Sydney NSW 2060
www.randomhouse.com.au

First published by Bantam in 2012

Copyright © Caroline Overington 2012

The moral right of the author has been asserted.

All rights reserved. No part of this book may be reproduced or transmitted by any person or entity, including internet search engines or retailers, in any form or by any means, electronic or mechanical, including photocopying (except under the statutory exceptions provisions of the Australian *Copyright Act 1968*), recording, scanning or by any information storage and retrieval system without the prior written permission of Random House Australia.

Addresses for companies within the Random House Group can be found at
www.randomhouse.com.au/offices

National Library of Australia
Cataloguing-in-Publication Entry

Overington, Caroline.
Sisters of Mercy / Caroline Overington.

ISBN 978 1 74275 042 2 (pbk.)

A823.4

Cover photograph of woman © Fabio Sabatini/Flickr/Getty Images
Cover background © Rick Elkins/Flickr/Getty Images
Cover design by Christabella Designs
Internal design by Midland Typesetters, Australia
Typeset in 12/18 Sabon by Midland Typesetters, Australia
Printed and bound by Griffin Press, South Australia

Random House Australia uses papers that are natural, renewable and recyclable products and made from wood grown in sustainable forests. The logging and manufacturing processes are expected to conform to the environmental regulations of the country of origin.

For Omi and Opi

Chapter One

I'll be honest and say I got a bit of a shock when I started getting letters from Snow Delaney.

The first of them arrived in April 2011, by which time she was already in prison.

Apparently Snow decided to write to me after her lawyer – or, more accurately, her old lawyer, the one she's now sacked – gave her copies of some of the articles I'd written about her case.

They must have got up her nose, those articles, because Snow accused me in that first letter of getting 'key facts' wrong and of being biased against her.

I wrote back, asking her to tell me where I'd gone wrong, and then Snow replied, and so on and so forth for more than a year.

Some people might be wondering what exactly Snow hoped to gain by writing to me, but I reckon it was pretty obvious: I'm a reporter, and she wanted to convince people that she's innocent of everything she's ever been accused of doing.

As to what I was doing making Snow my penfriend, well, I reckon that's obvious too.

I was trying to coax some kind of confession from her, so I could put the minds of some good people to rest.

I see now that's not going to happen. I got a letter from the State government a few months back, telling me I was officially banned from writing any more letters to Snow while she's in prison, and since I haven't heard from her I take it she's also banned from writing to me.

I'm annoyed, mostly because I believe that Snow had something to do with the disappearance of her sister, Agnes Moore, and now I've lost my chance to trip her up on that point.

At least one of my contacts in the New South Wales police force agrees that Snow knows more than she's saying. Cops, though, spend too many years watching tricky lawyers get dodgy people off the hook, and for them it's all about getting enough evidence to prove it in a court of law.

Evidence that's legally admissible tends not to be as important to reporters. For us, it's all about what makes sense – and what makes sense, at least to me, is that Snow Delaney needs to stay behind bars.

SISTERS OF MERCY

Mr Jack Fawcett
c/o *The Sunday Times*
Sydney, NSW, 2000

Dear Mr Fawcett,
You don't know me, although you seem to think you do.

My name is Snow Delaney. That's right, I'm the real Snow Delaney – the one who is actually not like the person you write about in your newspaper.

I've been reading your articles and I want you to know that you've got key facts wrong.

Like most reporters I don't suppose you care what the facts are, and you're probably so biased against me it doesn't even matter what I say, but if you're ever interested in finding out the truth you should get in touch. I don't expect to hear from you, though, because no journalist I've ever met has been interested in facts, only in sensationalism.

Yours sincerely,
Snow Delaney
Silverwater Prison

CAROLINE OVERINGTON

Dear Ms Delaney,

Thank you for your letter. I'm sorry that you think I have made mistakes in my articles about you. Please write back to tell me where I've gone wrong so I can, if necessary, issue a correction.

Yours sincerely,

Jack Fawcett

Journalist

The Sunday Times

SISTERS OF MERCY

Dear Mr Fawcett,

So, you decided to write back to me! I'm surprised because most of the journalists I've written to don't bother to reply.

You asked me what mistakes you've made. Where do you want me to start? For example, you wrote in *The Sunday Times* that nobody knows how I got the name Snow.

I'm sorry, but that's ridiculous – everyone knows how I got the name Snow.

You seem to think that I know stuff that I actually know nothing about. Like, you said I must have had something to do with my sister Agnes going missing, and that's complete rubbish. Why should I know anything about what happened to Agnes? I wasn't even there when she wandered off.

All in all, Jack, you've put yourself up like you're some kind of expert on me, but actually you don't know me and maybe you even owe me an apology.

Yours sincerely,

Snow Delaney

Silverwater Prison

Dear Ms Delaney,

Thank you for your letter.

You say that everybody knows how you got the name Snow but since I have no idea you'll have to fill me in.

You are quite right, I do believe that you know more than you are saying about the disappearance of your sister. I'm sorry that you think that's unfair, but you still haven't told me precisely where I have gone wrong in my stories so I can start working on my correction.

While you are at it, why don't you take some time to tell me how you are being treated in Silverwater because I'm also interested in your rehabilitation?

Yours sincerely,

Jack Fawcett

Journalist

The Sunday Times

SISTERS OF MERCY

Dear Jack,

God, you made me laugh just then. You're interested in my *rehabilitation*?

Don't tell me that you're one of those people who think prison is supposed to rehabilitate people, because if you are you have less of an idea how things work than I thought.

Prison doesn't rehabilitate. What prison does is teach people how to take drugs and how to be lesbians, and if you think I'm lying you should come here and see it for yourself.

Every single one of the women in here with me is zonked out of their head on Valium or methadone, and the ones who aren't zonked out are cuddled up doing open-mouthed kissing with each other. The weird thing is most of them weren't gay before they got here and I know that because they've got kids.

Anyway, don't pretend you're interested in me when all you're really interested in is getting a scoop, not that you're going to be able to get much of a scoop since you're confused about everything.

You want to know what you got wrong. Well, for example I saw in your article how you drove to my old home town of Deer Park and you went around to all the old neighbours asking about me. You talked to old Mrs Andrewartha who used to live two doors up and she said, 'Oh, we couldn't believe it when we heard that Snow was in jail.'

She can't believe it? I can tell you for free that *I* can't believe it, Jack.

She said, 'Oh, she was such a nice girl and she had that lovely name, Snow, and we always wondered where she got it.'

Do you know what I thought when I read that, Jack? I thought, 'How can Mrs Andrewartha still be alive? She was already an old bag when I was a girl!'

No, I'm joking, what I actually thought was, 'How can Mrs Andrewartha not know how I got the name Snow? Because it's pretty obvious.

My first name is Sally.

My middle name is Narelle.

My surname before I changed it, which old Mrs Andrewartha knows since she lived next door to my mother for forty years, was Olarenshaw.

I don't see how anyone needs to be told that when your name is Sally Narelle Olarenshaw, your initials are going to be S...N...O. SNO, Jack?

Snow.

So that's one mistake you made, but that's not the only one. You said, 'Snow had a pretty good time of it when she was a kid, living in a nice house on Station Road with her mum and dad, and going to a good Catholic school,' or something like that.

You said, 'It wasn't like her sister, who had to grow up in the orphanage,' and boo-hoo.

I've got to tell you, Jack, when I read that I thought, 'So that's how he thinks things work, is it?' I had a mum and dad so my life must have been perfect, and Agnes got left in an orphanage so she deserves all the sympathy?

That might be how things work in your world, Jack, but they aren't how things work in mine, and if you can't understand that maybe I just shouldn't write to you any more.

Yours sincerely,

Snow

Chapter Two

If someone had told me in September 2009 that I was about to spend two years investigating a missing person's case, I wouldn't have believed it. Missing persons cases aren't really my bag, and that's because it's hard to get stories about missing people in the paper, and *that's* because a couple of thousand people go missing every year and 98 per cent of them turn up.

Those who don't, generally don't want to be found or will never be found. It's that last group that you sometimes hear about, but only a handful of those cases are ever interesting enough to capture the public's imagination, such as when a kid gets taken from their bed, as happens about once every five years.

It was my editor at the *Times*, Tyrone O'Brien, who asked me to have a look at the case of Snow's missing sister, Agnes Moore. From memory, his exact words were, 'I'm sorry to do this to you, Tap –' my first name is Jack but my colleagues tend to call me Tap, since my last name is Fawcett '– but apparently a British tourist, an old lady, went missing in that dust storm we had a few weeks back. The cops want to put out an appeal for anyone who might have seen her, so can I get you to go out to the Rose Bay cop shop?'

I knew O'Brien wouldn't be asking if he didn't think the story had potential, so I jumped in a cab and headed out to the Rose Bay cop shop, which isn't actually such a bad place to visit on a sunny day. It's right on the water and there's usually the odd pelican standing around.

The press conference was held in what the cops call the 'ante-room' – a little room off the main hallway. I've been in it a thousand times. There was a female copper standing by the door handing out press packs, so I took one of those and pulled up a seat in front of the little stage. From memory, I was one of maybe seven reporters there that day. We sat around exchanging a bit of chit-chat, and then a detective from Rose Bay – his name was Garry Croft – came walking in, with Mrs Moore's daughter, Ruby Moore, not far behind him.

There were some old desks and plastic meeting chairs set up on the stage at the front of the room and Crofty, as we call him, helped Ruby into one of the chairs.

I flipped my notebook open and started to take a few notes, including how Ruby looked – which was exactly as you might expect for somebody whose mum was missing: wrung out, pale, stressed out of her mind. Her hands were shaking a bit, and she was wearing one of those Lady Jayne velvet headbands to keep her dark hair off her face. She's only little, so it was hard to see her face behind the forest of microphones. Ruby's from England and she obviously hadn't anticipated the weather: it was 38 degrees in Sydney that day but she had on a tartan-patterned skirt with a pin at the side, pantyhose, and a maroon turtleneck. She must have been sweating, and near delirious with jetlag, but she was doing her best to hold it together.

Crofty sat down beside her and he did his usual spiel. 'Hello, everyone, I'm Detective Senior Sergeant Croft of the Rose Bay local area command.' And then he said, 'This is Ruby Moore. Ruby has flown out from London to be with us today. Ruby's mother, Agnes Moore, was visiting Sydney in September and was due to fly out on 23rd September, which was the day of the dust storm. But she didn't fly out.'

There isn't going to be anyone in Sydney on the morning of 23 September – I'm talking about the year 2009 – who won't remember the dust storm: the whole city woke up to find the sky glowing pink. And when I say the sky, I actually mean the *whole city* was glowing pink: sky, ground, buildings, even the sand on the beach. I remember looking out my window shortly after five-thirty, which is when I set my alarm to go off, and thinking, 'Whoa!' And then, 'Right, so this is how the world ends.' Because that was how it looked, like the sky was on fire. But then I put on the *Today* show, and Lisa Wilkinson was saying, 'Don't panic, we haven't been hit by an asteroid or anything like that, it's just a dust storm,' and they were showing pictures of the Opera House and the Harbour Bridge and Bondi Beach and everything, bathed in this pink colour.

Detective Croft said, 'Of course, Ruby and her family are really hoping that people will remember exactly what they were doing that day because that was the day her mum went missing. Then he looked at Ruby and asked if she wanted to say anything. Ruby launched straight into her spiel in her upper-class accent. 'Thank you all so much for coming. Detective Croft is quite right: I am hoping that everyone will remember what they were doing on the day of the dust storm because Mum was due to fly out of Sydney that day but she was never seen at the airport, and we don't know what happened to her.

'The last sighting of her was when she left her room at the Sir Stanton Hotel on Market Street. She was seen on the CCTV footage in a hallway at around 5 a.m. and she was seen leaving the foyer and walking into Market Street at around 5.10. That's where we lose track of her. I understand people could not see more than a foot in front of themselves for most of the morning. And I realise that everybody in this situation says this, but it's completely out of character for Mum not to be in touch, and so all this is obviously very worrying for us.'

Detective Croft said, 'You've got photographs of Agnes Moore in your press packs, guys.'

I opened the manila folder the female copper had given me on the way in. There were two sheets of paper inside, stapled together: the first one had Mrs Moore's stats on it –

hair colour, eye colour, age – and the second one was a copy of a recent photograph, showing Mrs Moore all dressed up for a wedding. If you've followed the case at all, you'll know exactly which photo I mean: she's got a skirt-and-blazer suit on, made of a kind of brushed, burgundy satin, like a mother of the bride might wear, and a hat with some netting. She's holding up a plate with a big piece of wedding cake on it that's covered in an inch of white icing, and she's making a funny face, like she can't wait to stick her fork into it.

It's a really nice photo. In other words, your ordinary, happy British grandma, having a good time at a family wedding.

Once we'd had a few seconds to study the picture, Detective Croft called for questions. I tend not to jump in on such occasions, in case I give away what I'm thinking and, therefore, my scoop. So the first question was from one of my News Limited colleagues, a *Telegraph* reporter who wanted to know, 'What was your mother doing in Sydney, Ms Moore? Was it a holiday?'

That's where things got a bit more interesting, obviously. Ruby said, 'It was a holiday but it was quite a special holiday. Mum was actually in Sydney to meet up with a sister she hadn't met before . . .'

That stopped most of us reporters in our tracks.

Sisters who hadn't met before? What was that about?

Ruby said, 'I should explain: Mum was born in London but she was placed in an orphanage near Manchester fairly soon after birth. This was in 1940, the war was on, so it was probably for her own protection. She spent seven years in that orphanage and for a long time we assumed that Mum's parents must have been killed in the war, or perhaps her father had to go to war and hadn't come back . . . We didn't really know what the story was, but then, just a year or so ago, Mum received a letter from a lawyer here in Australia saying that her parents hadn't been killed, they had actually got married after the war and they'd come out here and raised a family – they'd had another little girl, a girl called Snow. So that was very exciting for all of us, the fact that Mum had a sister in Australia, and of course she made arrangements to come out and meet Snow as soon as she could.'

By this stage I had begun thanking my editor for asking me to attend the press conference. 'Sisters who hadn't met before' – that's obviously a good story all by itself, without the added drama of one of them now being missing. I was about to stick my hand up to ask a few questions but a reporter from *The Herald* got in ahead of me: 'And can I ask you what you think happened to your mother? You said she went missing in the dust storm, so are you thinking she got lost, or she fell or . . .?'

Ruby looked at Detective Croft, maybe to see if it was okay for her to answer a question like that, which essentially called for speculation. He nodded and she said, 'The police have asked me whether I think it's possible that Mum was frightened by the dust storm, but I can't honestly see that happening. Mum is the kind of person who takes everything in her stride. I don't think she would have been frightened, and anyway, from what I understand, the dust storm wasn't frightening. People were milling about in it, and marvelling at the wonder of it. So I suppose my answer to your question is, I think Mum must have got lost or taken a fall, and perhaps she's injured, wandering disoriented, and obviously the longer it goes on . . .'

If you watched any of the press conference – on the news, I mean – you'll know that Ruby broke down at this point. People say the media can be mongrels, and maybe that's right because the cameras went mad, but then we all waited for her to compose herself before jumping back in. One of the *Herald* reporters asked, 'And was it your mum's first visit to Sydney or had she been here before? Did she know the place at all?'

Ruby said, 'Mum spent many years in Western Australia – she met my father there – but she'd never been to Sydney. She had only been here for a few days when she went missing. So, no, I suppose I'm trying to say that she didn't know Sydney . . . this was her first visit.'

The first journo, the one from the *Telegraph*, jumped back in, asking what I wanted to ask: 'Your mum's sister, the one you're saying she just met up with . . . Did you say her name was *Snow*?'

Ruby looked over at Detective Croft, who cleared his throat and said, 'Yes, Mrs Moore's sister's name is Snow. That is S-N-O-W as in . . .' and he made flurries with his fingers, like snowflakes coming down.

I said, 'And is Snow here today?'

Detective Croft said, 'No, I'm sorry, Ms Delaney – that's her last name, Delaney – isn't actually here today. As Ruby was saying, the sisters met up a little ahead of the dust storm, and from what we can tell they had lunch at Ms Delaney's house in Bondi and then Agnes went back to her hotel on Market Street. She had a chat to some of the staff there, went back to her room, and settled in for the night. Then she came out at around 5 a.m. and wandered into Market Street. We've interviewed Ms Delaney, and she's been very helpful in letting us know when Agnes left the lunch, and we know what time she got back to the hotel and so forth. So at this point we're trying to trace whether anyone saw her after she left her hotel room. Market Street is obviously a fairly busy street in the CBD, and while the dust storm that day did make things a bit difficult in terms of visibility, we are hopeful that somebody might remember something.'

There were a few more questions after that, yielding not much more detail, and then Detective Croft said, 'Okay, guys, that's probably enough for now. You've all got your press packs and you've got the number for Crimestoppers . . .'

I went back to my office at *The Sunday Times* and straightaway put a call in to a contact of mine at the Rose Bay coppers – not Crofty but one of his colleagues, and no, I'm not going to give his name away because I'm a reporter and no reporter would do that to a source. I asked him if he could put me in touch with Snow Delaney. I had in mind getting a few quotes from her, and maybe a picture of the two sisters together if one existed, to jazz the story up a bit. But he put the kibosh on that request immediately, telling me that Snow wanted nothing to do with the media.

'She's a bit of an odd one, Tap,' is how he worded it. 'You'd think she'd be willing to do whatever she could to help drum up some publicity, but, well, she's cold like a fish.'

I said, 'Is she a suspect?'

He said, 'Nah, from what we can tell Mrs Moore left her house in pretty good nick. Look, we're keeping an open mind, but to be honest we're not thinking foul play. More likely the lady has taken a fall in the low visibility . . . But yeah, you'd still reckon the sister might give enough of a stuff to turn up at the press conference.'

I couldn't publish any of that, obviously, it being what we call 'off the record', but I wrote up what I had – sisters raised apart, finally coming together, and now one of them was missing – and the story got a reasonable run the next day. In terms of lighting a media storm, though, it didn't, and there was no real follow-up, I suppose because there wasn't much else to say.

It can't have been more than a week later that I was having a beer with my contact from the Rose Bay coppers. He said, 'You know we never heard a word about the British lady who went missing in that storm.'

'What were you hoping to hear?' I asked.

My mate looked grim. 'Well, pretty much anything would have been helpful. It's like she's walked off the edge of the planet.' And that's where things stayed, at least until 23 December, when the editor called me into his office and said, 'You know the lady who wandered off in the dust storm? The family's giving another press conference. Why don't you go along and see what's up?'

I'd been working on other things, so I said, 'Has there been a break in the case?'

The editor said, 'No, I don't think so, but the cops are saying a couple of other family members will be along this time, maybe the sister. Did you say her name was Snow? Maybe she'll be there?' So I went along, but it wasn't Snow, it was Ruby with her brother, Steven, and his wife, all of them out from England.

Now, it isn't a secret that the Moore siblings aren't close. I could go into the ins and outs of it – something to do with Steven's wife not wanting Ruby to bring a turkey at Christmas or some such thing – but they'd put all that on the back burner for the press conference. I could tell just from looking that they'd been doing it tough. Ruby had lost a fair bit of weight since I'd last seen her back in October, and it was weight she could not afford to lose. So she was sitting there, basically skin and bones, quite a contrast to Steven, who is one of those podgy English blokes who tends to turn beetroot-red in the face when he's under a bit of pressure.

Ruby was the first to speak, saying, 'Thank you all for coming,' which was a bit embarrassing since there were only three of us this time, down from around seven at the first press conference. I took that to mean the other reporters knew perfectly well that Snow wouldn't be there.

Ruby said, 'It's now been more than eleven weeks since we've seen our mother and we're obviously frantic. We're so close to Christmas and Mum absolutely loves this time of year. It's inconceivable to us that she wouldn't be in touch. It's completely out of character for her to just wander off...' and so on, like that.

Steven spoke next: 'What we need to know is if anyone saw anything out of the ordinary that day. We know there was a dust storm in Sydney and it kind of threw everything off kilter, but somebody must have seen *something*...'

His wife, Irene, was sitting beside him, not saying much.

Detective Croft handed out new pictures of Agnes, including one where she was helping a grandkid – it turned out to be Ruby's boy, Rocco – get a train out of its wrapping paper, and another where she was posed beside the Opera House, which had obviously been emailed before she went missing.

I went back to the office and wrote another article, saying the lady who disappeared in the dust storm was still unaccounted for and her grandkids were really going to miss her at Christmas. But I'm not even sure it got printed. I can't find a clipping in the files and an internet search didn't turn anything up, which is usually a good sign that it was cut.

I might have walked away from the story at that point – the editor obviously wasn't that interested, despite sending me down there – but then I found myself with some time on my hands in the slow period after Christmas, and rather than try to scratch a new story out of nothing I got on the blower and asked my contact at Rose Bay if the Moore family was still in town and, if so, whether I could contact them.

Police are sometimes reluctant to give the press access to families in crime stories, but Ruby had insisted upon seeing any reporter who showed interest in her mother's disappearance, so he gave me a mobile number for her, and I rang to introduce myself and ask if I could come out and talk to her a bit more.

Ruby told me she was staying at the Sir Stanton Hotel on Market Street in Sydney's CBD, which struck me as a bit odd because that was the hotel her mum went missing from. But as soon as I got there I understood: she had managed to get the manager to put a giant photo of her mum up on an easel in the foyer with a plea for anyone who might have seen anything to come forward. It was standing next to a polystyrene reindeer with a red nose that was obviously supposed to flash but was only managing to at intervals, and there was still the odd bit of Christmas tinsel here and there.

I sat down on one of the vinyl tub chairs in the foyer and waited. Three minutes later, Ruby came out of the lift, one hand extended, and the other clutching an expandable manila folder with the word MUM written on it.

'Thank you so much for coming, Mr Fawcett.'

I said, 'Thank you for meeting me,' and I suppose that was the moment our friendship started. We started talking in person, and later by email, and much of what follows, in terms of the picture I'm going to build of Ruby's mum, comes from the conversations we've had over the past eighteen months.

We looked around for a quiet place to sit and talk – not easy since it was still pretty early and the foyer was packed with business people pushing those fancy four-wheeled suitcases ahead of them, and waiting to check out. I had a peek through a set of glass doors and saw there was a ground-floor restaurant, and I thought, 'I'll get them to find us a quiet corner away from the people standing at the buffet, piling up their plates with melon slices and strips of bacon.'

Ruby put her 'Mum' folder under her chair, took the linen napkin off her plate and spread it over her lap. I got my little digital recorder out and put it on the table between us. The hotel was the type that employs trainee waiters from Bangladesh who are big on smiles and little on English. Our guy had an especially big, beaming white smile, and he approached saying, 'Good morning, sir and madam! I may get you some coffee and some tea!'

I ordered coffee and Ruby said, 'What kind of tea do you have?'

The waiter said, 'Yes, ma'am! We do have tea! We have peppermint, we have chamomile! We have Earl Grey, we have English Breakfast! We have lemon, we have licorice . . .'

Ruby waited patiently, and said, 'English Breakfast will be fine.'

The waiter left, and I delivered my pitch as straight as I could, saying, 'I'm going to be honest with you, Ruby. I'm happy to try to drum up some interest in the story but I don't know how successful I'm going to be.'

Ruby said, 'I'm grateful for your interest, Mr Fawcett, given how difficult it's been to get any attention at all.'

I put on my sympathetic face, the one I use for when people criticise the media. (It's not like I don't know how callous we sometimes come across.) 'We get a lot of reports of people going missing – thousands of them every year – and it's hard to get all of them in the paper.'

'I suppose I thought people would be as frantic as we are,' Ruby replied. 'It's as I said at the press conference: this is totally out of character for Mum.' She made a grim face. 'Goodness, I hear myself saying that and I can hardly believe what's coming out of my mouth. I feel like one of those actors in a crime drama. But I can't stress it enough, Mr Fawcett, this honestly *is* out of character for her.'

I said, 'Call me Jack.'

The waiter came back with Ruby's tea. He made a big fuss of putting everything down – cup, saucer, strainer, spoon – and he was beaming when he announced, 'You will be having the buffet breakfast!'

I looked at Ruby, who shook her head, no, so I told him we just wanted to talk in private. That seemed to confuse him, but he nodded and backed away, holding a napkin under his teapot. I waited for him to be out of earshot before I said, 'Ruby, I want you to tell me, as frankly as you can, based on your instincts, what do you think has happened to your mum?'

Ruby wasn't drinking her tea, just staring into it, and she had her fingers resting gently around the rim of her cup. 'Are you asking me if I think my mother is dead, Mr Fawcett?'

I was a bit taken aback. Obviously I was wondering if Ruby understood that, given her mum had been missing for weeks with no sign of her, she was most likely dead, but I would never have said that to her. 'I just want to know what you think has happened.'

'Of course I accept that she may well be dead, Mr Fawcett. *Jack*. I can see how bad this looks. Yes, there's a possibility that something has happened to her – that she's fallen, or tripped, and has a memory loss – but there's also a very good chance that she's come to harm.'

She reached down to pick up the 'Mum' folder from under her seat, saying, 'I actually brought along some photographs and other bits and pieces to show you how completely normal and lovely Mum is. She's just a typical grandmother, mad about the grandchildren, not the kind of person who would disappear without a very good explanation.'

She took out a couple of photographs of her mum playing with the grandkids: Agnes was holding Ruby's little girl, Stella, steady on a pony ride in one of them, and there was another where she was riding with Ruby's boy, Rocco, on some kind of rollercoaster.

I said, 'How many grandkids has your mum got?'

'Two of mine – they're upstairs with my husband, Philip – and my brother, Steven, has three boys. He and his wife have gone home to England now to be with them.'

'By the look of these photos, she dotes on her grand-children.'

'She does.'

I said, 'Okay, and what else can you tell me about your mum, Ruby? I've got in mind doing a bit of a feature article about her to try to get the public's attention, but I'm going to need your help to bring her to life.'

I could have kicked myself for saying that.

I said quickly, 'I mean, when you think about her, what would you say . . . what kind of person is she?'

Ruby looked a bit confused. 'Oh, well, she's Mum, isn't she? She's . . . I don't know! I've never thought to describe her. She's not a flashy kind of person. She's not at all interested in being the centre of attention. She'd be mortified by the fuss we're making.'

From memory, Ruby started to cry at this point and that sent the beaming Bangladeshi waiter into a spin. He'd been hovering over her shoulder, waiting for a break in our conversation so he could top up her tea. I signalled for him to come over and start pouring, but his hands were trembling so much he ended up splashing the tea all over the white cloth. He was saying, 'Oh, madam, I'm so sorry,' and Ruby was having to say, 'No, please, it's fine.' But at least the commotion was a diversion, and Ruby was soon saying, 'I'm sorry, I think I've startled him with all the waterworks.'

I said, 'Don't worry about it. Of course you're going to be upset,' and Ruby said, 'We all miss her so much.'

'Of course you do. So take your time . . . just when you're ready. We can take it slow. You said at the press conference that your mum spent some time in Australia when she was growing up? That she met your dad here? Can you tell me about that?'

Ruby took a tissue from where it was tucked under her sleeve, and blew her nose. She nodded. 'That's right. She was born in London in 1940 but for most of her childhood, until she was seven, she lived in an orphanage at Newton-le-Willows. And then the nuns who ran the orphanage came and told her that she was going to Australia.'

Ruby opened the folder that was now on her lap, and began sorting through the various bits of paper until she came across what looked like a photocopy of a page from an old newspaper.

'This is an ad from *The Times*,' she said, passing it across the table to me. 'My daughter, Stella, found it in the London Library. It was a couple of years ago now. She had to do an assignment on her family tree for school. Mum told her, "Don't do my family tree, Stella, do your grandpa. I don't know anything about my family tree." But Stella is the kind of girl who rises to a challenge.

'She got Mum to write down what she did know about her background – that she was born at the London Hospital for Mothers and Babies and raised at the orphanage at Newton-le-Willows, and then shipped out to Australia in 1947. Stella got in touch with the people at Births, Deaths and Marriages, and they referred her to the Red Cross and we were, in the end, able to find quite a bit of information.'

The piece of paper Ruby passed across the table to me comprised just three lines:

The Fairbridge Society proposes taking 120 children to Australia.

Rescued from a life of crime and misery here, for adoption by Australian families.

A sum of 800 pounds is now required . . . Will you help in this Good Work?

'Mum was practically jumping out of her skin when she saw that,' Ruby said. 'It's obviously an ad placed by the Fairbridge Society to raise money to send children from English orphanages to Australia. But Mum was a bit upset when she saw it. She kept saying, "The ad is wrong, Stella! I was never rescued from a life of misery! I was happy in the orphanage. I didn't want to leave it. How can they say I was rescued from misery?" And at first I thought she must have been glossing over things, for Stella's sake. I've read enough about the old English orphanages to know how awful they were. But Mum said no, she really didn't mind the orphanage, and the reason she didn't want to go to Australia was that she'd always been told her parents would be coming back for her one day.

SISTERS OF MERCY

'She explained to us that for as long as she could remember, the nuns had told her that the other kids were orphans, but she wasn't an orphan. They had said she had a mother and a father, but her father was fighting the Germans and as soon as the war was won he'd be back for her. So she told the nuns, "I'm sorry, I can't go to Australia! I have to stay here because my parents are coming back for me!"

'The nuns were very matter-of-fact and stern, as they were in those days, and one of them said to Mum, "Don't be silly, Agnes, your parents are *not* coming back for you. The war is over, and nobody has come, and your parents must be dead." That's what they told Mum, Mr Fawcett, that her parents were *dead*.'

I said, 'It sounds cruel, but it was pretty common. It happened to a lot of British kids after the war.'

'That's true, I know, we've been hearing all about it lately, but it was a complete shock to Mum, at the age of seven, to hear that her parents were dead, because she had spent all that time waiting for them to come sashaying into the orphanage to rescue her. From what I understand, she refused to believe it. She kicked one nun in the shins and ran and hid under a bed. They had to drag her out and, to their credit, they were very kind, telling her not to worry, it wasn't her fault, and what a marvellous adventure it would be to sail to Australia. And so before she knew it, she was being weighed and measured and inspected for lice, and being told that Australia was warm and lovely, and that there would be trees with sweet fruit everywhere, which they'd be able to reach up and pick as much of as they wanted.'

I'd heard a million stories like it, of course, and especially around that time, which was just after the Prime Minister, Kevin Rudd, had made his apology to what he called the 'Forgotten Generation'. Most of them were young British orphans who weren't really orphans, and who got shipped out to the colonies after the war.

I picked up the old advertisement from *The Times* again – *The Fairbridge Society proposes taking 120 children to Australia* – and I'll admit it wasn't exactly clear to me what the Fairbridge Society was. I'd heard of the Christian Brothers bringing child migrants to Australia but not the Fairbridge Society. Ruby explained that the society was a private charity, named after Mr Kingsley Fairbridge, who sailed to Australia for the first time in 1912. He had two thousand pounds in his pocket and was intent on buying land to build a farm for orphans. I've done a fair bit of research on him since, mostly at the Mitchell Library on Macquarie Street, which keeps files on the Forgotten Generation, and the land he found was near Pinjarra in Western Australia. It was remote as remote got in those days. He put up tents, and that was the start of it. Over time the Fairbridge Farm School grew until there were 3200 acres with cottages and a dining hall; farm buildings and a small stone chapel; a milking yard and a chicken coop; an orchard and an old red telephone box; and a rope swing by the natural pool in the river.

SISTERS OF MERCY

Ruby said that her mum remembered being given new clothes for the voyage to Australia, including a grey woollen blazer with the Fairbridge crest, and new shoes and socks, which was amazing to her because she'd only ever had one pair of shoes in the orphanage. She was also given what they called 'Mementoes from the Old Country' – an apple, a postcard with a red St George Cross for England, and a Bible, which Ruby had tucked away in her folder marked 'Mum'.

I asked if I could hold the Bible and Ruby nodded. It was a wonderful old thing from the British Bible Society, with a cover made of mother-of-pearl, and yellowed pages, some of which were loose. On the inside cover, someone had written:

> *Be strong and of good courage, be not afraid, neither be thou dismayed, for the Lord thy God is with thee withersoever thou goest* – Joshua, 1.9

I couldn't think what to say when I read that, but Ruby said, 'I wish she had that Bible with her now.'

I moved the conversation on, saying, 'Do you happen to know what ship your mum came out on?' And of course she did, it was the *SS Ormonde*, and that ship is going to be familiar to a fair number of people because it's the ship that a good percentage of all British migrants came out on after the war. Mrs Moore's voyage began in Southampton on 10 October 1947. Reading reports of it makes you feel like you were there: a brass band played for two hours before the streamers on the shore broke. The Fairbridge kids travelled first class, meaning they went from scraping by in the orphanage to eating in a dining hall with velvet chairs and a giant chandelier and a stag's head on the wall, and there were waiters in starched uniforms serving up creamed sole and buttered egg, and Leicester pie with wine jellies, and tea.

I asked Ruby how much her mum remembered of the voyage, and she said it was difficult to know how much she *remembered* and how much she *thought* she remembered, but some of the stories did turn out to be true. For example, Mrs Moore liked to tell the story of there being a boy on board the *Ormonde* screaming in pain, who had to be operated on right there on the ship, cut open by a woman who happened to have a sharp knife handy. The grandkids had shown some scepticism about that over the years, but it's actually true, there was a fifteen-year-old boy, Raymond Willocks, aboard the *Ormonde* and he was stricken with appendicitis. Dr Margaret Henderson – she was a PLC old girl from Peppermint Grove in Perth, and a graduate of medicine at the University of Melbourne – did the surgery.

The ship was four weeks at sea before landing at Fremantle, with stops at places like Colombo and Port Said on the way. I dug a press clipping from the *West Australian* out of the 'Forgotten Generation' files: it records the arrival of the *Ormonde* at Fremantle, on Saturday, 8 November 1947. The copy reads:

She had 1052 passengers, almost all of whom are intending settlers in Australia . . . including many children from orphanages in Scotland and England . . .

That obviously tallies with Ruby's story. It goes on:

They have been assisted by two Sisters, and four nurses . . . altogether, there are 291 children under the age of twelve years aboard the ship, and they were popular with the crew . . . that is shown by the actions of the seamen in paying for a prize, consisting of a packet of sweets, a bar of chocolate and postcard of the ship for each one of them.

According to the *West Australian*, two buses were waiting by the dock to ferry the Fairbridge kids to a reception at St Patrick's Hall, where they had to listen to what was probably a boring message from the Minister for Immigration, Arthur Calwell, booming out of the sound system, telling them they'd been given a new life in a new country and they should make the most of it. A troupe of Old Fairbridgeans played musical instruments, and then it was off to a picnic lunch at Perth Zoo.

'Mum definitely remembers the zoo,' Ruby told me, and I was immediately struck by her use of the present tense, as if her mother was just around the corner. 'Mum hadn't seen wild animals before, so it stuck in her mind. She also remembers the trip out to the Fairbridge Farm School in a yellow bus. It was hot, and there was no air-conditioning so they all had their elbows out, and they all got sunburnt, and they thought that was hilarious, having white skin and bright red elbows.'

I've had a look at some of the old pictures of the Fairbridge Farm School on the web: there used to be an old dirt drive, winding up and over a cattle grate that stopped dead in front of the main building. Ruby says her mum remembered the bus pulling up, 'and there was an old man with a flat cap standing there with a two-handled trolley, like a wooden wheelbarrow. He put all the orphans' suitcases on that trolley and he told Mum to kick her shoes off and put them in the milk pail, and none of the children wore shoes again, except to church.'

There's a good history of the school on the web too. New kids got new clothes for the farm – old clothes, for running around in – and they got new 'aunties' and 'uncles', who were basically people who lived on the farm and took care of them. Agnes got Aunty Mitty. 'And she was apparently the aunty that everyone wanted,' Ruby said. 'She chain-smoked morning till night, even when stirring the big pots of porridge, and she had all the children roll her cigarettes for her. She was big and fat and always up for a cuddle.'

I know from my own reading that life at the Fairbridge Farm School in the 1950s was pretty basic: kids lit a copper to boil water; they collected eggs and milked cows. They had the river pool; they had movie night in the old hall, with wooden seats, and girls on one side of the room and boys on the other, and that was about it.

SISTERS OF MERCY

'But as far as Mum was concerned it was paradise,' Ruby told me. 'The only thing that bothered her, really, was the haircuts – they had to sit on milk crates and let Aunty Mitty go at them with shears. And the flies. She says you wouldn't believe the number of flies.

'But for the most part, Mum can't say enough about Fairbridge. She loved it. Of course I've heard all the stories . . . I've seen that documentary, *Oranges and Sunshine*, and I know that some of the orphans that came here from Britain had a terrible time of it. But all I can say is, as far as Mum was concerned, Fairbridge was wonderful, it was a big adventure. She even told Rocco it was like . . . what is the daughter of Steve Irwin called?'

'Bindi Irwin?'

Ruby said, 'Bindi Irwin! Yes, that's what she told Rocco, that it was like being Bindi Irwin, climbing trees all day. And the only thing that troubled her – the only thing that really played on her mind – was the confusion she felt, having been told in the orphanage that she wasn't an orphan, and then being told, just out of the blue, that actually she was. So you can imagine her shock, finding out late in life that she'd been right all along, and that she wasn't an orphan, and then getting a phone call from a lawyer in Australia saying that her parents had also moved to Australia and that they'd had a little girl here, a girl they called Snow . . .'

Chapter Three

Dear Jack,

I haven't heard back from you since I wrote my last letter, so I suppose you're waiting for me to come up with a list of all the mistakes you made so you can correct them. You'll have to excuse my French but it's not exactly easy to pick out a few mistakes when the whole story you wrote was rubbish, starting with how you said my dad's name was Jim Olarenshaw and that he was from London.

My dad wasn't Jim Olarenshaw, he was *James* Olarenshaw and he got called Jim because that's what everyone does with the name James, but if you're going to be writing people's life stories you should at least get the basics straight, which means you should have said he was James and not Jim.

You said he was born in London and that's not true. He was born in Jarrow and that's hours away from London, and the reason I know that is because my father was one of the Jarrow marchers, and if you don't know what that is, look it up on the internet. It means he was one of those guys who marched from Jarrow to London when the ship company he worked for in Jarrow got closed down in the Depression and people were starving. He was only sixteen when he did that and he had to sleep on the ground in the freezing cold and there was nothing to eat.

You said that Dad joined the navy to get out of the Depression, but like I just told you he was only sixteen when he arrived in London and you can't join the navy when you're sixteen. Dad was supposed to go back to Jarrow, but what would have been the point of that, when his family had no money? So he decided to stay in London and work on the railways or do whatever work he could find, and he was in London when the war broke out and that's when he joined the navy. He was gone for four years and when he came back he married Mum, so that's something that you got right at least!

You said Dad came to Australia as a Ten Pound Pom and that was right, and you said he got given a house when he arrived but, just so you know, it wasn't a posh house, it was a railway house, which means a fibro house. And from what Dad told me, it hadn't even been painted when he and Mum tried to move in. They hadn't put down any footpaths in Deer Park and it was all mud. Mum couldn't walk across the mud because she only had one pair of shoes, so they had to go and find planks of wood and put them down so she could at least get in the front door.

You made it sound like my parents just stayed in that fibro house for free but that's not right because my dad had to buy the house off the railways and it was nothing fancy, it was three bedrooms with Venetian blinds like all the other houses in the street.

You said that Mum and Dad were living here in Australia for a long time with no children and Mum must have been rapt to find out she was having me because she was already forty when I was born, but that's not actually the way it was, Jack. There are some people who just don't like having kids around, and did it ever occur to you that Mum might have been one of those people? Maybe she wasn't trying for years to have a baby. Maybe she was trying hard *not* to have one and maybe I was a big mistake. Because if you want to know the truth, that was how Mum made me feel when I was a kid, Jack. Not like I was some lovely surprise like you said but the *big mistake.* Maybe she never said that in so many words, but she would say, 'Oh, I used to have a very nice job with the Postmaster-General, with my own desk and my own telephone and everything, but of course I had to give all that up when you came along, Snow,' and stuff like that.

Don't get me wrong, Dad would tell her off. He'd say, 'Oh, come on, Ros, you love being a mum! You don't have to go to work, you can stay home and lie on the couch all day reading *The Women's Weekly*.'

Mum would get stuck into him, saying, 'That's what you think it's like, Jim? Sitting around reading magazines? You have no idea.' And then it would be on for young and old.

You made it seem like my dad had plenty of money when I was growing up, but that's not true. He worked at the railways and that was a good job until I was born, but then he got laid off and he opened the shop, Olarenshaw Electrics, and he couldn't charge high prices in Deer Park because the customers were what we called the New Australians and they had no money. Or else they wanted things on credit and wouldn't pay. So we might have had food on the table but we never went out to a restaurant for dinner or anything like that. And if we did my mother would take a bottle of cordial in the boot of the car and I'd have to have a drink from a cup before we went inside because 'bought drinks' cost too much.

If I got a special treat it was lollies in a white paper bag and that was only on the days that Dad got paid, when he brought his pay home in an envelope with the coins rattling around in the bottom. My mother would count every cent and she'd know if Dad had been short-changed by even one dollar. This was in the days when mums would take all the money and give dads maybe a two-dollar note and a one-dollar note and that was supposed to last a fortnight, including smokes. I don't know what your idea of luxury is but we had no luxury when I was growing up. Like, if we had holidays at Christmas, it was in the caravan park at Ocean Grove. And I never had a TV in my bedroom or anything that other kids had, I just played hopscotch with bits of plaster board we scabbed from building sites. We didn't eat fancy at home, we had chops and peas and mashed potatoes, and if I got dessert it was jelly or tinned peaches with one scoop of ice cream from the tub.

I know what you're thinking – that that's still better than my sister had in the orphanage, but my mother wasn't a nice person to live with, Jack. She was strict with me – maybe as strict as people in the orphanage – making me go to bed early and do all my homework at a desk in my bedroom, and not because she wanted to teach me manners or to be good at school but because she didn't want to play with me or talk to me or do anything with me. So, seven o'clock would come around and it didn't matter if it was light outside – and it was sometimes light until nine o'clock in Melbourne – I'd have to go to bed. Once I said, 'Other mums let their kids stay up later than seven o'clock,' and Mum said, 'But I'm not other mothers, am I, Snow?' So basically it was about getting me into bed.

Besides not being able to stay up late, I wasn't allowed to answer the phone, which every other kid at my school was allowed to do, and that was because Mum couldn't stand to hear kids on the phone. If she rang somebody's house and their kids answered she'd say, 'I don't understand what possesses your parents to let you run to the telephone when it rings. Go and get your mother for me now,' or else she would hang up. And sometimes a ball would come over the back fence and my mother was one of those who wouldn't send it back.

I hardly ever had any friends come over because people just thought that Mum was mean, and so I mostly played by myself, which wasn't fun anyway because I wasn't allowed to make a mess or bang the door on my way out the house or get my good clothes dirty. I wasn't allowed to touch 'Mum's station' on the radio, and I wasn't allowed to take posters out of *TV Week* and stick them on my schoolbooks or on the walls like everybody else in my class, because that was messy too.

I was sometimes allowed to walk to the milk bar on the corner, but only if Dad had given me twenty cents. And I was only allowed to buy milk bottles and lolly teeth and other white lollies, because chocolate made a mess on my fingers and so did Smarties if I held them for too long. Once I came home with one of those bubble-gums with the tattoos inside and I put the tattoos on my arm with the kitchen sponge, and when my mother caught me she grabbed me and said, 'Let me tell you about the kind of girl that gets tattoos, Snow. Sailors and prostitutes – that's who have tattoos.' And she grabbed my arm by the wrist and scrubbed the tattoo off with the

SISTERS OF MERCY

Ajax. The funny thing about that story, Jack, is that if Mum was still alive I'd be able to tell her, hey, Mum, you were right, all the hookers in here do have tattoos – blue prison tattoos on their boobs and around their ankles – and some of them look like they did the tattoos themselves with a pin and a Biro.

I haven't told you yet that Mum was also basically an alcoholic, drinking gin every night, and while I'm at it you might as well know that she was also a racist. She couldn't stand the New Australians that were coming to this country, and I know that because once, when I was about seven or eight and I was standing at the dressing table and Mum was trying to get the knots out of my hair with her big brush, I asked if I could have my new friend Gertrude over to play. Mum stopped tugging at the knots and said, 'What kind of name is Gertrude?' I didn't know what she was talking about. She said, 'Is Gertrude one of the New Australian families?' And I didn't know – how was I supposed to know? – but Mum said, 'The trouble with all those New Australians that are coming, Snow, is how do we know where they're from?' She said, 'Gertrude sounds like a foreign name to me.' And if there was one thing Mum couldn't stand it was foreign things, like people growing potatoes in the back garden like the Turkish people on the corner, and hard brown bread like the German people ate, and people who had concrete lions at the gate, and people who spoke languages that weren't English. She'd say things like, 'You'd think they'd at least try to learn English, but they don't bother. I saw that poor little boy, Charlie Pasquali or whatever his name is, at parent–teacher night, having to translate everything the teacher was saying. His mum was sitting there with no idea what was going on.'

Dad would look up from the sport or the comics or whatever he was reading and he'd say, 'Charlie Pasquali might like that, Ros. He can tell his parents he's getting straight A's!'

But my mother wouldn't have it. 'How can it be good for Snow to be in a class with so many children who don't speak English? And who even knows what these migrants are saying when they talk to each other?' And then she'd start going on about how I should be in the local Catholic school and not the local State school, and Dad would say, 'But we're not even Catholic.'

Mum would say, 'It doesn't matter, it's not good for Snow to be mixing with people when we don't know what habits they have,' and Dad would say, 'I'm sure they're just like us, Ros.'

Mum would say, 'They aren't like us, they're different.'

Then Dad would get to joking, 'At least they aren't descended from convicts like the Australian kids!' And that would send Mum into a spin because she hated the idea that Australians were descended from convicts, she only wanted me to have friends who had parents from England like she was from England. Actually, I've just realised, Jack, that I'm writing to you from prison, so imagine if I'd ever had kids, they'd have been able to say they were descended from a convict!

But anyway, that's all beside the point because the real point I want to make is that you said the only bad thing that really happened to me when I was a kid was that Mum and Dad split up for a while. The way you said that like it was no big deal made me sick, to be honest, because that was actually a big deal for me, and if you want to know why I'll tell you why. My dad liked to play cards, and he had a friend who used to come with his wife on pay days to

SISTERS OF MERCY

play bridge with Dad and Mum. That friend was Russell Cooper, and his wife was Sybil or maybe Cecil, I can't remember.

Dad had gone from Victoria Railways by then and he had Olarenshaw Electrics on the High Street. Russell Cooper worked for him in that shop, so basically my dad was his boss and Russell Cooper was to me just another old man, meaning he looked old. He wore singlets under his shirts and his wife was also old like my mother, except she had gold in the back of her teeth, which you could see when she laughed. My mother wouldn't have been seen dead laughing like she did, she said it was common.

So there would be a knock on the door at seven o'clock every Thursday – this was after we'd had tea and washed up and when I was supposed to be getting ready for bed. Dad would open the door in his brown bridge cardigan with the big buttons that looked like walnuts. There would be Russell Cooper and his wife, and Mrs Cooper would be carrying a bottle of something like Moselle, or else she might have wine in a cask.

Mum would be in the lounge room setting up the vinyl card table – it was one of those that had metal corners and legs that folded up, and I loved to help fold it up – or she'd be putting out one of those trays with Planters Nuts and cabana, and the ashtrays would be out, with cigarettes to offer the guests. Dad would rub his hands and say, 'Now, who's for a drink?' And he'd have sherry for Mrs Cooper and Mum would have gin.

I was supposed to have had my bath and brushed my teeth and be ready for bed, but I was allowed to come down the hall in my dressing gown to get a Ritz cracker with a square of cheese, or else a piece of cabana on a toothpick, and I was supposed to give a kiss to all the grown-ups, including Mr Cooper, who was creepy to me.

The big game was seeing how many times I could sneak back into the room after I'd been sent to bed before Mum threatened to get the wooden spoon out. So I'd come down the hall and I'd say, 'I need the loo' or 'I need a glass of water' or 'I had a nightmare', but really what I wanted was to see what kind of adult thing was going on in the smoky bridge room. I remember Mum in there with her cigarette in one hand and she'd be keeping score on a tiny little pad of paper with a tiny little pencil, saying things to Dad like, 'Shut up, Jim, nobody's interested' when he wanted to talk about politics, which was all Gough Whitlam and the Dismissal in those days.

It was like that every pay day for as long as I could remember, until bang, one day there was no knock at the door, not that week and not for two more weeks, and not much was said about it, or not to me, anyway, but I noticed that things were a bit strange. And then, maybe it was a week or so later, I can't remember, I got up one morning to get ready for school and instead of finding my place set at the kitchen table with a bowl for Weet-Bix and a glass of orange juice, I saw my mother in the kitchen and she wasn't dressed. She had her dressing gown on, the quilted one that went down to the floor and had little satin buttons up to the neck. And I have to tell you, Jack, my mother wasn't the type to go wandering around the house in her dressing gown. She was the type to dress in a trendy way, maybe because she was older than all the other mothers and didn't like to be reminded of it, so when I was growing up she liked her flared jeans with the embroidery down the side, and she liked her platform shoes made of cork, and she wore her hair big, and had macramé vests and other things that I wanted to wear except I wasn't allowed.

Anyway, I said, 'Where's my breakfast?' and Mum didn't say anything, she was just standing looking out the kitchen window with a cup of instant coffee, and she was smoking, which she wasn't supposed to do in the kitchen because the smoke wasn't good for me as I had asthma. I sat down at the kitchen table and Mum still didn't move so after a while I said, 'Are you going to make me any breakfast?'

Mum said, 'Oh, I'll give you canteen money today,' which was amazing to me because I wasn't allowed to miss breakfast and I wasn't allowed to go to the canteen. And then Mum said, 'I'll just get the keys,' meaning she was going to drive me to school which, again, never happened. I always walked to school, or else I got the bus, and that was the same for all the kids in Deer Park. So I said, 'Are you going to drive me to school?' and Mum said, 'Yes, because I want to have a little talk to you.'

Straightaway I thought, 'Okay, I'm obviously in trouble,' and I was trying to think of what I might have done wrong. But then Mum said, 'Don't worry, you haven't done anything. Just get your school bag and let's go.' She made out like she was going to go out the front door and so I had to say, 'But aren't you going to get dressed?' because she was still in her dressing gown.

She looked down, a bit surprised, but then she said, 'Don't be silly, Snow, it's not like I'm going to get out of the car. I just want to have a bit of a talk to you.' And she walked out to the drive in front of the neighbours in her dressing gown and her slippers! Since

I was about ten years old, that was so embarrassing, and even as we were driving along in the old Datsun we had I could see people staring in at Mum in her dressing gown at the wheel of the car. I kept waiting to see what the big thing she had to tell me was but she obviously lost her nerve because she didn't say anything to me in the car.

I probably forgot how weird all that was once I got to school, but then when I got home that afternoon, there it was: the suitcase in the hallway.

Like an idiot, I said, 'What's that?' And Mum, who had pulled herself together and was now playing all easy-care, said, 'Oh, that's your father's, Snow, he's going away for a while.' And that's when I saw Dad, who was never usually there when I got home from school – he was always still at the shop. But on this day he was home and he was standing in the middle of the kitchen in the blue Yakka pants he always wore to Olarenshaw Electrics, with the Olarenshaw Electrics polo shirt on and his brown bridge cardigan with the walnut buttons over it, just looking sick.

I said, 'Where are you going, Dad?' because Dad basically never went anywhere and certainly not in the middle of the week, and he said, 'Well, tell her, Ros.'

Mum said something like, 'Don't make this harder than it has to be, Jim.'

Dad said, 'I'm not doing anything. This is *your* doing, Ros,' and I actually thought he was going to cry. I'd never seen Dad cry because dads didn't cry, not in those days.

Mum said something like, 'I thought we agreed,' and Dad said, 'I haven't agreed to anything,' and that must have annoyed Mum because she took me by the shoulders and said, 'Come here, Snow, and sit down.' But instead of pushing me into the lounge room, where I might normally have sat, she took me into 'the big bedroom', which is what I called Mum and Dad's room – because there were three bedrooms in the house: mine, one spare room, and the 'big bedroom' that was Mum and Dad's – and she made me sit on the edge of the big bed. That was again very strange because I wasn't allowed to sit or jump on that bed *ever*.

Mum sat down on the bed next to me and said, 'I want you to listen carefully, Snow. Your father and I have been having some problems.'

I said, 'What problems?'

Dad appeared in the doorway and said, 'Yes, Ros, tell Snow what problems we're having.'

My mother said, 'Jim, *please*,' as if that would make Dad shut up, and maybe it did because he took a packet of cigarettes from his shirt pocket, took out a cigarette and lit it and started dragging hard on it.

Of course by this time I had figured out what was going on and I blurted out: 'You're getting divorced, aren't you?' But there was no way Mum wanted to admit that because this was back in the day, when a divorce was still pretty taboo. She started saying, 'No, no, don't be silly, Snow. You're always jumping to conclusions. We're not getting divorced. Of course we're not.'

I said, 'Well then, what are you doing?'

Dad said, 'Yes, Ros, tell Snow what you're doing,' but Mum ignored him and said, 'We're just going to see if we'd be *happier* if we lived in different houses for a while, Snow.'

I said, 'How would we be happier in different houses?' Because kids don't want to live in different houses, Jack, they want to live in *one* house. Dad must have agreed with me because he said, 'Don't ask me, Snow, it's your mum's big idea.'

Mum was glaring at him and she said something like, 'What we've decided to do, Snow, is find out whether we'd be happier if we weren't living together *all the time*. If we were *still married*, but we lived in two houses.' And I have to tell you, Jack, my father laughed so hard that the smoke in his lungs came up and he started coughing, and he was saying, 'Oh, Ros, do you even believe your own bullshit?' which might have been the only time I heard him swear in front of my mum.

Mum ignored him and said, 'Listen, Snow, your father and I are not getting divorced. What we are getting is *separated*. It's different. We want to live in two houses for a while and see if we like it.' And then – and this is my favourite part, Jack – she said, 'It's not really something we're going to explain, Snow, because it's an *adult* decision.'

I've got to tell you, Jack, writing all this down, I'm trying to remember how I felt. I suppose I was just numb because I can't even really remember the point where Dad actually picked up the suitcase and walked out of the house, but it must have happened because at some point he was gone.

I jumped off Mum's bed and went into my room and slammed the door, and all that was going through my head was the word *divorce*.

Like, *divorce, divorce, divorce*.

I must have just sat in my room thinking that for ages because after a while I realised it was dark outside and Mum hadn't called me for tea, so I went into the kitchen and Mum was in there, practically in the dark, chopping this giant mountain of onions with the Staysharp knife that I wasn't allowed to touch. Her nose was red and her eyes were running, so I said something smart like, 'Why are you crying, Mum, if getting a divorce from Dad is such a good idea?'

I didn't expect her to whirl around quite as fast as she did. She just spun round and threw the knife onto the floor so hard that it bounced up and landed on its point, and she said, 'For God's sake, Snow, we're not getting a divorce!' And she picked up the cutting board with the onions and everything on it and swept the whole lot into the bin.

I got such a shock I just ran back into my room, and I was crying and crying. I must have fallen asleep on my bed because the next thing I remember I woke up and I was cold and Mum was in my room, standing there with a plate of toast with honey on it. She had a soft voice for a change and she was saying, 'Here, have this.'

I said, 'What's the time?'

She said, 'It's after midnight.'

Anyway, you know how you wake up sometimes and you can't be sure whether or not you had a dream and then you remember you didn't and everything's real? That's what it was like waking up the next day, going into the kitchen and finding my mother standing there, drinking her instant coffee and having her cigarette near the window like she wasn't supposed to do because of my asthma. My place was set for Weet-Bix and the glass of orange juice was there again. I pulled back my chair and my mother must have heard me because she turned and I noticed she had drawn her lipstick around her mouth and it looked bad like a clown. She had a lot of eye make-up on too so she must have been crying all night and was trying to hide it.

Mum said, 'Oh, good morning, Snow,' and when I kind of mumbled she said, 'Don't be cross, everything's going to be okay. It's just going to be a bit different.' She said, 'Let me make it up to you. Tell me what you'd like in your lunchbox and I'll make it for you. What would you *really* like?' And when I said I didn't want anything she said, 'Well, let me give you some money for the canteen,' making it two days in a row that I was suddenly allowed to go to the canteen.

She said, 'I think I'll drive you again today, Snow. You'd like to be driven to school again, wouldn't you?' And I was starting to think that the whole divorce thing wasn't that bad, since I was getting special treatment, nice treatment, for a change. But then, while she was driving, Mum made a point of making eye contact with me in the rear-vision mirror, and she said, 'You know, there's no reason to tell anyone every little detail of our personal lives, don't you, Snow? People love to gossip, but remember what I told you, it's not good manners.'

I could see what she was getting at, which was that I wasn't supposed to run into school and immediately tell everyone our private business, that Mum and Dad were getting a divorce. But I was only about ten when all this was going on, so how was I supposed to keep it to myself? I couldn't wait to get to school and blurt it out to everyone, but then the first girl I told – 'My parents are getting *separated*' – wasn't exactly shocked, she just shrugged and said, 'You know it means you won't see your dad again?' Which was something that shocked me maybe as much as what Mum had told me about wanting to have two houses.

I said, 'Of course I will.'

She said, 'Okay, then where is he now?' And that's when I realised that I didn't know where Dad had gone when he left the house what felt like ages ago.

The first thing I did when I got home was say to Mum, 'The kids at school said I won't see Dad again.' To begin with she was furious that I told people, but then she said, 'It's rubbish, he's coming next week,' and I suppose it was about a week later that Dad called to say he'd come and pick me up for a visit 'so you can see where I live'.

I can't tell you how weird it was to answer the phone and have Dad on the other end, mainly because I don't think I had ever spoken to Dad on the phone before. He never went anywhere, so why would I talk to him on the phone? He was always at home and now he was calling to speak to me because he didn't live there any more. But anyway, the day came for him to pick me up and I noticed he didn't pull into the driveway like every other day. He stayed out on the road and honked the horn and I had to run down the driveway to see him.

Dad pushed the passenger side door open for me, and do you know what he said when I got in, Jack?

Not, 'How are you, Snowdrop?'

Not, 'I've been missing you.'

He said, '*How's your mother?*'

I said, 'She's fine,' because what else was I supposed to say? She looked fine to me. But Dad said, 'Has she talked to you about me?'

I said, 'No,' because she hadn't, but it didn't matter, it set up the pattern for us for the next few years, where every time I saw Dad he would say, 'How's your mother?' I would say, 'Fine,' and he would say, 'Does she ever talk about me?' and I would say, 'No.' Because she never did.

We drove around to where Dad was living and it was basically a run-down bungalow behind some lady's house, and the old lady didn't like kids, so later on I'd call her the old bag, but not to her face. She'd given Dad practically no furniture. There was a single bed with flannel sheets, and a TV on wooden legs, and one of those ancient toasters with the sides you have to take down so you can get the toast out.

I said, 'You've got better things than this in the shop.' And that was true because Dad had toasters and jugs at Olarenshaw Electrics and they were at least new, and all this stuff was old.

Dad said, 'Yes, but this isn't my home, Snow. I can't bring my things here. I'm renting.' And I said, 'Why don't you just come home then?' And he said, 'It's not what your mum wants, Snow.' I said, 'But it's your house,' and he said, 'It doesn't work like that. I can't put you and your mum out in the street.'

I guess you won't be surprised to hear that it wasn't long after Dad moved out that I came home from school and found old Russell Cooper standing in the lounge room and, you guessed it, there was Mum, who had obviously been waiting for me, saying, 'Oh, here's Snow! Come here, Snow, there's somebody I'd like you to meet. You know Russell. Say hello to Russell.'

I couldn't say hello to Russell, the main reason being that I knew perfectly well who he was – Dad's employee, Mr Cooper from the bridge nights – and I had never addressed him, or any adult, by their first name in my life. 'Russell' had always been 'Mr Cooper' to me and I couldn't see why that was suddenly supposed to have changed. But he stuck his hand out, and next thing I knew we were all sitting around the kitchen table with everyone feeling a bit sick.

Mum said, 'I've made a nice tea for the three of us, Snow.' And even though I knew the answer, like a smart-arse I said, 'Isn't Mrs Cooper coming?'

Mr Cooper looked at my mother and said, 'Not tonight, Snow, no.' And then before I knew it he was tucking a napkin into the collar of his shirt, like he was suddenly lord of the manor, and he picked up his cutlery and held it upright in his fists like some kind of caveman. Mum announced that she had made a meatloaf, which I loved but she only ever made on 'special occasions', and she served it up on a good platter, and she put the good salt-and-pepper shakers – the wooden ones with the pewter base – on the table too.

The tea was supposed to be for the three of us but Mum didn't seem to be able to sit still, she kept dancing in and out of the kitchen, fussing over side dishes and forgetting to take off her apron when she finally sat down. Mr Cooper ate everything she put in front of him and then wiped his plate with a piece of buttered bread and said, 'Well, Roslyn, that was delicious,' which stunned me all over again because I never heard anyone call Mum 'Roslyn' – she was Ros to my dad, or Ros-the-Doz.

To make things even stranger, Mr Cooper also said, 'Now, let me help you with the dishes.' And he got up and followed my mother into the kitchen. When I went in there, carrying my own plate, I saw them standing very close together over the sink.

You probably want to know how soon after that Mr Cooper came to live with us, but all I can remember is that it wasn't long before

Mum was calling me into her bedroom one afternoon after school to sit on the 'big bed'. She gave me the spiel that all the kids with divorced parents were getting: 'You like Mr Cooper, don't you, Snow?' And she was all fidgety and anxious. 'Wouldn't you like to see more of him? Because I'd like to see more of him.'

In case you can't guess how that sounded to me, Jack, it sounded like it sounds to all kids, which is just gross. I knew what Mum was getting at – her and Mr Cooper wanted to be boyfriend and girlfriend. That isn't the kind of thing you want to think about when you're ten.

I said, 'I don't want Mr Cooper living here,' but nobody cared much about what kids wanted in those days. It was all, 'Oh, it's for adults to decide,' and, 'There's no point staying together for the kids,' and, 'Oh, kids just get used to it,' and all that rubbish. So Mr Cooper moved right in and suddenly I had this strange bloke living in my house and no Dad around. And as if to rub it in, Mr Cooper brought all these strange habits with him, like sitting on the back porch and cleaning his toenails with the sharp end of my father's steak knife, and walking through the kitchen in socks and underpants and a shirt that Mum had ironed that barely covered him up. And he brought daggy things with him, like Scotch glasses with the face of Elvis etched into them that said 'The King!' which we were supposed to put on display.

Worse than that, he tried to make friends with me – that was another 1970s kind of thing, for adults to try to be friends with the kids. But it was obviously a bit pointless because I never could stand him and didn't want him around. So he would say, 'Why don't you and I go and do something fun, Snow?' And I would say, 'Because

SISTERS OF MERCY

I don't want to do anything with you.' And he would say, 'I'm not trying to replace your father, Snow . . .' And I'd have to say, 'That's because you're *not* my father.'

He'd say, 'But you need to understand that there are rules in this house . . .'

I'd say, 'This isn't your house.'

He'd say, 'I understand that, Snow, and as I say, I don't want to replace your father, but don't you think that we can be friends?'

I thought, 'To be friends with my mum's boyfriend? That's not going to happen!' And thank God after a while he at least gave up trying to win me over and just got on with being all lovey-dovey with Mum, which included going out on what they called 'dates' – which was so embarrassing because 'dates' were actually dancing up the pub, where people could see them together and know that they weren't married.

One particular night they got dressed up in fancy costumes so they could 'hit the town', as Mr Cooper loved to say, and I couldn't believe it when he came out of the big bedroom to show me what he was going to wear, saying, 'What do you think, Snow?'

He was standing side-on so I could see how he'd drawn sideburns onto his face and how he'd stuck some kind of grease in his hair to make a quiff. Then my mother came out of the big bedroom and she was wearing a fifties skirt with a net petticoat, and her hair was like a beehive and she said, 'It's a fifties night! Come on, take our picture, Snow!'

We had an old Polaroid in those days, but the idea that I was going to use it to take pictures of Mum dressed up to go out with Mr Cooper was ridiculous. I just got up and went to my room.

I heard my mother saying, 'Oh, come on, Snow, can't I have a bit of fun?'

Mr Cooper said, 'Don't worry about it, Roslyn, she'll come around,' and there was a sound like Mum was crying, but they still went out and left me there with the TV on and no babysitter except for Mrs Andrewartha's phone number written on a piece of paper, in case, I don't know, the house caught fire or something.

Snow

Chapter Four

I've been trying to remember how long I sat with Ruby Moore during our first interview at the Sir Stanford. It's the kind of thing I can usually figure out from the length of the recording on my digital device, but we kept talking long after I'd run out of batteries on that, and long after I'd run out of paper in the notebook as well.

I remember the hotel staff coming into the dining room at some point to start clearing away what was left of the breakfast buffet – greasy strips of bacon and the gone-cold eggs – and start re-setting the tables for lunch. I remember that not many people came in for lunch so the big steel buckets of prawns with the chunks of lemon were soon getting cleared away too.

To the hotel's credit – and Ruby tells me they were pretty fantastic through all of this – none of the waiters ever once asked us to move, and they only really bothered us every hour or so with a question about whether Ruby might want some more hot water for the tea, or whether I was sure that I didn't want another coffee.

Ruby's mobile phone went off once during the interview and she grabbed it, which reminded me how desperate she was to hear something – anything – if not from her mum then from the cops. But it was her husband, Philip, who was upstairs with their kids. He was asking if she was okay, and if he could do anything, and what did she think about him taking their kids over to Luna Park, since they were going stir-crazy in the hotel room?

Ruby said that would be fine, and the kids came down in the lift. I was struck by how much Stella looked like her mum, and how Rocco was a double for his dad.

I stood up when Philip came in – he was very tall. He shook my hand and thanked me for coming, in that formal way British people have. It was warm outside – it was still December – and Philip and the kids were pale and wearing what looked like new, ironed shorts with pleats in the front from somewhere like David Jones.

Philip asked a couple of questions about the best way to get to Luna Park, and I told him that the ferry was enjoyable, and they'd get a good view of the Opera House and the Bridge. I told Rocco that Luna Park had some fun rollercoasters, and he said, 'I went on a rollercoaster at Alton Towers.'

I told him I was pretty sure the rollercoaster at Alton Towers was better than what they had at Luna Park, but Rocco was mostly looking forward to seeing the Harbour

Bridge in any case, which he said had six million rivets holding it together. He was clearly like a sponge when it came to remembering things.

They headed out the glass doors into the hotel foyer. We watched them go, and I couldn't help thinking that Ruby's mother had done just that: walked out those doors and got swallowed up into the red mist and never come back again.

This might not be obvious but I was conscious of the fact that I'd need to have a conversation with Ruby at some point about whether her mum had met with foul play. The idea that she was still wandering around in Sydney, lost, might have seemed reasonable in the early days, but not after three months. Something must have happened to her. But, having just seen Mrs Moore's grandkids skip out the hotel foyer, I suppose I didn't feel quite ready to raise the subject so I turned back to Ruby and said, 'You were saying that your mum loved living in Australia when she was a little girl?' And Ruby, who was doing her best not to get teary again, said, 'That's right. Mum's incredibly proud of having been brought up in Australia. She was only seven when she landed here and she didn't meet my dad until she was seventeen, so she spent a good decade here, and she's got wonderful memories of it, such as the time she saw the Queen.'

I said, 'Here in Australia?'

Ruby laughed. 'I know, I know, meeting the Queen in Australia! You'd think she'd remember seeing sheep or kangaroos or spiders or snakes, but Mum remembers seeing the Queen and Philip on their trip to Perth, two years after Elizabeth took the throne. There was supposed to be a church service but there was a polio outbreak, so the Queen didn't get off her yacht, and the Fairbridge kids were left to wave at her from the wharf. And Mum *swears* that Prince Philip picked her out, pointed at her, and gave her a little wink. She tells the story all the time: "He looked right at me and winked at me!"'

'She sounds like a card,' I said.

Ruby nodded. 'She is. She's the joker.'

I said, 'How long did your mum stay at Fairbridge, Ruby?'

'Until she was sixteen,' Ruby replied. 'She was sent into domestic service at that age. I'm not entirely sure where, only that it was a large property that Mum calls "the Hadenfelds".'

From my own research, I'm pretty sure that 'the Hadenfelds' must be Mr and Mrs Winston Hadenfeld, who in the 1950s had a massive property near where the Lyons meets the Gascoyne River, a five-day mail run from Perth. It's not there any more – the land was purchased by the industrial giant, Monsanto, some time in the early 1980s – but when the Hadenfelds owned it, the land size was 46,000 square kilometres, so it was bigger than the village of Bucklebury, where Ruby's from.

'The way I understand it, Mum had to travel there by bus and it took days to reach the place,' Ruby told me. 'She said, "I'd get off the bus and get put on another coach and we'd travel for a day, and then I'd be checked into a women's motel with a chaperone, and it went on like that for almost a week."'

Finally Agnes was dropped at what looked like the intersection of four dirt roads, all leading to the horizon, and she was standing there in the heat in her hat and gloves when a horse and carriage appeared for what was the final leg.

'Mum was covered in dust and the first thing she wanted when she finally arrived was to have a bath, but she was sent straight out to work,' Ruby said. Domestics at the Hadenfelds in those days dusted and did laundry; made damper and billy tea for the shearers; cooked eggs in skillets on open fires; scrubbed the floorboards in the main house and swept the veranda, which was four metres wide and seventy metres around; sewed patches into torn clothes; and picked fruit, bottled and preserved it.

'It was obviously hard work, but I do remember Mum telling me that there were parties every month and they were wonderful,' Ruby said. 'People would come by horse and cart, or by tractor or bus, some of them from homesteads hundreds of miles away. Food would have to be flown in, including fruit and vegetables that Mum had never seen before. Melons, for example.'

'It sounds glamorous,' I said.

'It was,' Ruby agreed, 'but there was obviously a downside for Mum: nobody would go home! They couldn't drive for three or four hours at night when there were no lights on the roads, she told me, and also there were kangaroos everywhere. So there would be extra beds to make and extra breakfasts to prepare. And she's really funny about having had to do all that when she was a girl. I remember Steven and I were complaining to Mum once about all the other kids having home-made cookies and why didn't she ever make home-made cookies? And Mum put her hands on her hips and said, "Oh, Rubes, please believe me, I've done my time with the flour and the apron and the rolling pin. I've done it over and over again."'

The Hadenfeld property – the formal name was Normanswood – was a sheep farm, and shearers would arrive in big numbers at the start of every shearing season.

'Mum was told to look down at her shoes while she was doling out their breakfast,' Ruby said. 'But the shearers were big men, and the domestics loved them and Mum was really pretty. Apparently Mrs Hadenfeld used to say to her, "Those looks of yours will get you in trouble."'

Most families have got a bit of a story about how the parents met and, according to Ruby, it was love at first sight for her mum and dad.

'Dad was the ringer, leader of the shearing pack,' she said proudly.

'Mum says she'd been eyeing him off over the porridge pot for a few weeks, building up all these fantasies of where he came from. He looked like the Australians: tanned, with what Mum called a big Ned Kelly beard. She didn't know he was British until he opened his mouth and the accent came out.'

SISTERS OF MERCY

John Moore wasn't just British, he was what the British call 'posh'. He went up to Oxford – that's how they say it, he 'went up' to Oxford – at the age of twenty in 1930 and, like pretty much half the athletics team, he was picked for the Olympics in Melbourne in 1956.

'He ran as the third man in the relay race,' Ruby said, but unfortunately the team didn't place, and he didn't get a medal.

'Dad was due to fly home after the Games but wrote to his folks, saying he wanted to stay longer. They were all for him having an adventure.'

John Moore went by rail from Melbourne across the desert to Coober Pedy to look for opals, went from there up to Lightning Ridge to pan for gold and, when he heard that jobs were going for shearers on a large property called Normanswood in Western Australia, he headed straight there.

'As far as I've been able to work out, he must have arrived at the Hadenfelds in around October 1957,' Ruby told me, 'because Mum says she was seventeen when they met.'

Fraternisation between the domestics and the shearers was banned, but Ruby's parents must have fraternised because, not six months after they met, Ruby's mum was having to tell Mrs Hadenfeld she was pregnant.

'She was dismissed on the spot,' Ruby said, 'as was my father, but they didn't care.'

'Because they were in love?'

'Because they were in love,' Ruby agreed. 'They were in love, and both of them by then also wanted to go home, which for Mum was always Britain. I hope that doesn't offend anyone: Mum really did love it here in Australia, and her memories of the place are all happy ones. She was forever telling me stories about Australia when I was a kid . . . She was absolutely addicted to *Neighbours* when that was on. When Scott and Charlene got married, she could hardly speak for a week, she was so swept up in the emotion of it all. But Britain was home.'

We talked for a while longer and eventually Ruby's kids bounded back into the hotel, desperate to talk about Luna Park. Her husband let them race over to say hello. Rocco sat half-on and half-off his mum's knee, and picked up one of the sugar packets, which he began sucking on. Stella's main interest seemed to be playing with a long strand of hair.

I decided to call the interview to a close for that day. Ruby looked exhausted, so I asked if it would be okay if we re-convened the next day and she agreed – she was set to fly back to London the day after that.

I arrived at the Sir Stanford at around 11 a.m. the following day, and I was pretty relieved when Ruby told me she couldn't face the dining hall again. She said, 'I think I've got a touch of cabin fever. I've been holed up in the plane, and now in this hotel. Do you mind if we head out for a bit?'

We went into Market Street and down the road to the David Jones food hall. Not exactly the quietest place to talk but at least it gave Ruby a chance to stretch her legs.

Some bar stools at the Salad and Wine Bar became free so we grabbed them. The waiter took the linen napkins off our plates and said, 'Will you be having wine?' I looked at the two glasses already standing where we were sitting and I was about to say, 'Not for me,' when Ruby said, 'That would actually be lovely.' So I joined her, and we got talking about the love affair her mum had with her dad.

'Practically the minute they found out Mum was pregnant with Steven, they flew home to England,' Ruby said.

I said, 'Excuse me, she *flew* home to England?'

Ruby looked surprised at my reaction – obviously it hadn't occurred to her what a radical idea it would have been for a young couple to hop the Kangaroo Route then.

'People were still arriving by boat in those days,' I said.

'But Mum probably didn't want to get the boat,' Ruby said. 'She'd already been to Australia on the boat and, anyway, she loves to fly!'

I'm tempted to say that God alone knows what it would have cost, but Google gives you a fair idea: a flight between Perth and London in the 1950s involved five stops, including two overnight in Singapore and either Karachi or Tripoli, and the fare was three times the average *annual* salary.

'There are photographs of Mum and Dad on that trip,' Ruby said, 'and one in particular I remember: Mum in a one-piece bathing suit, sitting by some hotel pool, wearing cat's eye sunglasses. You can't really tell that she's pregnant.'

I couldn't help wondering what John Moore's folks made of the idea that he was coming back to London with a girl he'd met in Australia, who was already expecting their heir, but when I put that question to Ruby, she laughed.

'I know, I know, we Brits can be a bit funny when it comes to class!' she said. 'I have wondered what Granny Moore made of it, but then Mum was pregnant so the main thing was to get her married to Dad as quickly as possible!'

I said, 'How did your mum cope with all that class business? Strikes me she'd have taken it in her stride.'

Ruby said, 'Mum will tell you . . . she's never had any problem "pretending to be posh" as she puts it. Granny Moore is dead now, but basically everyone got on.'

We had ordered grilled fish, and as it arrived I asked Ruby whether her mum ever went back to work after Steven – and then Ruby herself – was born. She shook her head. 'She didn't, no. She was lucky, in that she didn't have to work. Dad went into business, making and delivering shipping containers, and they bought a house at Bucklebury.

'Obviously Mum wasn't scared of hard work. I mean, we all know that taking care of little children *is* work, but the point is, she was perfectly happy to be at home with us. We had stables, with horses. I think she quite liked playing lady of the manor, even if she did it tongue-in-cheek.'

It was tender territory, so I stepped cautiously into my next question. 'Do you know how your mum was feeling about coming back to Australia for this visit, Ruby? How she felt about having to come to meet her sister, I mean?'

Ruby said, 'Oh, she was fine! My boy, Rocco, *he* was a mess but Mum was fine! Rocco has always made a point of studying everything about Australia, knowing that his granny grew up here, and he can tell you, Australia has nine of the world's top ten most poisonous snakes, or six of the most poisonous spiders or whatever it is.

'His vision of the place is obviously of some wild land with all these dangerous animals, so when we went to Heathrow to see Mum off, he was hanging onto her hand, very anxiously, and he was saying, "Remember not to go swimming with sharks, Granny, and don't step on any snakes, and don't touch any spiders," like those were the kind of things that Mum might do!

'And Mum made a great show of saying, "No, no, it's not like that any more, Rocco, that was when I was a girl. Australia is all grown up now – it's like London. Nothing will happen to Granny so don't you worry." And now of course she's disappeared in Australia, and I have no idea what to tell him.'

Chapter Five

Dear Jack,

I realise it's not polite to write to somebody before they've had a chance to write back to you, but that last letter I sent, it got me thinking about other things that happened to me when I was a kid that I'm still pretty upset about. The first being that every time somebody decides to get divorced it's 'Oh, we want it to be civil, we're going to try to get along for the sake of the kids,' and then it straightaway goes pear-shaped.

So, pretty much from the minute Dad was out of the house, Mum was saying she wouldn't be able to send me to the local Catholic College for high school like she'd always wanted because Dad wouldn't pay the bills. She said that was going to be my bad luck because the local high school was rubbish.

Like I said before, Dad used to say, 'But why do we have to send Snow to the Catholic College, we're not even Catholic?' And, 'What's wrong with the State system anyway?' He would have gone along with it while he was still living at home but once he was out he was saying, 'Why should I pay for that? Why not get your new boyfriend to pay?'

Mum would say, 'We don't want Snow to run off the rails,' and, 'We don't want Snow mixing with the wrong type,' by which she meant the New Australians, which was hilarious because many of the New Australians, especially the Italians, were Catholic so they would have been at the Catholic school.

Dad kept saying that my mother was living in his house with another bloke and if he wanted to live there he could 'cover the bloody bills' and things like that, and I had to listen to all this for months, and I couldn't tell anyone at Deer Park Primary where I was going for high school because I didn't even know.

Anyway, my dad eventually went up to the Catholic school and paid the fees himself.

I was supposed to be rapt to have such an 'opportunity', whatever that meant, but I hated that school. It was strict and it was still using the strap on girls, and the first week I was there a teacher broke a ruler over the back of a girl's hand because the hem of her skirt didn't touch her knees.

Lucky for me I was a pretty good student and I never got the strap, but I did give the teachers some headaches, and Mum too, especially when I got my first boyfriend.

He wasn't at the Catholic school. Actually, he wasn't at any school when I met him because he was much older than me, and that freaked everyone out the way it always does.

I know you're going to want to know all about him so I might as well fill you in on what a disaster it was. I was thinking before that

I wasn't going to tell you about him because then you'd try and find him on Facebook and interview him, but he was a bastard so I don't care if you do track him down.

You can tell him that from me.

So anyway, his name was Vincenzo Martinelli . . . and yes, I'm serious!

He was a wog, a New Australian, whatever you want to call it, and my mother's worst nightmare, with a hotted-up car and crazy horn and mag wheels. He wore singlets that showed off all his chest hair, and shoes with no socks.

He was the full catastrophe in other words.

Somewhere in the boxes of stuff I've got stored away, I would have thirty school books with Vincenzo's name scrawled all over them, which makes me laugh now but I had a real crush on him then, and we all know how that ends.

I was thirteen when I met him and it was actually Mum's fault that I started going around with him because she was the one who let me go on the train by myself to see *Grease* with John Travolta and Olivia Newton-John.

The movie had just come out and hardly any of the Catholic school mothers wanted to let their kids go and see it because there was no cinema in Deer Park in those days so if you were going to go you would have to go to the city on the train. Also, there was a bit in the film where a girl got pregnant and wasn't married, and that was still taboo and not completely normal like now.

Nobody was surprised that my mum was going to let me go because, after all, she had Mr Cooper living with her and they weren't married.

SISTERS OF MERCY

It felt like I'd been badgering Mum for about three months to let me go when she said, 'Okay, you can go, but only if you go with Mrs Halfpenny's girl.'

Mrs Halfpenny was a friend of Mum's from when she worked at the Postmaster-General's, and they had their babies at the same time. I didn't really know Mrs Halfpenny's daughter very well because they lived on the other side of town, but Mum was forever going on about how responsible and mature she was – not that I cared, I just wanted to see *Grease*.

Mum said, 'Mrs Halfpenny's daughter will meet you at Spencer Street station and you'll walk from there up to Bourke Street, and I want you to go straight in the cinema and come straight back out and get straight back on the train and come straight home.'

I said yeah, yeah, whatever, and the minute she dropped me at the train station I forgot all about that.

Trains that went through Deer Park in those days were the old Red Rattlers with the compartments inside, and you could smoke in some of them. The train came and I walked along until I found a compartment that was empty and took the whole thing for myself. But I didn't have it to myself for long because Vincenzo Martinelli got on at the next stop, which was Sunshine, and kind of looked in and saw me sitting there and came straight in and sat down next to me.

In case you think it was love at first sight it wasn't. The first thing I thought was 'Greasy wog', because that's what he looked like with his gold chain with a gold horn thing on it. I had been warned by Mum to stay away from greasy wogs because they were always looking for 'skip' girls that were supposedly sluts.

We were barely away from Sunshine station when Vincenzo started on me, saying, 'What's your name?' and 'Where're you going?' and 'How old are you?' and 'Where are your parents?'

I knew I wasn't supposed to talk to him but I told him that my parents were separated and probably getting divorced, which was about as dramatic a thing as I could think to say to anyone.

Vincenzo, who anyway I always just called Vincent, made this sad face and he said, 'Oh, that's bad, that's bad,' and he was shaking his head and took a cigarette from his packet and put it in his mouth, still shaking his head. Then suddenly he asked if I wanted one. I didn't smoke so that was my first cigarette, and it wasn't like you see on the movies with me coughing, it just made my head spin.

We talked all the way in to Spencer Street station, where Mrs Halfpenny's daughter – I can't even remember her name – was standing waiting for me like Miss Goody-Two-Shoes, and all through the movie I was thinking about how Vincent had said, 'I'm going to be waiting for you when you get out.'

I was shaking when I came out, expecting to see him there, but he wasn't at the cinema and my stomach just sank. I walked back to Spencer Street station with Mrs Halfpenny's daughter just going on and on about the movie. But then when the train pulled up he was suddenly there, saying, 'Bet you thought I wasn't coming.'

I made like I didn't care but when he sat right next to me in the compartment and our legs were touching I didn't move away, and after about ten minutes he put his cigarette out and went to kiss me. I jerked my head away from him so fast that I cracked it on the window, and Vincent said, 'What's the matter? Don't you want anyone to see you kissing a wog or something?'

SISTERS OF MERCY

I said, 'That's got nothing to do with it,' and Vincent said, 'Then maybe you're frigid.' I didn't want to be frigid so when he said, 'Get off the train at my stop, come on, I won't rape you,' I said okay and we got off.

He had his car parked at the station, and it wasn't like driving in your parents' car, it had one of those smelly Christmas tree things, and the steering wheel was covered with sheepskin. We drove for about ten minutes and then we pulled up into the drive of this house, and Vincent went around the back and let me into what he said was his bungalow.

There was one of those couches covered in that old bobbly fabric that everybody had in those days, and it was all sticky from whatever he'd spilled on it. There was a TV sitting on a cardboard box, and all these posters of half-naked men on the walls, which was a bit of a shock since I thought blokes were supposed to have pictures of naked women on the walls. But not the wogs, they had half-naked bodybuilders on the walls.

We sat on the couch and Vincent was rubbing my knee and saying, 'You don't know how beautiful you are, do you?' and all that stuff that blokes say when they're basically trying to get into your pants. I was brushing him away because that's what girls are supposed to do, and he was pretending to get sick of me saying no, and I was going on about how much trouble I was going to be in for not being on the train. So he said, 'Alright, I'll just take you home.' He kind of dragged me up onto my feet and shoved me out the door.

He was driving pretty fast and he kept going on about why didn't I want to kiss him and badgering me about how old I was, and somehow we got to the idea that I should go around with him, officially. But then he was asking about Russell Cooper, saying, 'Is your mum's boyfriend a big bastard? Is he going to knock my block off when he finds out we're going around together?'

I said, 'It's not like he's my dad.' And Vincent said, 'You better not tell anyone we're going around together because if anyone finds out the cops will come and bash me.'

I probably don't need to tell you that I got into so much trouble when I finally got home that day, Jack. My mother had the wooden spoon in her hand – not actually a wooden spoon but a stick thing that she *called* the wooden spoon – and she was yelling at me for being out of her mind with worry, and what was I playing at, and where had I been?

I made up a big lie, saying, 'Oh, I missed the train. I waited for the next one but it didn't come so I had to get the bus instead.' And my mother was saying, 'Do you think I came down in the last shower, Snow?'

I got grounded for two weeks, but there comes a point where you can't really ground a kid who won't be grounded and I had no intention of staying in because Vincent was ringing me up all the time and saying, 'Come out.'

It was driving Mum crazy because the phone would go all the time and I'd just snatch it up and Vincent would say, 'I'm in the phone box across the road,' and I'd run out and get in his car. It wasn't long before he wasn't even trying to hide. He'd just pull up outside the house in his Monaro and sound the comedy horn and I'd run out.

Mum was yelling at me, and calling Dad on the phone saying, 'Do something, do something!' And I could just picture what Dad was saying on the other end of the line: 'What exactly would you like me to do, Ros?'

Mum said, 'She's underage!' And Dad must have said, 'So call the police,' because Mum, who was one of those British people who can't stop thinking about what the neighbours might think, was saying, 'I can't do that, then the whole neighbourhood will know!'

Mr Cooper was weighing in, saying rude things like, 'Why does your greasy friend want a girlfriend who's still in school, anyway?' And, 'Can't you see he's using you?' which, when I think of it now, wasn't such a dumb thing to say, but I wasn't listening, at least not until what was bound to happen happened. I got pregnant.

Obviously my mother went off the planet about it, going on about 'The money we've spent on that school . . . the opportunities you've been given . . . have you any idea how hard it's been for me?' And then, 'What do you think you're going to do now, Snow? You can't have that baby. You're only fourteen years old – they won't even give you a single mother's pension.'

I was so full of myself, I said, 'I don't have to worry about that because Vincent's going to marry me.' And I actually believed it, Jack. I really did! But word for word what he actually said when I phoned him was, 'How do I even know it's mine? You could be having sex with anyone.'

At first I thought I must have heard wrong, or maybe his mum was listening and so he was saying what she wanted to hear, because he also kept saying, 'You have to have an abortion,' and, 'You're giving me stress and I have an ulcer. If it bleeds, I'll die.' And, 'My mother will have a stroke. She's not well. You can't do this to her.'

I said, 'I don't want to have an abortion!'

Vincent said, 'My father's an old man and this'll kill him.'

The next time I called him, he wouldn't come to the telephone. But you know who did, don't you? His mother did and she spat venom at me. '*Putana, putana*, skippy, skippy, leave my boy alone!' Like I'd tried to trap him or it was all my fault and it doesn't take two to tango.

So then I had to tell my mother I'd have the abortion, and if you think she said, 'Oh, Snow, don't worry I'll look after you. Come on, have a little cry,' then you're wrong because she didn't. What she did was make that 'I told you so' face and then said, 'There's only one place that deals with girls like you.' She meant Bertrand Wainer's clinic on Wellington Street in Richmond, which probably isn't there any more but is where all the girls from the Catholic College had to go, and all I can say is at least she drove me there, and at least she kind of helped me get through the people with their ugly posters of dead babies, and at least she waited for me to come out, and drove me home and put me to bed. But if you think she was any nicer than that, you'd be wrong.

I fell asleep when I got home, and then I woke up at, I don't know, nine o'clock, and I was hungry and groggy from whatever they give you, and my mother was in the lounge room watching *Homicide* or something like that, and Mr Cooper was standing at the ironing board, ironing my Catholic College uniform. Seeing me at the doorway in a long T-shirt, with mascara streaked down my face, you'd think my mother might have said, 'Oh, come on, let's get you something to eat,' or something nice, but all she said was, 'Go to bed, Snow. You've got school tomorrow.'

SISTERS OF MERCY

I ran back into the bedroom and pulled the stuffed animals over me so I could hide underneath them, but my mother stormed after me, saying, 'Don't you tantrum around the place, Snow. What you've done is terrible,' and then she was going on about how I better not tell anyone because 'if word gets out, you'll have a reputation worse than the one you've already got'.

So that was that, and the weird thing about all of it was that I'd forgotten most of it, wiped it from my brain basically, until they brought it all up at the trial. I'm guessing you were in court that day, but anyway, it was around the time, maybe just before the judge was making his big speech about what a terrible person I am, at that bit where they let all the experts in to try to convince him not to lock me up and throw away the key. One of the psychologists said, that 'episode' – he meant the abortion – set me up for the trouble I got into in my life.

I thought at the time, 'Well that's kind of social worker talk,' but now that I've had some time to think about it I don't actually disagree with him, Jack. Because it was like that psychologist said: I was feeling, how did this happen? He said he loved me and who will love me now?

The psychologist said, 'Oh, it's no surprise that Snow then went looking for that affection anywhere she could find it.' And I have to tell you, it was nice to hear something like that in the court, because up until that point it had basically been every witness was there to say what an evil person I am. Finally, there was somebody who could see that, whatever I was supposed to have done, *it wasn't my fault*.

Snow

Chapter Six

The first thing police will do in a missing person's case is try to trace the person's movements in the twenty-four or forty-eight hours before they disappeared.

In the case of Agnes Moore's disappearance, that meant talking to staff at the Sir Stanford, and it meant talking to Snow.

From what I understand, police knocked on her door in Bondi something like a week after the dust storm, which sounds like a desperately long time but remember there was at least a day during which Agnes was supposed to be on the plane, then some time during which enquiries were being made with airlines and then with the hotel, plus the routine time that goes by, while the police wait to see if somebody who has disappeared might just show up.

In any case, the detectives who knocked on Snow's door or, more accurately, rang the buzzer, asked if they could come in, and Snow apparently said, 'Why, what's it about?'

When they explained that her sister hadn't got on the plane, Snow said she knew that because her niece – meaning Ruby – had called.

My contact in the New South Wales police tells me that the police who visited that day didn't go inside; they stood on the porch to ask their questions. Snow said her sister had arrived at around 1 p.m. and she left at around 3 p.m. and that tallied with what police knew from the CCTV at the hotel, which showed Agnes going back to her room that night.

There might be people who say police should have dug a bit deeper there and then, but remember their attention at that time wasn't focused on what Agnes had been doing before she went missing but rather after she stepped into the dust storm.

I remember asking Ruby, back at the lunch we had at David Jones, what kind of contact she'd had with Snow in those first days after her mum went missing and she told me much the same story as my contact at Rose Bay: Snow wasn't exactly rude, but she wasn't much help either.

'Mum had left me with a list of important numbers in Sydney – the number for her hotel, and Snow's number, and so on – and as soon as I figured out that she wasn't getting off the plane, and I couldn't reach her by phone at her hotel, I called Snow,' Ruby said.

'She picked up, thank God. But when I introduced myself, she simply said, "Oh, hello." Not, "Oh, my goodness, you must be my niece," or anything like that. Just, "Oh, hello."

'I explained the situation: that Mum hadn't got off the plane and hadn't been in touch either, but she offered no help at all. I thought that was . . . well, perhaps not odd, but certainly a little rude. I'd made it plain, or thought I had, that I was quite frantic. I'd said, "I haven't heard a thing from Mum, she wasn't on the plane," and Snow just said, "Oh?" Just like that: "Oh?"

'I asked her, "Do you happen to know where she's gone?" She said, "Maybe she's sightseeing." And I had to say, "But that would be so out of character. She normally keeps us up-to-date with what she's doing." Snow said, "Maybe she's gone on a trip to the Great Barrier Reef? She said something about wanting to take some trips." And I suppose if there was a moment when I was truly alarmed, that was the moment, because, as far as I could remember, my mother hadn't expressed any desire to "take trips" while she was in Australia, certainly not trips that weren't on her itinerary. In fact she had made a solemn promise to Rocco that she would *not* go to the Great Barrier Reef because, like most kids, Rocco was a big Steve Irwin fan and he was devastated when Steve was taken by the stingray. He made Mum *promise* that she would not take that risk. And yet I was being asked to believe that she'd decided to do precisely what she'd promised Rocco she wouldn't do?'

Frustrated by her inability to get any assistance from Snow, Ruby contacted the local police, who suggested she lodge a missing person's report.

'They gave me a link to a form I could fill out online,' Ruby said. 'I had hoped for a little more urgency than that but the police told me there was a process to follow, and it didn't help that I was still in London. I explained that Mum had by then been missing for something like thirty-six hours, and the police seemed to think that was no time at all, and in fact told me to call back in twenty-four or forty-eight hours, as if that might somehow make a difference.'

It was painful to hear Ruby recount that story. We'd both stopped eating and the food on our plates had gone cold. I pushed mine back and said, 'Probably they thought, "She'll turn up any minute and we won't hear from this lady again,"' and Ruby nodded and said, 'Probably. They certainly seemed surprised when I was on the phone again the next day, still trying to find out what happened. And by then I'd called the British embassy in Canberra, and I'd called Australia House in London too, but I really couldn't seem to get anyone to take it seriously.'

Frustrated by what must have seemed like the snail's pace of the investigation, Ruby flew to Sydney to meet the police, and it was shortly afterwards that she gave the first press conference at the Rose Bay cop shop.

I asked Ruby if she'd tried during that first visit to get in touch with Snow and she said, 'Yes, of course. I called her and told her I was in town and asked her if I could see her but she made it plain that she wanted nothing to do with me. She said something to them along the lines of, she never wanted to meet Mum in the first place and now there were all these relatives ringing up and she wasn't the type to welcome that kind of intrusion.'

I could see that Ruby was absolutely perplexed by that. It sounded pretty cruel to me too. I said, 'Did you ever have her address?'

Ruby said, 'I do. Mum gave it to me before she left.' And she fished it out: 27 Bat Street, Bondi.

I sat thinking for a minute. I live in Bondi, and have done since before it got all trendy and expensive – meaning before they started making *Bondi Vet* and *Bondi Rescue* and before Lara Bingle and all the hipsters moved in. I know Bat Street reasonably well – it's one of the streets that overlooks the beach.

'It's not more than twenty minutes by taxi,' I told Ruby. 'If you want to go out there, I'm happy to accompany you. I'll even knock on the door.'

I don't deny I had an ulterior motive. I was thinking that if Snow let us in, I'd get one of the stories I'd been trying to get all along, which was the sister of the missing British tourist appealing for anyone with any information to come forward.

Ruby slipped straight off the David Jones stool onto her feet and we both put our napkins down. I quickly paid the bill saying, 'Don't worry, Rupert can afford it.' We jumped in a cab and, on the way there, Ruby said, 'Do you think this is a good idea? She might think we're stalking her.' And I said, 'It's the kind of thing I do all the time, so don't worry.'

SISTERS OF MERCY

The minute I saw the house, I recognised it. Most people in Bondi will know which one it is: it's the massive one that stands halfway along Bat Street, on the low side of the street, near the south end of Bondi Beach, the one that is painted bright pink, like fairy floss. The one that's got all the pink turrets sticking up. It's old and broken down, like the kind of place that must have had a story behind it – even before it became notorious as the house that Snow Delaney lived in.

The first thing that struck me, once Ruby and I had got out of our cab, was how hard it was going to be to get through the front gate. The house sits well back, and there's an old cyclone fence around it. Paterson's curse had grown wild over it – twice as high as the fence itself, and thick – so it was impossible to see through it.

There was a gate with one of those cheap white plastic intercoms, but you couldn't even tell if it worked. I buzzed and nothing happened. I tried to see whether there was a way around the back but there wasn't, so I took hold of some of the thick weed trunks and used them as a kind of climbing frame to pop my head up over the fence. The garden was full of those huge cobwebs the size of bed sheets that hang between the trees in Bondi, with those big spiders with fat backs and the St Andrew's Cross bouncing in the middle of them.

I called out, 'Yoo-hoo, anyone home?' And you know how sometimes you get a sense that somebody is there but they don't come out, like maybe you think you've seen a curtain move but you wouldn't swear by it? It was a bit like that at Snow's place.

I debated for a minute whether to hurdle the fence and knock on the door, and knowing what I now know I should have done, but there didn't seem any urgency then.

I let my feet fall back down to the footpath and dusted myself off and said, 'Well, if she's home, she's not answering.' Ruby looked disappointed but not surprised and we were about to head back to the bus stop when a cheery-looking bloke across the road, who'd been painting his front fence, straightened himself up and said, 'Can I help you folks?'

I said that I was from *The Sunday Times* and he didn't seem surprised to hear it, saying, 'We had some other media people here a few weeks back . . . Do you mind telling me what's going on?'

'We're looking for the lady who lives here, do you know her?' I explained.

He shook his head. 'I don't, but my wife sometimes says hello. I'm pretty sure she's a nurse.'

Chapter Seven

Dear Jack,

I really don't understand you. At first you were all, 'Tell me where I went wrong with my stories about you.' And then I write back and tell you and you don't even bother to reply.

Maybe I shocked you too much telling you about how my own mother drove me to get an abortion. Maybe you're Catholic and you think people who have abortions have got to be sinners. That's what they thought at the Catholic College in Deer Park, and I know for certain that some of the nuns knew that I'd had an abortion because when I went back to school they avoided me in the halls.

I didn't care, and pretty much from the time I turned fifteen, I just wanted to finish school and move out of home as fast as I could. But first I needed to get a job and I had no idea what I wanted to do, other than leave school. We had a careers teacher who was supposed to help, but the only big ideas she had was: finish year 10 and go and be a teller at the State Bank, which would have been boring, or else learn to type up to a hundred words a minute with

85 per cent accuracy and there might be a job as a secretary somewhere. Or go and give your resume to the local hairdressers and see if they need an apprentice.

That might have been fine for some of the girls I went to school with, but I couldn't see myself standing at the bank window taking cheques from old ladies and I couldn't see myself sweeping hair up from salon floors, both of which would have meant I probably would have had to stay in Deer Park when what I wanted was to get *out* of Deer Park.

Just so you know, I *did* think of being a journalist, maybe at the *Sun* newspaper, which had the comics I liked, or else at the paper Dad liked to read in the afternoons – *The Herald*. But the principal at the Catholic College said, 'Oh, you wouldn't be able to do that, your English isn't good enough. If you don't want to go to the State Bank, why don't you try out for nursing instead?'

I can't say I was that interested, but I also had no other ideas, so I got the pamphlets from the careers teacher and put in an application form for the nurses' college at Coburg, and they said, sure, you can start training in January next year. So that was basically how I decided to be what I am.

I don't know what nursing training is like now but in those days it was pretty easy. There was a bit of learning from books and then six weeks of what they called the 'prac', which was basically being a nurse but not getting paid the full wage because you hadn't graduated.

I did my prac at the old Sunshine Hospital, and there wasn't that much supervision. They basically let us loose on wards that were filled with people who were coughing and dying. We did what used to be called 'rounds', which meant taking the patients' blood pressure and giving injections and handing out pills and changing bandages.

I know that people say I'm hard as nails, and I'm cruel and whatever, but you can ask anyone I trained with, I was the most squeamish of all the new nurses. I didn't want to do anything that might hurt somebody. Like, the first time I had to give a patient an injection, it was to an old, old man and he had that skin that was thick like leather, and brown and spotty from being in the sun for seventy years. He was sitting in one of those blood-taking chairs they have, with the wide armrest, and he was wearing one of those cotton robes that was open all down the back and he was pretty much bald except for white fluff on his head. I was supposed to stick a needle in him and get some blood out so I said, 'I'm sorry, Mr Whatever-His-Name-Was, but I need to do this.' He said, 'Oh, that's fine, love, don't be scared,' but I couldn't stop shaking. I was doing that thing where you try to get the needle in the right spot, pointing at the vein, but it wouldn't go in.

The old bloke could see how I was shaking and he said, 'Just push it in and don't worry.' But I couldn't do it, and then I got the wrong spot and blood came pouring out, and I panicked and pushed the emergency button and the matron came and shook her head like I was a complete idiot. She said, 'Just do it like this, Snow,' and jabbed the old bloke really quick, and really hard, and he cried out, and his mouth was left hanging open. I was shocked but the matron said, 'You need to be in control, Snow. No mucking around, just get things done,' and before long it was me who was just jabbing old people and letting them cry out and not even worrying about it, because you get conditioned to it and you're busy and you know it doesn't really hurt. Plus it's always better when it's quick, and to say, 'Let's get it over with.'

My first job after I finished training was at oncology, which is the cancer ward. If I had still been squeamish that would have been even worse because it was doing things like peeling back bandages for people who had skin cancer and bits of their flesh would come away, and no matter what you did you couldn't get it to stick back on.

You could still smoke in hospitals in those days, and plenty of people did – and yes, I mean on the cancer ward. One old bloke used to beg me to hold his durry up to his tracheotomy – the hole they'd made in his windpipe – so he could get some nicotine into him! That was nothing: we had patients who had lost both their legs and three fingers on each hand and they'd *still* want to smoke.

I stayed on oncology for about six months and then, when I was in my last year of training, I got sent up to geriatrics, where basically it was my job to feed old ladies who had no teeth and who were lying there on the wards all day with cataracts over their eyes, pretty much blind. It was hard to get them to eat because most of them had basically given up on living, and I didn't blame them. It was pretty obvious that nobody cared about those people. Everyone they'd ever known was dead, except maybe their kids who would come in on Sundays or else on what we called the 'duty' visits on Mother's Day and maybe Christmas Day. Then they'd just sit there in the visitors' chairs, trying to make small talk – 'Oh, little Kevin has made the final of the district spelling bee!' – and I'd see them sneaking glances at their watches and wondering how long they'd have to sit there before they could get up and leave and get on with their lives.

Maybe you're wondering why I'm telling you all this. It's because I think you should know what nurses know, or what the honest ones know, which is that it's just rubbish that people care about their families, because the minute they get old or sick the first thing they want to do is shut them up in some kind of institution and keep them locked away. As long as they're fed, and there's somebody there to change their filthy bed sheets and clean their teeth, that's all they care about.

But anyway, after two years of training I was a qualified nurse looking for something to specialise in. Some girls I'd done training with were talking about going to Emergency and 'saving lives' and some wanted to go to midwifery to deliver babies, but I wasn't interested in either of those things. Believe it or not (and nobody believes it), even back then I had a big social conscience and what I wanted to do was go and work with retarded children – especially those children like Annie McDonald, who everyone was talking about at that time. And in case you don't know who she is, she was a famous retarded person, and she'd been in the papers, and there had been stories about her on the news, and the story basically was that she looked retarded but she was a normal person on the inside, meaning she had a normal brain but she couldn't walk or talk, she could only dribble so nobody knew that she was normal on the inside.

Somehow she'd been rescued from whatever home she'd been living in for years and years, with nobody ever talking to her or reading to her, and then there were stories about how there were other people like her, also stuck in homes for the retarded, and suddenly the government was talking about ways to get them all out. Every week there were ads in *Nursing* magazine – jobs for people to go into homes for retarded people and see how many of them were also normal on the inside – and one of those ads was for nurses to join the staff at Caloola, which was a home for retarded people in Sunbury. I went to one of the information sessions and they said, 'We're looking for people who can help us find out which of the patients at Caloola might be able to live in the outside world.' I thought, 'Yes, that's what I want to do,' because that was me back then, a big bleeding heart. At least until I actually started at Caloola, and had the bleeding heart knocked right out of me.

Snow

Chapter Eight

Some people seem to think that journalists have unlimited budgets to just travel around but, let me tell you, with all the problems newspapers are facing these days, it's difficult to get the editor to fork out even for a trip to Melbourne.

That said, there was a time when I was that keen to find out what had happened to Agnes Moore, I would have put my own hand in my pocket to fund a trip down there.

Luckily I've got the kind of editor who will back me when I'm on a story, and when I told him that I wanted to go to Melbourne to do research into Snow's background – this was after she'd gone to jail, obviously – he somehow got the expense claim through.

I got a morning flight into Tullamarine and I asked the driver of the taxi if he knew where Sunbury was. He said, 'I'm from Sunbury,' which is the kind of thing that always seems to happen to me. So then I asked him, 'Do you know Caloola?'

'Do you mean the old mental hospital?' I said yes, and he said, 'Of course I know where it is.'

He drove me right up to the gates, telling me all these gruesome stories, most of them probably false, about patients who used to live at Caloola: murderers and rapists and people who ate their own faeces, and I don't know what else.

I paid the fare and stood at the iron gates, looking up at the building. It is pretty grand. It's made of bluestone, and it's got big windows and stone archways and lawns with fig trees, and climbing roses.

The history of the place doesn't make for such pretty reading. I downloaded a copy of the official one, the one that Sunbury Library keeps on file, and it goes into all the gory detail: when Caloola was first opened back in 1864 it was just one big building called the Home for Neglected and Criminal Children, and it was for orphans but also for little kids whose parents basically didn't want them – kids who used to get called 'waifs' and 'strays' and 'delinquents'.

It would never happen now but the cops used to take them to Caloola. It was just like Dickens: they slept on the stone floors and there was no heating but plenty of rats and disease. The place soon got itself the nickname of 'The Sunbury Slaughterhouse', because so many of the kids who ended up there died of malnutrition or smallpox or from eye infections that nobody treated.

Caloola even had its own undertaker to deal with all the bodies.

SISTERS OF MERCY

As I understand it, the sign for the children's home came down in 1879, but it was soon replaced by one that was worse: The Sunbury Lunatic Asylum. The first patients came from the goldfields at Ballarat, but before long they were taking patients from all around Victoria, and new buildings were going up to accommodate them.

Of course, we're talking now about a time when people who had disabilities – people with Down syndrome, for example, or people with cerebral palsy – were treated like they were insane and they got put in the same institutions as people who were actually crazy, so Caloola was soon bursting.

There weren't many drugs designed for mental illness, so pretty much everyone was locked into a straitjacket, and the other major treatment was 'thump therapy', where male nurses would go around at night, thumping people to make them go to sleep. There was also a 'Dark Room' – a tiny space, blacker than night – for holding particularly unruly patients, often for weeks on end.

This went on for years and years, until finally the screaming got too much for the good citizens of Sunbury, who claimed to be able to hear it coming down the hill. They formed a group – it was called the Sunbury Citizens' Advocacy Group and a version of it might still exist – to lobby the government to open up Caloola to some kind of scrutiny.

A report in *The Age* from 1985, which you can find on the Caloola home page, quoted a member of the group saying, 'I can't sleep at night, thinking about what might be going on in there. We need to go in and find out! We hear all kinds of rumours about patients being held in straitjackets, and we hear these terrible screams.'

A Victorian minister for community services at that time was a bit of a citizens' action group hero, because rather than tell the group that he'd get somebody to have a look into it, he empowered the Sunbury Citizens' Advocacy Group to enter Caloola to conduct its own investigation, and their report caused a sensation when it was leaked to *The Age*. I can see why. There's a copy of it still on file in the Victorian parliamentary library, and it basically says that patients at Caloola in the 1980s were living much as they had done in the nineteenth century. They were stripped to their underpants, tied down to chairs, and made to eat with their hands because the staff thought they couldn't be trusted with cutlery.

None of them had their own clothes – they were given clothes from a communal pile of laundry – and many had been given no explanation for why they were even in Caloola, let alone how long they were supposed to stay there.

I took a few notes from the report. 'We were disgusted by what we found at Caloola,' it said. 'It cannot be right for a person to be fed, clothed, sheltered, and left like a penned ox for sixty years. The waste of human lives is immoral.'

The minister hopped straight on it, promising first of all to bring the number of patients in Caloola down from 1000 to around 500, and he promised to train a 'new generation' of nurses to try to 'change the culture', and perhaps find out whether any of the patients who were stuck in there could actually live in the community. He called this 'the program of normalisation', and Snow was one of the first nurses to sign up for it.

I wondered how much Snow knew about what was going on at Caloola before she went to work there, and about the kind of things she had seen. I assumed that she wouldn't want to think about it any more, let alone talk about it, but as there was only one person who could answer my questions, I wrote to her, and it turned out she couldn't wait to fill me in.

Chapter Nine

Dear Jack,

So you want to know what it was like to work at the old loony bin, do you?

Caloola.

I haven't thought about the place for years. Trust you to head out there and have a bit of a stickybeak. I wish they'd let me out to go with you. I could have given you the full tour.

The job I applied for was a Normalisation Aide. In case you don't know, that was a new position for nurses who didn't want to do things the old way, and who wanted to do things the new way, which was to treat the people in the loonie bin with respect!

We were going to find out which patients were smart underneath all the dribbling and shaking they did.

You probably won't believe this but I was pretty naive. I bought into all that politically correct stuff in those days, but then I was only a few years out of the nursing college.

SISTERS OF MERCY

I remember sitting in some lecture and nodding, all earnest, while they told us that we wouldn't be calling the patients spastics or retards any more, we'd be calling them 'people with intellectual challenges' or else 'people who are handi-capable', if you can believe that!

We wouldn't be thinking of ways to just shut them up and keep them quiet, we would be thinking of ways to get them to communicate. I couldn't wait to get started because I was actually thinking to myself, 'I'm not just going to be feeding people mashed potato and wiping their bums, I'm going to be helping these people.'

And then I met them, Jack.

I don't want to sound smart, but honestly it did only take about a week for a person with those kinds of ideas to get a real wake-up call.

Let me tell you about the first day I walked into the place. I would have been about twenty, with two years of nurses' training, and then six weeks of lectures on 'normalisation' still in my head. There was a big stone arch out the front of Caloola with the year 1864 carved at the top, and I remember looking at that arch and thinking, 'This is one of the last old cruel places, and I'm going to be making a difference.'

And just as I was thinking that, a crazy lady with Albert Einstein hair came out of nowhere and chested me.

I got such a shock, mainly because I could tell straightaway that she was a patient and I couldn't work out why she was on the loose. She was wearing a canvas smock – I'm talking now about one of those cream-coloured ones made of that hard material that the patients can't tear up and shove down the toilet – and shoes with no laces, but she was also wearing boxing gloves.

I'm not kidding, she was wearing boxing gloves, and it looked to me like they were taped on.

So I was standing there with this woman, thinking, 'What the hell?' And waiting to see what she was going to say. But she didn't say anything to me, she just looked at me with her mad eyes – she didn't take her eyes off me the whole time – and then she put the boxing gloves up, not in a punching way, but with the thumbs facing me, like she was making cat paws. Obviously we hadn't been taught anything in nursing school about how to deal with that so I just kind of stood there. Then I realised she wasn't going to move, so after a while I started sort of edging my way around her and under the arch and into the reception.

Later on, when I was in the staff room being introduced to everyone as one of the 'new nurses' with the 'new program', I said something like, 'I noticed one of your patients, the woman with the boxing gloves . . .' And one of the big male nurses – they were mostly male nurses and they were all big, because who else was going to be able to handle people on the mental ward? – said, 'Oh, that's Madam Ali.'

I said, 'Madam Ali? What's a Madam Ali?' And the male nurse said, 'You know, like Muhammad Ali?'

I couldn't work out what he was getting at, so I said, 'She's a boxer?' And they all thought that was so funny. The male nurse was laughing and saying, 'She's not a boxer! But she's got to wear the boxing gloves every day, and because she wears the boxing gloves we call her Ali, like Muhammad Ali.'

I still didn't get it so I said, 'But why does she have to wear the boxing gloves every day?' And the male nurse said, 'Because if we take them off she'd try to take her eyeballs out, and yours too if you're not careful.'

Maybe you're wondering if I started to have second thoughts about that time, but I didn't, I was outraged like only somebody who is straight out of college can be outraged. Everybody thought this woman was funny and the best way to treat her was to put boxing gloves on her. I was thinking, 'Okay, so they were right about Caloola, it's got some nasty people working here,' because basically I couldn't believe how they could be so cruel to somebody with a mental problem, and laugh at her like that.

So that should give you an idea of how much I had to learn, Jack. I had *a lot* to learn.

Anyway, I decided on my second day at Caloola to pin up a piece of cardboard on the noticeboard to show people that because I was one of the new Normalisation Aides, I would be doing things differently, and maybe they could do the same if they wanted to make Caloola a place where we were all proud to work, and blah blah.

I got a big piece of cardboard and a permanent marker and I copied a list of 'values' from one of my normalisation lectures, and I can still see it. It was something like:

We respect:

- The right of every individual to achieve their maximum potential.

We behave:

- With respect toward the patients in our care.

We are accountable:

- For the decisions that we make.

I took that card in and put it up in the staff room with little balls of Blu Tack and tried not to care when people came along and put graffiti on it and changed it to read: 'And remember, don't feed the animals' on the bottom, because all of us Normalisation Aides had been told that there would be opposition to what we were doing and to just ignore it and soldier on.

Part of my job was to introduce these new communication boards that were all the rage then. They're like boards with big letters on them in squares, and the idea was you'd prop them in front of a patient and you'd hold the patient's arm by the elbow and let their finger dangle over the board and you'd see what kind of message they'd punch out.

I asked one of the Caloola managers what was the best group of patients to give the communication boards to, and she said, 'You can try it on whoever you like, Snow, and we very much look forward to watching.' I could tell that she was being sarcastic but I thought that was typical because she was 'old thinking' and I was 'new thinking', and as soon as the 'old thinking' people saw what us 'new thinking' people could do, they'd all jump on the bandwagon.

I asked one of the male nurses to help me get a group of patients together so I could demonstrate how to use a communication board. He was grinning at me nearly as much as the manager I'd asked, but at least he agreed, and said, 'Sure, let's get some of the Front Ward patients together.'

SISTERS OF MERCY

Although I didn't really know it then, the Front Ward patients weren't disabled, but they were completely crazy. I don't know if the male nurse went out of his way to get the freakiest patients he could find, but when I got to the classroom he'd set up there were ten men there and they were all grinning and mewing like cats, and all of them had those white, white three-day-growth beards that you see a lot of in mental hospitals because nobody would have wanted to go near them with a razor.

I tried not to worry about it, and I went around and handed out the communication boards. I told the patients what they were for and how they were supposed to use them and I said how I was looking forward to hearing what they had to say and not to be frightened because, once we all got the hang of it, they would be able to use them to communicate and how exciting would that be?

I was walking around putting one board on each table in front of each patient and then I saw that the boards were landing on the floor just as fast as I was putting them down. The patients were throwing them down, thinking it would be great fun to get me to pick them all up again.

Then one of the patients started hitting another patient on the head with his board and that was soon the new game, one patient using his board to belt all the other patients.

The male nurse and the others who had been standing at the back of the room, arms crossed, waiting to see what would happen, were falling about laughing, but I was determined not to let them get to me so I kept on saying, 'Now, come on, this is government equipment, it's very expensive, and I've ordered it especially for you. It's important that you treat it with respect.' But by this time the patients were taking their communication boards and putting them in their mouths or throwing them around like frisbees.

Some people might have given up at that point but not me. Oh no, I couldn't let the whole normalisation thing go. I'd been told a hundred times not to expect miracles and that things would take time to change so maybe it was just a matter of taking it one patient at a time. So I picked out one patient – his name was Hugh, and he was pretty young, maybe twenty, and he couldn't go anywhere unless he was in one of those chairs with the padded headrests – and I sat with him for, I don't know, maybe a year, trying to get him to punch out just one letter on the stupid communication board.

No, okay, I'm exaggerating, it wasn't a year, but it felt like a year that I had my hand under his elbow and his arm dangling down over the communication board, just waiting, waiting, *waiting* for him to tap a letter, any letter. And it just never happened, Jack, and I don't say that to make a point, it's just the truth.

Not once in all the time that I sat with Hugh, or with any of the other so-called smart patients at Caloola, did any of them make their hand like a beak over a water bowl, like they'd told us they'd do, and poke at a letter. But that was obviously not the result I was supposed to report back to my supervisors at the Health Department because when I did report that back, they basically said, 'You must be doing it wrong.'

I was absolutely sure that I was doing it right but they still felt the need to send some expert over to Caloola to give me more training. So then there were two of us sitting with this one patient, waiting for him to punch out something like, 'I am Hugh,' and to my absolute amazement, he actually did.

SISTERS OF MERCY

My supervisor was rapt, saying, 'See, it just takes time!' But I'm not stupid, I could see that the expert was helping him, meaning I'm pretty sure the expert was guiding his hand toward the letters.

I won't bore you with any more examples, except to say that I gave up on the communication boards not long after that, and started on some other programs, such as seeing if the patients could dress themselves instead of being dressed, and you'll be pleased to hear that that was nearly as successful as the communication boards.

I'd go onto the wards with a great pile of clothes in my arms and I'd sit down in a chair next to some drooling woman and I'd say, 'Now, Mrs Mulligan – or whatever her name was – today you're going to get dressed on your own.' And I'd hand her a pair of woolly socks and she'd put them over her hands and wave them at me, like they were sock puppets, and I'd say, 'No, no. Socks go on your feet. Here, let me do it.' And then I'd have to put on her socks for her, which defeats the whole purpose.

None of this would happen without an audience of other nurses who had been at Caloola for years, who would hoot and carry on, because who was I to think that I knew how to do everything better than they did? Now I'm thinking back on it, I get how it must have looked to them – all of us young goody-two-shoes types coming in to tell them how to do things – and I don't blame them for getting patients to play tricks on me, which they did, *all the time.*

For example, they asked me if I wanted to see one of the patients do a magic trick, and when I asked what it was the nurses said, 'We call it Hide the Pea.'

I said, 'Sure, that would be great, let's play Hide the Pea.'

101

They said to the patient, 'Go on, do your Hide the Pea trick.' And he pulled down his pants and stuck a pea from his dinner plate into the eye of his penis and then he started laughing. It turned out he wasn't a patient at all, he was another nurse, called in to set me up, but like I said, I had been told to expect all this and not to give up.

I don't know how long I'd been there when I hit on my next big idea – taking patients into town to get haircuts so they wouldn't have to wear the same bowl cut for years on end. I remember telling one of the managers, 'I'm sure the local hairdresser would want a bit of extra business,' and again she seemed to find it very funny because she said, 'Very good, Snow. If you want to take some patients into town for a haircut, you hop to it. Let's see what happens.'

Of course I couldn't do it on my own so I rounded up some other staff, and I got one of what they called the Sunbury Citizens' Advocates who were volunteering at Caloola to help me, and off we went, five patients and five nurses or other aides, into town for haircuts.

I probably don't need to tell you it was a complete disaster. First the patients wouldn't sit still on the bus, I suppose because they hadn't seen outside the walls of Caloola for, what, ten, twenty years, who even knew? Then the hairdresser, who had been all for it on the phone, looked horrified to see us because I suppose until you see five mental patients together you don't really know what it's going to be like.

There was no way to stop the patients roaming around her salon and picking everything up, and one of them tore a page out of the *Cosmopolitan* and put it in his mouth. And then when we got back to Caloola there was a message waiting at reception that a pair of scissors was missing, which sent a chill right through me.

SISTERS OF MERCY

But did I give up? No! Next on my list of things to try was lessons in money, because if any of the patients at Caloola were ever going to learn to live 'in the community', which was after all the point of the whole normalisation program, they'd have to learn how to use money and maybe even how to earn it.

The best jobs for disabled people in those days was to sit in wheelchairs under the clocks at Flinders Street station and sell copies of the *Herald*, but that program only lasted until a gang of punks turned up and bashed one of our patients who was half-blind and in a wheelchair. They also stole his money tin.

From there it was onto the football program, which was the simplest idea of all: let's round up twenty patients and take them to the footy, maybe once a month. Not to the real footy at the MCG, but just down the road to Sunbury Oval to watch the local team play. How hard could that really be?

Pretty hard, as it turned out, and especially after one of the Sunbury Citizens' Advocates, who was supposed to be helping me, lost sight of one of the patients for something like five minutes and by the time we found him he had a little girl cornered in the toilet block, and her mother threatened to sue.

Perhaps you're thinking, 'Well, maybe the problem was you, Snow. Maybe you were out of your depth and didn't know what you were doing.' And that's fine, you can think that, but the truth is, it wasn't me that was no good, it was the whole normalisation program that wasn't working, and the reason it wasn't working was because the people we had at Caloola *weren't* normal. They were crazy, or they were retarded, and all the social work mumbo-jumbo in the world wasn't going to change that fact. Once I'd finally come to accept that I found myself on the side of the other nurses, the old-timers, just trying to keep the people at Caloola on track and under supervision, so they didn't hurt themselves or anyone else, and whatever it took to achieve that was fine.

But did the do-gooders in government get that? No, in fact they came to Caloola one afternoon to tell us how normalisation was being rolled out everywhere and pretty soon all the mental hospitals would be closed and all the mental patients would be living in the community.

I stood up at that meeting and I said, 'You must be kidding. You're talking about putting people who eat their own poo out onto the streets? Can you imagine any of the patients we have here living next door to you?'

The do-gooder got nervous and laughed and said, 'Oh, it won't be like that. They'll be home with their families,' and that made me laugh because, like every nurse, I knew perfectly well that none of the patients at Caloola had any families who actually wanted them home, and maybe you think I'm exaggerating but it's true.

Sure, we had plenty of people who didn't mind *visiting* their relatives in Caloola – just like on the geriatric ward, we sometimes had a lot of visitors, especially on Sundays – but they didn't want to take their crazy relatives with them when they left. They wanted to come in at around midday and park their cars and come up from the car park with their picnic blankets and cut sandwiches and a thermos of tea. They'd set themselves up under one of the gum trees, and wait while we nurses came out with their mad relatives and sat them down, and we'd usually supervise, to make sure the mad relative didn't go through the visitor's handbag and steal their wallet.

SISTERS OF MERCY

Then, after about an hour, the family would pack up and leave, and I knew how they were feeling: they were grateful to be able to get away and leave their problem with us, because they knew, deep down, that they couldn't do what we did. And they didn't want to do any of it. I suppose the reason I'm telling you that is to explain to you that for all the nasty things people said about Caloola – it was like a prison for people who hadn't committed any crime, blah blah – we actually kept those people safe and we kept them fed and they could smoke and they could watch TV, and that was about the best anyone could expect.

Anyway, I'd better stop soon because it's going to be lights out, but before I sign off, just so you know, I left Caloola the year before they closed it, so I wasn't one of those who had to get turfed out. And also, whatever people say about Caloola, one good thing came out of that place: it was where I met Mark Delaney.

Snow

Chapter Ten

To my mind, it's not possible to tell the story of how Snow ended up in prison without also describing the kind of man she picked for herself, back when she was still in her twenties and working at Caloola.

She calls that man Mark Delaney, and that's fair enough – that became his name – but it's not the name he was given at birth. Mark's first name when he was born was *Marcel*, and his last name was Friedgut, but for reasons we can all probably understand, he hated that name and changed it pretty much as soon as he found out that he could.

The picture I'm going to build of him is mostly sourced from files held by the old delinquent boys' homes he ended up in. All make clear that while Mark liked to describe himself as a 'Bondi boy' that wasn't true: he was born in a tent on a hillside near the Snowy Mountains Project in New South Wales. His mother was a prostitute who went up there to service the migrants arriving in waves to help build the thing.

SISTERS OF MERCY

The way Mark liked to tell the story to his social workers, his mum fell pregnant with him while she was on the game, and since there was no single mother's pension and no legal abortion up there on the hillside, she had to convince one of her clients to marry her. The person she chose wasn't Mark's natural father (she probably didn't know who his natural father was), he was a migrant who had come out after the war to work as an electrician.

His name was Hans Helmut Friedgut.

Documents from Births, Deaths and Marriages in New South Wales show that he married Mark's mum, Joan, in April of 1950, and that Mark – in those days, he was still Marcel – was born in July. The couple and their new baby stayed up on the mountain until the Snowy project finished, and then came down so Helmut could find work.

They settled first in Albury, and then in Shepparton, where Mark's mum got a job in the cannery. She also pumped out three more sons, none of whom looked like Mark. One of the pictures I found clipped to his old Baltara Boys' Home file shows a short kid with a carrot top, and a couple of gashes to the forehead, probably from beatings that old Mr Friedgut used to hand out to him.

The Friedgut kids, by contrast, and by which I mean the kids actually sired by old Hans, had olive skin and black hair and they were as big as bears. From the reports I've read, they regularly beat the crap out of Mark on the grounds that he wasn't a real brother, a fact obvious to all of them.

By the age of ten, Mark was in trouble at school. He'd already been to at least four of them, because the family was always on the move, but this time he was being expelled for lashing out at other kids with sticks, biting and kicking the teachers, and throwing furniture around the classroom.

If expulsion was the punishment for that at school, I don't want to think what old Mr Friedgut did when he got hold of him.

By the age of twelve, he'd done his first stint in the Baltara Boys' Home, and he was only just out of there when Friedgut dropped dead from a heart attack, leaving his mum a widow.

His mum went back on the game for a while (she had four boys, after all), and started drinking and taking drugs, and she was committed to Caloola in 1963.

By most accounts, Mark was the only one of her sons who stayed close to her. He made regular trips over the years to see her in what he called 'the loony bin'.

One staff member who worked at Caloola in the 1970s, who didn't want me to use his name in connection with the place, says he remembers Mark as short and fat, with a sandy-orange mullet and stars tattooed across his knuckles. It doesn't exactly make him sound like a dreamboat.

He also had a decent criminal record, which I've been able to access through Freedom of Information.

Before he even met Snow, Mark had six convictions for possession, mostly of small amounts of marijuana, but also speed; plus three fines for drink driving (including two loss of licence); one conviction of being in possession of a controlled substance without a prescription (Valium); and, more troublingly, a conviction for 'exposure', which is what they used to call it when men flashed in public.

In case you're thinking he calmed down after they met in the late 80s, he didn't. The record shows that he was arrested at 3.35 a.m. on 15 December 1995, for example, after becoming involved in an altercation at the Bondi Hotel, during which he crushed a glass in his fist and required stitches.

At 4.10 a.m. on 19 September 1996, he was arrested outside the Golden Sheaf in Double Bay, bleeding from grazes on his elbows. Security staff said he had walked from the hotel onto the street with a drink in his hand and, when challenged to return his glass, he chose instead to put the security guard against the wall by the throat.

On 14 April 1997, he verbally abused a female bartender at the Esplanade Hotel in Melbourne's St Kilda – no record of why he was there, since he was living with Snow in Bondi by then – and, when asked to leave the premises by the back door, he staggered down the laneway and was later seen in the taxi queue challenging other patrons to fight him.

Given the picture I'm painting it's probably worth asking why Snow was smitten, pretty much on sight.

I've read all the reports the various psychologists have done on Snow since she's been in prison, and they all come to the same conclusion: that Mark got his hooks into her when she was still young enough to be vulnerable. She'd been raised in what they used to call a 'broken home', with her father mostly absent; she didn't like her step-father; she'd had that abortion; and her first attempt at some kind of professional success had fallen in a heap with the failure of the normalisation project at Caloola. So she was badly in need of being 'rescued'.

Reading those reports I wasn't convinced. Couldn't it simply be that Snow saw a kindred spirit in Mark, I wondered? A bloke as strange and cold as she is? Had anyone asked *Snow* how she saw things? I wasn't sure that they had, so I wrote to her, putting the obvious question: what did a girl like you see in a bloke like that?

Chapter Eleven

Dear Jack,

I've ripped into you a few times for getting stuff wrong, but at least you've never said that I met Mark Delaney on the Front Ward at Caloola, as if he was a patient there like some other reporters I could name.

I mean, I did meet him on the Front Ward but he wasn't a patient. His mum, old Joan Friedgut, was a patient and she'd been there for twenty years, maybe more, before I even arrived.

You're probably thinking, 'How could Mark's mother be "old Joan Friedgut" when he was called Mark Delaney?' But it should be obvious that anyone called 'Friedgut' would want to change their name. You're supposed to say it Fried-*Goot* not Fried-*Gut*, but I can tell you that nobody called old Mrs Friedgut Friedgoot, she was always Fried-guts.

Mark thought it made him sound like a wog, which was another good reason to change it.

Mark's mother wasn't a wog, she was Australian, and when I got to Caloola she was already there and nobody seemed to know why exactly, meaning what the actual psychiatric diagnosis was, but she was pretty much zonked out the whole time with drugs we had to give her.

I saw you made a big point in one of your articles of saying that it was interesting that Mark's mother was in Caloola, and I know what you were getting at. You were trying to say, 'Oh, well, Mark's mother was in Caloola and she was psychotic and don't these things run in families?'

That might be true for schizophrenia and maybe for depression but Mark was not a depressed person. He had a drinking problem and he couldn't control his temper when he was drunk, but both of those things were pretty normal when you consider what he had to put up with when he was growing up.

Anyway, you wanted to know how we met so I'll tell you: Mark would come up to see his mum at Caloola and I'd be there on the ward, simple as that. Why he came up to visit his mother I don't know because like you made clear in one of your articles, she was a prostitute before he was born and the only reason she married that old Hans Friedgut was because she couldn't figure out who Mark's father was.

In case you don't know how I know that Mark's mother was a prostitute, he told me. It was back when he was still a visitor at Caloola and I was brushing his mum's hair and I asked, 'What did your mum do before she ended up here?' And he said, 'She was a whore.' I nearly dropped the brush because that's not the kind of thing you hear every day, and then I said, 'Oh, Mark, you shouldn't say that. Maybe she wasn't nice to you – my mother wasn't nice to me either – but you can't call her a whore.'

He said, 'No, she was a *whore whore*,' meaning an actual prostitute, and that shocked me because I didn't know any prostitutes and now I was standing there brushing one's hair. Anyway, Mark told me that his dad was probably one of his mum's customers and she'd told him once that she wouldn't have bothered to have him except by the time she found out it was too late to have an abortion. So she'd looked around instead for somebody who might want to marry her, and there was old Friedgut waiting by the tent for his turn.

He told Mark's mum he was from Bosnia or maybe Croatia, but with a name like that I'd say he was German and he didn't want to admit it, because Germans were a bit on the nose after the war, not that it matters what he was other than a drunk who smashed holes in every wall of every house they ever lived in.

People like to bag Mark, call him a thug with a big criminal record, but when you know about him – that he was in and out of boys' homes when he was a kid and that his mum was a crazy person and his step-dad used to beat him up all the time – what do people expect?

I'm not trying to say he never did anything wrong because the record is there for anyone to see, but he had a bad start in life and that has to count for something. Back when we first started going out, Mark would tell me stories like the time his step-dad told his mother to stop feeding him and he got so hungry he started stealing lunches from the other kids at whatever school he was going to then. The teachers told welfare and the welfare workers went up to the school and asked Mark, 'Where's your lunch?' He had to say, 'I don't get any.'

Then the welfare people had to go and talk to his mum and they saw all the other fat Friedgut kids running around, and his mum was shaking and crying and they tried to talk to old Mr Friedgut, saying, 'You have to feed all of them. You can't starve one of them.' And Friedgut said, 'Why should I put food in his mouth when he isn't mine?'

But Mark got his revenge because when old Friedgut had his heart attack Mark was the one who saw him go down on the kitchen floor. He saw him lying there on his back with bubbles coming out of his mouth, and he was reaching up to Mark, like 'help me, help me', but there was no way Mark was going to help him.

Pretty soon after that, Mark was back in Baltara and then later he was in the Tamworth Boys' Home. I don't know what you know about that place but they used to make the new boys put cardboard boxes on their heads when they arrived, so the other boys could kick and punch them. By the time he got out, his mum had gone crazy, but he always went to see her at Caloola. He visited her for twenty years and he was there on the day she died, and I know that because I was there, on the ward, and I walked by and saw he was crying. His mum's eyes were wide open and she was staring up at the ceiling, and Mark was sitting near her bed. I sprinted across the room, took her by the arm and tried to find a pulse, knowing it was hopeless. I said to him then, 'What happened? Did she just go?' And he could hardly talk about it.

Maybe people will say, 'Oh, please, you just want us to take pity on him,' but he didn't want pity.

I sat next to him with his mum not breathing in the bed beside us and I said, 'It wasn't much of a life she had, anyway,' and he agreed with me and a couple of days later he was back to collect his mum's things, not that there were very many of those, and he said, 'I wonder if a girl like you would go out with a loser like me?'

It was a bit of a shock to hear him say that because his mother had just died and I did think to myself, 'Be careful, Snow, this isn't something you want to get involved in, because he's just missing his mum,' but the look on his face was like a big kid and I thought, 'Well, how bad would it be to go out on a date with him just now when his mum has died? Maybe a bit creepy but not too creepy.' So I said, 'Yes, okay.' I was glad I did because it cheered him up straightaway. And then, even after just seeing him a couple of times, I knew that he was Mr Right.

What did I see in him? Who can say what anyone sees in someone? You either like somebody or you don't. I hadn't had that many boyfriends – not after what happened with Vincent – so it felt pretty good when Mark came with a bunch of red roses for my birthday and did other nice things. We went to St Kilda to look at the beach and we talked about how we'd both got duds for mothers, and after a while I was just thinking about him all the time.

The problem we had was that he was living in Bondi and he'd only been coming down to Melbourne to visit his mum. If we wanted to talk on the phone when he went home we had to make STD phone calls from phone boxes and we were always running out of twenty-cent pieces. One of us would have to move and I thought it might as well be me because what did I have in Melbourne except Mum, who was still going around with Mr Cooper, and Dad, who was working in the shop?

Mark came down to help me pack up my things and we got the bus to Sydney and I remember the driver stopped at the border at Albury so we could stand with one foot in Victoria and one foot in New South Wales, and I got all excited to see cars with New South Wales plates, and street signs in a different colour, that's how innocent I was.

The bus dropped us at Central station – a really nice old stone station, not like Spencer Street – and Mark was great: he got my suitcase from under the bus, and hauled it down to the next corner so we could get the bus to Bondi, and then he carried it all the way up to Mrs Bannerman's house.

I'd never met Mrs Bannerman before that. Mark had told me he lived with an old lady called Mrs Bannerman, and that she had been a friend of Mark's mother from the Snowy Mountains days. He said that whenever old Mr Friedgut beat Mark's mum up too much, she'd take Mark and the other kids and they'd go to Mrs Bannerman's because she had a boarding house, and they'd stay there until he sobered up and came and got her.

Mark liked it at Bondi: there was a milk bar on the corner where he could get a milkshake and he liked the beach, so when he found himself with nowhere to live after his mum went into Caloola, he gave Mrs Bannerman a knock on her door and explained the situation, and offered to do odd jobs around the place. She took him under her wing and let him live with her, and that was in the 1960s so he'd been there more than twenty years before I arrived on the scene.

I remember walking down the hill to the house – it was so humid my clothes were sticking to me – and I remember Mark saying, so here we are, and the place looked like it was falling down. People say it was huge but I had come from Caloola, remember, and Caloola was that much bigger so it didn't look 'huge' to me – just big and old and ugly.

Mark had a key to the front gate so we went through and down this path toward the back of the house, and there was a huge crater in the back yard big enough to sink a car in. I asked him what that was about and he said it had been there since some Japanese sub had shelled Bondi, and if you don't believe me go and look it up, it actually happened, the Japs did bomb Bondi.

I said, 'But why did it just get left like that?' And Mark said that Mrs Bannerman's husband had gone on for years about how he was going to fill it but the lazy bastard's idea of filling it was to fill it up with junk. And it was *filled* with junk.

I was standing pretty close to the edge of the crater. Mark said, 'You want to be careful you don't step too close. The sides give way.'

I said, 'It's like a tip in there,' and it was, with old metal and washing machines and everything all strewn together.

Mark said, 'You think there's a lot of stuff now, back when I moved here, there was ancient stuff that you don't even see any more: an old ringer, for getting water out of clothes, and the old wash bowls with jugs that have flowers and shit painted on them.' And he said a lot of that stuff only got taken away because some people from that show, *The Sullivans*, came and knocked on the door one day saying, 'We heard you have things from before the war, and can we have a look?'

Mrs Bannerman told them, 'You can have a look but only if you take it away,' because she still had boarders in those days and it was dangerous, so they came back with trailers and scooped out what they wanted, but didn't fill the crater in and pretty soon it was full of junk again. Anyway, we picked our way around the crater, with Mark saying, 'Hey, Aunt Beth, are you around?' There was no answer but then we got to this spot behind the passionfruit vines and there was this woman standing there.

You should have seen what she was wearing! She looked like a wizard, or a witch or something, because she had a heavy burgundy robe made of some kind of velvet – maybe velour – and bits of it had worn away, leaving all these shiny patches and it looked heavy and hot and the hem of the thing was filthy.

She had a pile of dead hair, the same colour as the dress, all bunched up and pinned in a bun on the top of her head, and her face was lined like an elephant's. She was brown like the wood of a tree and she must have been able to see us, we were standing right in front of her, but she didn't say hello or anything, she just stood under that passionfruit vine, grinning.

Mark said, 'Hey, Aunt Beth,' and walked over to her and clicked his fingers in her face, and she barely even responded. Since I'd been in Caloola and knew a few things, I was thinking, 'Uh oh, there's nobody home,' because there was nothing behind those eyes.

Mark kept saying, 'Hey, Aunt Beth, this is Snow.' But Aunt Beth didn't say 'Hello' or 'How are you?' or 'Welcome' or even 'Snow, did you say Snow?' which is what everyone says when they first get introduced to me. And I was about to say, 'Well, hi,' but then Aunt Beth looked at me and said, 'I can do all my exercises from physical culture!'

That made no sense obviously, but next thing I knew Mrs Bannerman got down on the ground and lay in the dirt and started cycling her legs above her head, like she was doing the bicycle.

SISTERS OF MERCY

Mark was saying, 'Don't do that, Aunt Beth.' But it was as though she couldn't hear him, because she stayed on the small of her back, in the dirt, cycling. And then she rolled over onto her side and scrambled to her feet and said, 'Star jumps!' And she started doing star jumps. Then she said, 'And leg kicks!' She had her hands on her hips and was high-kicking – not easy in that robe she had on – and then she said, 'And now marching!' She started marching up and down, like she was in some kind of band, and Mark kept saying, 'Will you stop, Aunt Beth?' But it was like she couldn't stop. She was saying, 'Fit as a fiddle!' And her arms were pumping, and the dead hair bun on her head was bouncing, and I'll be honest, she was as demented as any person I'd ever seen, and I'd seen a few.

Finally Mark said, 'Don't worry about her, just come inside.' So we picked our way across all the junk and around the massive pit and went into the house through the front door. I can tell you, it was as rundown inside as it was out. The boarders were long gone and there was mould on the walls, the floorboards squeaked, there was rust in the sinks and rings in the baths, and foam coming out of the chairs. There were dinner plates on stands, including one with the marriage of Charles and Diana, and they were all dusty, and there were lace curtains that had never been washed because the holes between the lace were caked in dirt. The curtains were so stiff they would have stood up on their own.

Mark said, 'Don't tell me, I know! She's a crazy old coot.'

I said, 'What does the doctor say?'

He said, 'She doesn't want to see a doctor, and I don't need a doctor to tell me that she's a screw loose. You saw yourself.'

I said, 'She probably needs to see somebody.'

But Mark said, 'Good luck with that!' And that was fair enough because even though I tried a few times over the years to talk Mrs Bannerman into going to see a doctor with me, she wouldn't listen. She'd stick her fingers in her ears and say la-la-la.

I said, 'Are you sure it's going to be okay for me to live here?'

Mark said, 'Like she'd even know?' Which was probably true – she wouldn't have known if I was there or not. He took me through the kitchen to his bedroom – our bedroom – on the ground floor near the front of the house. I said, 'Where does your Aunt Beth sleep?' And he said she had a room upstairs but she never used it, and now that I think of it I don't think I saw her in the house more than once or twice in the whole time I was there. And if she ever saw a person, even down in her patch under the passionfruit vine, she'd run off with whatever robe she had on flapping behind her.

Mark told me, 'She wants to sleep outside.'

I said, 'Are you kidding?'

He said, 'No, in that bungalow, whatever you want to call it, out near the passionfruit. It's got holes in the ceiling but that's what she likes.'

I was pretty keen to see inside that bungalow, but it wasn't like Mrs Bannerman was ever going to invite me in since she'd never even said hello to me, so I crept around the crater one day and poked my head in there, and I saw it had stained-glass windows, and wedged into the window, at the height of the sill, there was what they call a day bed, which was where she must have curled up like a cat and slept.

Mark's bedroom was a bit different, since it had a big brass bed that made me feel a bit jealous when I saw it – why did he need a big bed like that, when he told me he didn't take girlfriends around to Mrs Bannerman's? But then I thought, 'Maybe it's been there since the place was a boarding house.'

The only other thing Mark had was a milk crate for a bedside table, and maybe he could tell that I was looking a bit worried about it because he said, 'You can make it nice if you want.' So later that week I went to Kmart and bought a new doona, sheets, pillows, pillowcases, towels, a lamp, pots, pans, plates and cutlery for the kitchen. I had money saved from when I'd been working at Caloola, which was just as well because Mark had no money, though it wasn't his fault because as I was soon to find out Mark had a gambling problem. That's an addiction, like a sickness, and it was hard for him to work because he had this obsession with needing to be at the pokies. He was always thinking, 'If I'm not there at the machine when the numbers come up, how can I ever win?' And yes, he would take my money and put it in the pokies, but that's because he was always thinking of money as an investment in the jackpot he was going to win one day.

It was because Mark didn't work that I had to find a new job pretty much as soon as I got to Sydney. Mark didn't see the point, saying, 'Why don't you just go on the dole?' because he'd been on the dole for years, but I don't think people should get money for doing nothing. I mean, Mark's situation was obviously different to mine: he had his addictions, not just gambling but the choof as well, and that was because he'd had a lot of pain in his life. Thinking about it now, he probably shouldn't have been on the dole, he should have been on the disability pension, but he wasn't. He was registered with the CES – Centrelink, they call it now – for the dole plus he could get money out of Mrs Bannerman's bank account on pension days so he could handle all the bills for her house.

Anyway, I made some enquiries and found out that there was a home for geriatrics up on O'Brien Street in Bondi, and since geriatrics was where I did some of my training they hired me straightaway. Mark couldn't get his head around that kind of work, saying, 'That old person's smell is disgusting.' And maybe it is, but we needed the money. I realise that maybe I'm making it sound like I was working my guts out and Mark was at home on the bong and on the TAB account, but that isn't the way it was. He was pretty good about fixing up some things in the house that needed fixing. Like, when I complained about the state of the front garden, he walked down to the old hardware store on Hall Street – it's gone now, turned into a café – and bought a pair of shears and got stuck into the trees, and started clipping them to look like animals. I mean, he started by just clipping them and then he stood back and said, 'Look at that, Snow, it looks just like a lollipop.' And then he decided the lollipop should be an emu, and before long we had two emus in the front, and another tree shaped like a kangaroo.

He was rapt when some old bloke from across the road hollered out, 'You're doin' a good job there, mate!' He even talked for a bit about starting a business, doing manicured trees, because people would actually stop in the street and hold their kids up to look over the fence. We'd hear them saying, 'Look at the tree, cut like a kangaroo. Isn't that clever?' He started cutting back the Paterson's Curse that was all over the fence, but I told him to stop because I liked the jungle feel and the purple flowers.

SISTERS OF MERCY

Maybe you're thinking, 'Well, that's all very well and good but what else did he ever do? Sit at the pokie machines and suck on his bong?' But like most people who have got these problems, he'd have times when he was great. Like when the Olympics came to Sydney, and everyone was signing up to volunteer. He was right into that. I admit, we both decided to volunteer mainly to get those uniforms – Mark seemed to think they would be worth something one day – and because he wanted a shot at running the torch relay. Those torches were apparently going to be worth something one day too.

I filled out the forms and we both got accepted, basically because everyone was being accepted, and we both got the uniform – I loved mine, and I still have it in a box somewhere. If you weren't in Sydney for the Olympics you missed out because it was brilliant. I was a volunteer on the torch run – we had Jane Flemming on our part of the road – and I was keeping the crowd back so she could stick to the line they'd drawn. Mark was at the main stadium at Homebush, taking tickets and doing crowd control. It was fantastic, just fantastic, and we got invited to the volunteer party, and all the government big-wigs were there, coming out to shake our hands.

But anyway, it was a week or so after the Olympics that I found out about Mark having this affair. Apparently it started at one of the Olympic volunteer pub nights. This woman was trying to hit on Mark and get him to do the 'Macarena'. I'd been saying to her, 'Forget it, no way is Mark the type to do the "Macarena". He'll punch his fist to "Khe Sanh" but he's not going to dance.' But this woman got him on his feet and she was putting his hands on his hips and doing all the movements, and he was shuffling and grinning and trying to pretend like he didn't like it.

Later I said, 'You seemed to be enjoying yourself, Mark,' and he couldn't wipe the smile off his face.

We had an argument when we got home and Mark was saying, 'No, no, there's nothing to it.' But a week later I came home from work and that same woman was sitting on my couch. Mark had his hands in her lap, and it wasn't like they weren't trying to hide what they were doing, because they didn't get up and run when they saw me, they just sat there, grinning like idiots.

I got such a shock I went out to the kitchen and starting bashing pots and pans together, basically because I couldn't think what else to do. But I could hear Mark talking quietly and when he finally came into the kitchen he said, 'I'm a man, Snow, and I've got needs like a man.'

I said, 'What am I supposed to do? I've got nowhere to go,' because at first I thought, 'If she's here, I must be out' – she was younger and all that – but Mark said, 'No, no, I'm not going to throw you out, but I want to do my thing with her too.'

I said, 'What's that supposed to mean?'

He said, 'Nothing changes.'

And I said, 'But are you going to have sex with her?'

And he said, 'I already have.'

I wanted to hit him with a pot, but he looked so happy, like a kid with a new toy, so I went into the lounge room and I sat down in the armchair and glared at his woman, and Mark said, 'Come on, Snow, just say hi.'

I said, 'Hi,' like as short, as obvious as I could that I wasn't happy about the fact that this woman was in my house and was having sex probably in my bed. But she didn't care, and they started smoking pot and getting on with each other and that's a bit boring when you're the third wheel, so I went to bed and when I got up she was at least gone.

I still gave Mark the cold shoulder, but he just kept saying, 'That's what men do, Snow, they can't control themselves. It doesn't mean that I don't want to be with you.'

I said, 'How am I supposed to believe that? It's not like we're married, and you can throw me out any time.'

He said, 'Don't start all that,' because I had been going on about why we weren't married for quite a while by then and Mark would always say, 'It's no different being married,' and I'd say, 'There's a big difference,' and he'd say, 'What would change?' and I'd say, 'My name for one thing!'

Mark said, 'If you want to change your name go ahead and change your name, I can't stop you. I might even change my own name.'

I asked him what he was talking about and he said he'd always hated the name Friedgut, and let's face it who wouldn't, and not just because it sounds strange but it was old man Friedgut's name. So I rang Births, Deaths and Marriages, and they said, 'Anyone can change their name, just come in.' So we went in, and I said to the girl behind the glass, 'He wants to change his name.'

The lady behind the counter said, 'Fair enough.'

I said, 'Does he have to know his real dad's name, or what?'

She said, 'He can call himself anything he wants, it's a free country.'

Mark said there was a motorbike rider in America that he liked whose name was Delaney and would it be alright if he picked Delaney, and the lady said, 'Okay, Marcel Delaney,' and he said,

'No, I get called Mark, so I want to be Mark on the forms too, or does that cost more?' And she said it didn't cost more.

She said, 'I'll get the form, you fill it out, you pay the fee, and you're away.' So we did that, and then she looked at me and said, 'Are we doing you at the same time?' I didn't know what she meant, so she said, 'You're his wife, aren't you? You're a Fried Guts too?'

Mark said, 'No way am I ever getting married. What's marriage, just a piece of paper.'

The lady said fine, but I said, 'I want to have the same name as you,' and he said, 'Well, change yours too, if you want.'

I looked at the lady behind the counter and said, 'Can I do that? Can I be a Delaney too?'

She said, 'You can be Humpty Dumpty if you want.'

So I said, 'Okay, give me the same forms.' And I filled them out and that was that: I was Snow Delaney. And I remember we left Births, Deaths and Marriages, and as soon as we got back to Mrs Bannerman's I got on the phone to tell Dad. I said, 'I've got news, I'm not an Olarenshaw any more!'

He said, 'Don't tell me you married that Mark bloke,' or something like that, because it's no secret that Dad didn't much approve of Mark, although how he came to any conclusion about him I don't know since they hardly even saw each other. But anyway, I said, 'No, no, Mark doesn't believe in marriage, but now we've got the same name so it's nearly as good!' I could tell he didn't see it that way, though.

Anyway, that's when Dad said, 'Well, we've got news too, Snow,' and I remember thinking, 'Who is this "we" he's going on about?' And then he said, 'Your mum and me, we've gotten back together.'

SISTERS OF MERCY

I was that shocked I nearly dropped the phone. Straightaway I smelled a rat because Mum hadn't paid the slightest bit of attention to Dad for twenty years and now they were back together? I said, 'So what brought this on?' And that's when he just cracked up crying, saying, 'Your mum's got cancer, Snow, she's come back because she needs me.' I wanted to know what had happened to Mr Cooper, but apparently he ran off as soon as he got the news that one of Mum's boobs was going to have to come off, so with no shame at all my mother had got on the phone to Dad and said, 'You have to come back, I need you.'

I don't have to tell you how I felt about it. I said to Dad, 'So, let me get this straight: she turfed you out, moved another bloke in, and then when she calls you in a crisis and says, oh, please help me, you run straight over there?' And do you know what he told me, Jack? He said, 'What can I tell you, Snow? Your mother is the love of my life.'

But didn't I already know that? I knew that from how Dad used to come and visit me in Deer Park after my mother moved Mr Cooper in, and all he wanted to know was, 'How is she, Snow? How is she?' It had actually got to the point where I refused to talk to him about it. I'd visit my father for Christmas, or Easter or my birthday, or I'd call him on Father's Day, and he'd say, 'How's your mother doing?'

I'd say, 'Why don't you ask her?'

That was a bit cruel because she wasn't talking to him, but why should I have had to act like a telephone between them? And why did he stay stuck on her for years and years when he could have just done what everyone does and take up with somebody else? I'm sure he would have had offers, because he had that shop, Olarenshaw

Electrics, so he wasn't a dole bludger, and there were plenty of old single women around in Deer Park, at the bowls club and everywhere else, who might have wanted to marry him. But when I asked him why he didn't take up with one of them, he said, 'I got married once, and it was for life.'

But anyway, they were back together and even worse Dad was saying, 'Snow, you've got to come and see her.'

I said, 'Why do I have to see her?'

He said, 'She's got cancer. She's going to have treatment. You're a nurse, you understand these things.'

I didn't want to do it, but the fact is I loved Dad, and if he loved Mum what was I supposed to do about it? And thinking about it now, there was one other thing that Dad said around that time that I probably should have picked up on but didn't, and it only makes sense now that I'm thinking about it.

He said, 'You don't know what we've been through together. Your mother has had to do some hard things in her life. I wasn't always there to help her.'

I had zero interest at the time in asking Dad what he was talking about, but anyway, I went down to Melbourne to see them. Mum had already started chemo by the time I got there and was bald and wearing a scarf. I had a look through the medication she was taking, and it seemed to be pretty much what cancer patients were then being given to buy them a bit more time.

I asked her how she knew she was sick, meaning how did they pick up the cancer? She said, 'Oh, I'd gone down to the haberdashery to pick up some material for some curtains and bang, I fell over, flat on my face on the floor.'

SISTERS OF MERCY

She said, 'I don't know how long I was out, Snow, but when I came around, the old lady whose shop it was had put some wool under my head and was fanning me with a Butterick pattern. All I could see were these lovely faces looking down at me.'

She said, 'Honestly, Snow, it was like Muldoon's picnic, what with the butcher and the green grocer next door. They said, "You fainted," and I reached up and there was a bump the size of an egg on my forehead. They insisted on calling an ambulance and just as well because when I got to hospital they ran the tests, and they found the cancer.'

She told me she'd booked in to see her doctor while I was there so I went with her to see her doctor and it was all pretty straightforward: Mum would get treated, and then she'd probably have a few good years. Not that Dad wanted to believe that. All through the chemo and for a few months afterwards, he was saying, 'She's still clear, Snow! Doing great in remission! I think we've got this beat!'

They didn't have it beat because about a year after the Olympics, Dad phoned up, saying, 'You have to come, Snow,' and I didn't want to go because of the whole fiasco with Mark and the woman he brought home from the pub not that long before, but I could tell from Dad's voice that Mum's cancer was back. So I asked my boss if I could go and see her and they were absolute bastards about it, saying: 'You don't have leave, you can't go indefinitely.'

I said, 'My mother's dying,' and one of the managers actually had the hide to say, 'But you can't tell me how long that's going to take, can you? And we can't cover you forever, you know.' So I quit on the spot.

It was September 2001, and I remember that because it was only a week or so after those attacks in New York and there were a lot of cheap flights around. Dad picked me up from Deer Park railway station. He would have been eighty by then, still wearing those Yakka pants with the crease down the front, the ones he wore every day of his life at Olarenshaw Electrics.

I said, 'How is she?'

He said, 'Not good.'

When we pulled in to the drive at Deer Park, he said, 'I don't want you to get a shock.'

It takes a lot to shock me, Jack. I've worked on cancer wards, remember, so I knew what to expect. My mother was lying in the lounge room in a hospital bed that my father had rented so she could be propped up to eat. The two metal sides were up and my mother was lying flat under a blanket, so thin she hardly made a mound. She was either deeply medicated or sound asleep, because she didn't stir.

I looked at the clipboard hanging from the base of the bed: blood pressure, temperature and medications, none of it looked good. I said, 'What does the doctor say?'

Dad said, 'He doesn't say much, Snow! That's one of the problems. He won't give me any idea as to when your mum might be better!'

I thought to myself, 'He must be joking. What does he mean, when she might be better?' There wasn't a chance in the world that my mother was going to be getting up off that sick bed, but Dad either couldn't or wouldn't see it. I said, 'You need to send her to one of those palliative care places, or else she's going to die here and you're going to be left to deal with the corpse.'

SISTERS OF MERCY

He looked at me like I'd said the worst thing in the world. But honestly, Jack, death and bodies, they aren't anything to me. I've seen hundreds of them: people dying over weeks and months, suffering no matter how much morphine you put into them. I've gone on to wards at Caloola and found corpses of people who had died in the night – I even found Mark's own mum, dead as a doornail in the bed that day.

Dad shook his head and said, 'No, no, the minute you go into one of those homes you start dying.' So I gave it up and said, 'Alright, you do what you want,' and flew back to Sydney, where Mark was waiting for me.

He said, 'So, how did it go?' And I said, 'Well, she's going to cark it,' because what else was I supposed to say? It wasn't like Mum and me had been close.

And oh, here's a funny thing, Jack: I remember I'd been back about a day when I noticed that old Mrs Bannerman was gone. I don't mean that *she* was dead but she wasn't out in the bungalow and she wasn't out doing calisthenics under the passionfruit vine, she wasn't anywhere. I asked Mark about it and he told me that a woman had been knocking on the door, claiming to be Aunt Beth's niece, and that Beth hadn't wanted to see her, but then she'd changed her mind and gone to visit her.

I said, 'I didn't know that Beth had a niece.'

Mark said, 'I didn't either, but that's what this woman told me, that she was Beth's niece, and when I told Beth that she'd been here, she said, no, I'm not interested in that, but then a couple of days later she put on her hat and told me she was going to visit her.'

I thought, 'Well, that's a bit dodgy, can she even catch a train or is she too demented?' I said, 'How long has she been gone?' But that's not the kind of thing that Mark will always notice, especially if he's on the choof or on the punt, so he basically said he didn't know. I thought, 'If Mark's not worried about Beth – and she's his sort of aunt – then why should I worry? She's not my aunt.'

As to what else I found when I got back to Bondi – no, it wasn't another woman sitting on my couch this time, thank God! – it was actually something nice. Mark had been out in the back yard, shifting all the junk that had got stuck in the big crater behind the back door. He'd dragged it all out, and he was finally putting up the deck I wanted.

I said to him, 'What's all this?'

He said, 'You were good to me when my mother died, and I wanted to do something good for you.'

And *that* was the kind of person Mark was, the kind of person who'd do something nice like that, without me even asking. He hired a concrete mixer from Ray's up at Bronte, and he bought decking timber, and decking oil, and big square terracotta pots, and he worked until that area behind the door there was all filled in and covered over. Then he oiled the decking timber, and picked up an old kettle barbecue. And once he was done, we sat out there with a mozzie coil burning, and things were pretty good. But I suppose I'd only been home a week when Dad called and said, 'Snow, Snow, you've got to come,' because of course Mum wasn't getting better, she'd taken a turn for the worse. So it was back on the plane and back to Deer Park.

It didn't take long after I'd got there. Mum dying, I mean. She wasn't conscious for more than three hours a day, not that it mattered since she didn't speak to me. I stayed mostly in the kitchen, scrambling eggs for Dad, who refused to go to bed to get a proper night's sleep, saying, 'No, no, I want to be here with her, in case something happens,' and then she died while I was asleep.

I woke up at around 5 a.m., which was pretty early for me, and the sun was hardly even up. I went down the hall and there was Dad with his head resting on her body. He wasn't saying anything, but like with Mark's mum, I could tell by looking that she was gone.

We had the funeral at Tobin Brothers in Altona. There were six rows of those horrible plastic seats but hardly any were taken. I'm fairly sure one of the women in the front row came because she was one of those people who read about funerals in the newspaper and come to eat the free sandwiches.

My father gave a long eulogy, full of stories about how he'd come to Australia with Mum and how they'd had me, and how happy they'd been in Deer Park and what a privilege it was to have nursed her. He didn't make one mention of the fact that she booted him out of the house and kept him dangling on a string for twenty years. And at the end of the service, he gave everyone a little Scratchie because 'Ros loved the Scratchies. Always thought she'd win the jackpot.'

I scratched mine, and didn't even get $2.

Of course I asked Dad what he was going to do now that Mum was dead. The house in Deer Park was practically falling down, the carpets hadn't been replaced in twenty years, it was way too big for him.

I said, 'Why don't you move out to one of those retirement villages?' But he said, 'Why would I do that, Snow? I want to stay in my own home.'

I said, 'How are you going to be able to cope?'

He said, 'I fended for myself for years. You'll notice I didn't starve to death.'

I said, 'But you're eighty now, Dad.'

He said, 'No, no, I want to stay in my own house,' which was a bit frustrating, because if he'd moved out I would have been able to sell that house and, sure, it might not have been worth much, maybe only $300,000 or $400,000, but it would have at least meant that I wouldn't have had to find another job because I could have managed that money for him. But as it was, with Mark's gambling, I did have to find another job and that was how I ended up at Emu Cottage.

Snow

Chapter Twelve

The locals wouldn't want to admit it but there are quite a few similarities between Bondi, where Snow lived before she went to prison, and Manly, where she was working at Emu Cottage.

They're both by the beach, and they both have at least nine gelato bars, three of which are going broke.

It isn't easy to move between the two places, however: to get from Bondi to Manly, you've got to get a bus up Bondi Road to Bondi Junction, then a train to Circular Quay, and then a JetCat across to Manly, and then it's a fair walk up a steep hill to Emu Cottage, on Emu Lane.

I know how far it is because I made the trip out there pretty much as soon as I found out that Snow used to work there. Emu Cottage wasn't a geriatric home like the one she worked in before her mum died. It was a day-care facility for disabled children. It's closed now but it wasn't too difficult to find. It's on Ocean Road and it's a timber cottage like the other ones on the street, but if you look through the windows you can see that the old pictures are still on the walls: there's a big giraffe painted in one room, and a whale in the other.

There's a ramp out the front with bright yellow aluminium handrails, like you see at childcare centres, but it's not for prams, it's for wheelchairs.

As far as I understand the chronology of events, Snow started working there early in 2002 as a senior nurse. That might sound good, but the money wasn't great – Snow and all the others were taking home around $540 a week – and Mark was by this time in the grip of a serious gambling addiction. The Star City Casino had opened in Sydney, and he was without doubt one of their best clients, eligible for all kinds of free drinks, provided he kept turning up.

The money Snow was making obviously wasn't sufficient to feed his habit because he was also taking stuff out of the old house – and off the street – and selling it on eBay.

It seems that Snow was at Emu House for about a year, and by most accounts enjoying it, when a minister in the State government announced the funding had been cut.

I've had a bit of a dig into the newspaper files at News Limited and there was a bit of coverage of that decision. One story, which was in *The Sydney Morning Herald*, had the parents of a boy called Robin who had fallen into a swimming pool as a toddler and had lain on the bottom for several minutes before he was found. The paramedics got him breathing again but he had severe developmental – and behavioural – problems.

The *Herald* story quoted his mum, saying, 'Robin comes to Emu Cottage three days a week and I don't know how we'd cope if we didn't have a place for him here. He has friends here, and they can do so much more for him than we can do at home.'

The story said the Emu Cottage parents were planning a march on Parliament House and there was a bit of coverage of that, with the disabled children in their wheelchairs and parents chanting, 'Don't Take Our Emu Away!' and parents holding up the signs saying, 'No School For Me = Discrimination!'

There's always a belief that these kinds of protests actually achieve something, but it costs a lot to run a place like Emu Cottage: it needs staff, a manager, facilities, insurance, and so on, and closing it would have been about money.

Some reporters asked the Minister for Community Services where the kids were supposed to go once Emu Cottage was gone. She said, 'We're going to fund a pool of new foster carers to take children into their homes for a few hours each week, to give the parents a bit of a break.'

They also wanted to know what was going to happen to the staff, and the Minister said they could apply to become one of the foster carers, which is precisely what Snow Delaney did.

Chapter Thirteen

Dear Jack,

You might think that I've never noticed how you don't have a good thing to say about me, but I *have* noticed and I don't think that's actually very fair because I have done good things in my life, including the work I did at Emu Cottage.

I mean, parents would come into that place with their kids in their wheelchairs and they'd leave them with us, and that might be the only break they'd get all week. We'd take the kids out on the Emu Bus to feed the seagulls at Manly or whatever and it was actually pretty fun.

When I first heard the rumours that the funding was going to be cut I thought it must be some kind of joke, because parents would actually tell us, 'I couldn't survive if I didn't have a couple of days' respite every week. I'd go out of my mind.'

I knew what they meant because it was hard keeping those kids occupied all day and we were being paid to do it in eight-hour shifts, so imagine those parents, getting no money and having them

24/7. They didn't know what to do to kill time except to sit them in front of the TV and hope they didn't scream too much. The look on their faces when they dropped them off at Emu, it was relief. They'd say, 'I just feel that he – James, or whoever he was – enjoys being here so much more,' when what they meant was, 'When he's here, he's not my problem, he's your problem.' And I don't say that because I'm judging them, because it was boring and frustrating looking after those kids.

And it's not like those kids give anything back. They don't smile and they don't laugh and one mother even told me, 'He's never spoken to me, let alone called me Mum.' Plus it's not like the child is growing up into something interesting. They're going to stay in their wheelchairs and their big nappies forever, and the bigger they get, the worse it is because you have to hoist them in and out of bed, and roll them over and change them.

When the disabled girls get to puberty they get acne that they pick and scratch so then they look ugly. They get periods and you have to manage that because they have no idea what's going on, and people take advantage of them, so you have to watch them like a hawk so they don't end up pregnant.

I remember the director of the cottage saying, 'Maybe it's a bluff, maybe they just want us to try and get the costs down,' but none of us could see how we could get the costs down because we already had only one bus for fourteen kids and we'd been cutting corners on the meals, giving everyone a slice of bread to try to bulk them out a bit.

We saw the Minister in the paper saying, 'Oh, but it will be much better for the children if they can stay at home with their parents or be out in the community,' and of course I was thinking, 'Now, where have I heard all this before? That's right, at Caloola.' Because it was all the same argument, and all the same pretending about how it was about human rights when it was actually about money.

The Minister was saying she'd get the Department to help the parents by getting foster carers to take the kids for them for a few hours a week, and some emails went around asking staff if they were interested in training as foster carers. I was thinking to myself, 'Good luck finding anyone,' because it's not like an ordinary foster carer is going to be able to take a kid with the kind of disabilities that we had at Emu Cottage.

But it didn't take me long to figure out that I was going to be much better off as a foster carer than I was working at Emu Cottage, because according to the emails they sent out, they were going to be paying $150 a day for people to take just one disabled kid in, which was more than I was making for one eight-hour shift at Emu.

People might think that sounds callous, but what's callous about it? I was making $540 a week as a nurse with fourteen kids at Emu, and they wanted to pay me more than that to look after one kid in the comfort of my own home. I would have been stupid not to take the offer. Plus, I'm a nurse, so having a kid with problems in the house wasn't likely to faze me like it might faze other people, who might think, 'Oh, I couldn't do it. What if something went wrong, and I was to blame?' I'm not scared of handing out medicine, and I'm not scared of putting in a stomach tube for a kid who can't feed himself. I'm not scared of a kid having a fit. I know exactly what to do.

The only problem I had really was that Mark would have to be convinced to let me get on with it. I think I told you in one of my letters that I started out squeamish when I was first on the wards, and it's like that for everyone. It takes a while to get used to people who are sick, or who have problems eating and going to the toilet and so on. But if he wanted me to keep on bringing in money so he didn't have to work, he'd have to get used to it. So I told him about Emu Cottage closing down and I said, 'But we can take one of the kids here and they'll pay me for doing it.'

The first thing he said was, 'But I don't want a retarded kid running around here.' And, 'Don't you have to be a Christian or something?' And that's what a lot of people think – that if you're a foster carer and you have disabled kids, you must be a Christian. But you don't have to be a Christian, and you don't have to be a nurse. You don't have to be anyone special because basically the welfare department will take anyone. Think about it: they've got all those kids who used to be in institutions so of course they'll take anyone to be a foster carer – and if you don't believe me you should go out and have a look at some of the places where foster kids live.

Mark said, 'But what am I going to have to do? Do I have to touch them or feed them? Because I'm not doing that.'

I said, 'You won't have to do anything because I'll make a room at the back of the house for them, and all you'll have to do is have the Working with Children check,' which is the police check that everyone has to have before they can work with kids. Mark said, 'Well, you can forget it then, Snow, because I'm not going to be able to get one of those police checks, am I? Because I've got a record.'

Of course I knew he had a record – I'd been home plenty of times when the phone had gone and it would be the cops, saying you better come and bail him out – and he was right, that might have made the

Department say, 'Oh no, we don't want him.' But I was pretty sure I'd be able to explain to them about his background in the boys' home and how he nursed his mum, and maybe it would make them think he'd be a good carer, because he'd have an understanding of institutions. So I was basically upfront with the Department. I said, 'Mark can get a bit stupid when he's been drinking but he's quit that now.' And besides, how many people do you think were lining up to take these children, Jack? Don't bother answering that because I can tell you: there was *nobody* lining up to take in disabled children. If you don't believe me you should talk to the parents and they'll tell you: 'We've been trying to get respite for years and years and when you finally find somebody who can take your child, even it's for a few hours a day, you never give them up.'

Anyway, I filled out all the forms and set about clearing up the house, and we had what they call a 'home visit', where the social workers came around and looked at the house. I remember thinking it was just as well that Mark had done the deck because there was no way we would have been approved with that hazard in the backyard. But we did get approved and it was in 2003, I think, that we got our first kid, a boy. I think his name was Brian. The parents dropped him off at around eight o'clock in the morning and he got picked up eight hours later. I can tell you, it wasn't as easy as I'd thought it was going to be because he was an Asperger's kid or something, and he screamed from the minute they took him out of the car until the minute they came and took him away again. And when he wasn't screaming he was being violent, and throwing his food around.

An hour into it, Mark went to Star City and didn't come back all day, but then, ping, two days later the Department put $150 into our bank account, and Mark said, 'So that's it, one hundred and fifty bucks, and they don't tax you?'

I said, 'It's an allowance, so no tax and it doesn't affect the dole.'

He said, 'So, if we'd taken two of them they'd have given us three hundred bucks?'

I said yes and so that was it, we were in business, and before long we had half a dozen kids coming for a day here and a day there, and it was actually pretty good in terms of the money we were making. But then it wasn't great, because we never knew how many kids we were going to get, and we had no say over the kind of kids that were coming, so we didn't know if they'd be what Mark called 'screamers' or good, quiet kids.

I rang the Department and said, 'Can't you give me a few more Category Two kids?' because Category Two is the worst kind of disability, like kids who are just vegetables. They're easier to look after because they don't do anything, but you get more money for them because they're so disabled.

The Department said sure but most of those kids have been relinquished by their parents so you'd have to take them full-time not part-time. I thought about that, and I said, 'Okay, fine, let me know when one comes up,' and I was waiting for that to happen when they rang one day and said, 'Snow, that boy you have with you today, we're wondering if he might be able to stay overnight. His mother's refusing to collect him.' I said, 'What do you mean she's refusing to collect him?' They said the mother phoned up and basically said, 'I'm sorry, I can't do it any more,' meaning she was sick of the way he'd thrash around and kick and swear, and sick of never being able to leave him unattended, sick of not being able to go to work, sick of lifting him everywhere, in and out of bed, in and out of the bath, in and out of the car, sick of changing his nappies, sick of turning him in his bed three times or else he'd get bedsores. She'd been saying 'I need some respite' for about three years, and getting maybe four hours a week.

She'd taken to dropping him at the Children's Hospital once a week just to get a break, claiming he was sick, but they woke up to that pretty quick and they said, 'You can't bring him here, we're not a respite centre,' and finally she'd just snapped and said, 'No, I'm sorry, I can't do it any more.' The Department said, 'Sure, okay, we'll take him off you for the day' and they dropped him off with me but then the mum said, 'I'm sorry, but I'm not going to pick him up.' You might think you can't do that, but plenty of parents who have got disabled kids do it, and you might think that the Department would have called the cops, but that's not how it works. What happens when a mum won't pick up her kid from hospital is, the Department has to quickly go to court and get an order saying he's been abandoned.

They said, 'Can he stay with you while we get an order?' I said sure, and I put some sheets on a bed and put him in it, and it was awful. He was yelling and screaming and thrashing around and Mark was going off his tree. I kept telling him, 'It's only for one night, and we'll get $400 for the overnight stay.'

The next day Mark said, 'I'm not doing that again,' but I said, 'What about if we had one that wasn't a screamer – what if we had a quiet one, or even two quiet ones – and we had them for a few days? That would be six or eight hundred dollars a week.' And he said, 'Okay, let's do it.'

SISTERS OF MERCY

It wasn't exactly cheap or easy to get the house ready to take disabled kids overnight. We had to put up a ramp and rails out the front and clear out a room at the back of the house to use as a bedroom, but once that was done, we got approved for overnights pretty quick, and that's when we decided to call ourselves 'Delaney House'. Delaney House for disabled kids. It's got a bit of a ring to it.

I told the Department that we didn't want 'screamers and dribblers', as Mark called them. We wanted Category Two kids that wouldn't make a huge amount of fuss and noise. The Department was thrilled because most people say they don't want vegetables — they actually want kids they can play with or something.

We weren't expected to do it for nothing because who'd do it for nothing? It was our business. And the Department was rapt. The number of times one of their social workers said, 'Oh, you're doing such a great job at Delaney House. If only everyone was like you.' And maybe you don't know this, but the Department actually gave me a prize for doing all that foster work, which means, now I think about it, that I might be the only inmate in Silverwater who has an award from the government. That was in 2008, after we'd been taking those kids for about five years. I got an invitation in the mail, saying, 'The Governor of New South Wales requests your attendance at a gala event,' and it was all to celebrate the work the foster carers were doing.

I got on the phone to RSVP and the official I spoke to said, 'Oh, why don't you bring your husband with you?' I had to say, 'We're not married, but anyway he can't come. I can't leave the kids unattended at Delaney House, they need to have somebody there caring for them.' So Mark said he'd look after the kids, and the waiters at Government House served tea and sandwiches, and the Governor made a nice speech, saying, 'We all remember when families who had a child with a severe disability had to put them in an institution and I'm so glad those days are over.' And she said, 'Aren't we lucky to have these carers, who take them into their homes to give the parents a break?'

Then she said, 'So give yourselves a huge pat on the back and a big round of applause for the difference you're making in the lives of these children. Hip, hip, HOORAY! Hip, hip, HOORAY!'

Whatever people say now, it was pretty difficult not to feel a bit proud of myself that day, Jack, and it was a nice party they put on, with sandwiches and scones and jam and cream, and fruit with custard in little glasses. Then, when I got home to Bondi, Mark said the local paper, the *Wentworth Courier*, had called and they wanted to do a story about the fact that we'd been given a prize.

I called the number he'd written down and they sent around a reporter and a photographer who took a photo of me sitting out on the veranda with one of the children (not with their face, because you're not allowed to show their faces) and the story was all about how we'd take kids nobody else would, and the headline on it was, 'The Carers Who Can't Say No'.

They quoted me saying it was an honour to have the kids, and so yes, it was all very nice, but then I could have killed Mark, because just when I went inside to get a cup of tea for the reporter and a plate of jam tarts, he moved in on her, probably trying to chat her up, and when I came out I heard him saying, 'We're making $2100 a week.' I had to cut him off, saying, 'Mark, you know you're not allowed to talk about the allowances the children receive,' because actually, when you think about it, the money wasn't for us, it was for their food and other things that the kids needed.

Anyway, like I told the reporter, and like I'm telling you, we didn't do it for the money, or not only for the money. We were actually trying to help, and everyone was praising us and say how proud they were of the work we were doing, my dad included, and I know that because when I rang him to tell him about the prize he said, 'It's great what you're doing, Snow. You've really made something of yourself.'

And that's why I got such a shock when he died, and his lawyer rang to tell me that he'd never basically trusted me enough to tell me the truth about anything.

Snow

Chapter Fourteen

When Snow Delaney refers to her dad's lawyer, she's talking about a man called Doug Grenfell, who has his own little practice in Deer Park.

I remember calling him after Snow got arrested and telling him what I was after: 'I'm doing an investigation into the disappearance of Snow Delaney's sister, and I was hoping you'd be able to help me.'

He asked if I'd come down to his office. It meant another trip to Melbourne, but it was one I was happy to make.

Doug Grenfell and Sons is on the fourth floor of a building above a Video Ezy store. I got the train there from the city, and couldn't help noticing that the whole town had been taken over by what Snow's mum would have called New Australians. I walked past a falafel kitchen, and past a Vietnamese bakery, and past a $2 shop with Chinese writing all over the windows.

There was no lift up to Doug Grenfell and Sons, so I had to traipse up two sets of stairs, avoiding where I could holding on to the blue banister, which had bits of chewing gum stuck underneath. Grenfell doesn't have a secretary so it was a matter of waiting in one of the vinyl chairs until he got off the phone and came out.

We shook hands and he said, 'I can't tell you how happy I am to hear that somebody has agreed to take a look at this.' He took a seat behind the Formica desk, and I could hardly see him there, with what looked like three months' worth of work in manila folders towering all around him. For all his disorganisation he was a nice bloke – a good bloke – something you don't see all that much with lawyers. He asked me if I wanted a coffee and I said yes, and it was Nescafé, from a polystyrene cup, just how I like it.

'So do you think Snow had anything to do with it?'

That was the first thing he said in relation to Agnes being missing, and I had to answer honestly and say, 'I think so but I can't prove it.'

'It's just too much of a coincidence,' he said, 'that Agnes was at Snow's house, and now she's missing. But when I called the police to tell them that, they said Agnes had left the house in a perfectly good state of health, and there was no reason to think that she ever spoke to Snow again.'

I said, 'But you don't believe it.'

'You bet I don't.'

I asked him to tell me exactly when and how Snow found out that she had a sister called Agnes, and he sketched the basics for me, saying, 'It gives me no pleasure to tell this story. I knew Jim Olarenshaw for more than twenty years. He was a friend of my father's. I knew his wife, and I knew Snow. She was younger than me – ten years younger – but I knew that Jim was devoted to her when she was a little girl.

'I was there for Jim when his wife died, and I saw him resisting Snow's efforts to put him in a nursing home, telling her flatly that he'd managed for years on his own and could do so again. I was one of the people who used to visit him after his wife died. He'd taken to feeding rosellas that came to sit on the wires of his old Hills hoist in the afternoon, and some afternoons there would be hundreds and hundreds of birds out there. It wouldn't surprise me if some people thought he was a bit nuts.'

He wasn't nuts, that's for certain, but I'll let Doug Grenfell tell the story.

'At some point in the late 1980s, or the early 1990s, Jim was given an old computer – not a Commodore but one of the competitors – and the first thing he did was take it apart to see how it worked. Given that he was an electronics engineer – electronics was what he did at the Victoria Railways, and he had that shop, Olarenshaw Electrics – he easily spotted a flaw in its design.

'There was some problem with the ways the wires or charges interacted with each other – I don't pretend to understand it – and Jim quickly figured out a way to solve the problem by creating a new circuit that made the motherboard more stable. He sold that invention to the computer company for a significant amount of money. I know because I handled the paperwork.

'I was a junior solicitor in those days and I remember being pretty impressed that this old guy – Jim would have been in his sixties then, so ancient to me – had pulled off this coup. He asked me to use the money to buy three blocks of land at Ocean Grove, out on the peninsula. And here's the thing: he never told anyone about it, not his wife, not his daughter, nobody.'

I couldn't quite see the logic there but Doug Grenfell could.

'He didn't trust the bloke that Snow had hooked up with,' he said, leaning back in the office chair with his own Styrofoam cup of coffee in his hands. 'That Mark Delaney bloke, he didn't trust him. And he wasn't with Ros – that's Snow's mum – at that time, so there was no reason to say anything there either.'

It's not entirely clear whether Snow's dad ever visited the land in Ocean Grove, although I suppose he must have done. Doug told me he had power and water connected only because the council ordered him to do it. All rates for the property, and other notifications, were sent to the offices of Doug Grenfell and Sons.

'The land increased in value over time but Jim never showed any interest in liquidating those assets,' Grenfell explained. 'Not when he moved back in with Ros while she was being treated for cancer, and not when he was diagnosed with cancer himself, seven years after Ros died. The reason, probably, was that Jim's cancer was already advanced when it was discovered. The only treatment was palliative, designed to ease him into the grave.

'I advised him around that time to give up the old house in Deer Park, but he had no interest in doing that, not until a palliative-care nurse told him he had no choice. He stayed home until she ordered his transfer by ambulance to hospital just a few days before he died.'

From what I understand, there were plenty of people who wanted to see Jim Olarenshaw before he went to his maker – friends from the bowls club and so on – but the person he most wanted to see, besides Snow, was Doug Grenfell.

'I'd been his solicitor for years, so I wasn't surprised to be summoned to his bedside,' he told me, 'but I was very surprised by what he had to tell me. I was sitting in the visitor's chair next to Jim's bed, and we were going through the list of things in the will. I said, "I've got down here: the house in Deer Park and its contents; the car; and the three blocks of land at Ocean Grove," and he nodded. I said, "In a way you're lucky, Jim, having only one child. There's going to be quite a bit of money, but at least there won't be any disputes."

'And that's when Jim raised his finger and said, "No, that's not right."

'I said, "What's not right, Jim?" And he was very clear about it. He said, "There isn't one child. There's two."'

Chapter Fifteen

Dear Jack,

Remember when I first started writing to you and you told me to point out where you'd gone wrong in your stories? Well, I'm going to tell you now that one of the things that really annoyed me was how you kept saying, 'Oh, Snow found out when her dad died that he'd left half the family fortune to a sister she'd never met,' but that's not right, Jack. That's just wrong.

What actually happened was, I'd been visiting Dad every four or six months in that year before he died, and I was always worried that something would happen to him because I was living in Sydney and he was in Deer Park and I couldn't get to see him that often because I had the kids at Delaney House.

I wanted him to move out of the old house, but he kept telling me not to worry and that his neighbours dropped in on him. I was right to be worried, though, because just after his eighty-ninth birthday, he slipped in the kitchen and hit his head. He managed to call an ambulance and he got taken to Footscray and District Hospital. He said he felt fine but they insisted on doing a body scan and, just as they'd done with Mum, they found cancer. He called me from his bed to say, 'Better come say your goodbyes. I've got the big C, and it's gotten hold of everything.' And I thought, 'Right, okay, I'll book a flight for next week,' and next thing I knew, Doug was on the phone saying, 'He's dead.'

It annoyed me that he hadn't told me how bad it was and I didn't even get the chance to say goodbye.

I don't know if you've ever had to bury one of your parents, Jack, but if you haven't, let me tell you it's not much fun. You've got to track down people you haven't seen for years, and you don't know where to find them. You've got to book the funeral home and put a notice in the newspaper, so a bunch of people you've never met can come and eat the sandwiches you've paid for. And the funeral home that Dad wanted to use carried on like it was McDonald's, trying to get me to upsize everything: are you interested in brass handles for the coffin, or just the cheap and nasty ones? Would you like flowers at the end of every pew or only on the coffin? Would you like hot food served afterwards, or just the tea and sandwiches?

I told them: 'It's just me. There are no other children, no grandchildren, no other kin.' They said, 'Oh, you never know, people come out of the woodwork.' And do they ever: there was a crowd of at least fifty at the service, blokes long-retired from the railways, old ducks who used to get their toasters from old Jim at Olarenshaw Electrics, blokes from the Station Hotel, a couple of geeks from some computer group he must have been involved with, all chewing away on the egg-and-lettuce sandwiches and helping themselves to cups of tea.

SISTERS OF MERCY

I'd booked the funeral home for an hour, which was the shortest time you could book it for. A few of the old-timers looked like they might have stayed all day but I wasn't interested in hanging around at Tobin Brothers. I wanted to go back to the old house at Deer Park for one last look around, because the first thing I was going to do once the probate on Dad's will went through was sell it.

Everyone says this, but I was never able to walk into that old house as a grown-up without thinking about how small it was. Even my room, which had seemed huge when I was a kid, you couldn't actually swing a cat in.

I poked my head into a couple of Dad's old cupboards but there was nothing interesting to see. I got a jumbo garbage bag from his kitchen drawer and made a bit of an effort to sort through the piles of Yakka trousers and the cardigans. Then I thought, 'To hell with it, I'll get the Salvos to take what they want and the tip can have the rest.'

I opened the fridge in the hope of finding something to eat, but everything was rotten and the birds that Dad used to feed were parked in the trees outside, screaming, so I went out with a broom and waved it around, saying, 'Get out!' And, 'Go, you won't be getting any food from me!' I looked around for a few things I might be able to sell on eBay: the TV, the DVD player and that kind of thing, and then I went to sleep in my old single bed.

The next day I made my way to Doug Grenfell's office in Deer Park. You'll know Doug Grenfell, he was Dad's lawyer and it's no secret that there's no love lost between us. It was obviously a big day for me but I was also thinking, 'I won't ever have to come back,' because my idea was to sell the Deer Park house and never visit Melbourne again.

When I got to Doug's office, I remember Doug looked weird, like he'd been waiting for me with bad news. He asked me if I wanted a glass of water and I said no, and waited with my handbag in my lap for him to say, 'Okay, well then, here's the will, and once you've got the death certificate organised we'll get the house at Deer Park on the market, and six weeks from now you'll have the money.'

But that wasn't what he said. What he said instead was, 'I have to tell you, Snow. There's a complication.'

Now, I know I don't need to go through the whole story, Jack. You know it all, but I couldn't get what Doug meant by 'a complication', and so like an idiot I said, 'Is it a good complication or a bad complication?' Like there's ever a good complication! Doug said, 'It might well be both, depending on how you feel, Snow,' which made no sense. And then he said, 'Alright, here we go: just before he died your father told me that you're not an only child after all. You have a sister.'

You're going to be wondering how I reacted to that, Jack, and I'll tell you how I reacted to that.

I laughed!

I laughed because it was so ridiculous. Honestly, my first thought was, 'Pull the other one, Doug.' And then, 'Is this really the time to be cracking jokes, when I've just buried my father?'

But Doug didn't laugh, so then I thought, 'Is this bloke trying to rob me? Is this some kind of weird stunt, designed to get me to carve off a slice of the fortune and hand it over to Grenfell and Sons on the premise that they'll take care of everything? Because that's not going to work.'

But then Doug said, 'I'm sorry, Snow, I know it comes out of the blue.'

SISTERS OF MERCY

It was slowly dawning on me that this was no joke, and I said, 'You're not kidding, are you?'

Doug said, 'No, I'm not kidding. You do have a sister. And it's a bit exciting, isn't it? A sister, after all these years!'

I don't need to tell you that 'exciting' wasn't really the word that I was thinking of. I was thinking of words like, 'this is ridiculous', but then it dawned on me that the reason Doug was even telling me was obviously because Dad had left this sister something in his will.

I said, 'Well, spit it out, Doug. Who is this woman and how much money do I have to give her?'

And that's when he said, 'You have to give her half, or at least you have to *offer* her half and see if she wants it.'

Did your mother ever to tell you to close your mouth or you'll catch flies, Jack? Well, that's what somebody needed to say to me. My jaw was on the floor.

I said, 'Half?'

Doug said, 'Half.'

And I said, 'Of the whole lot?'

He said, 'Of the entire estate, yes.'

I said, 'Which is how much?'

That's when Doug dropped his second bombshell. 'Oh, well, we need to get some estimates on the value of the various properties, but I'd say it's somewhere in the order of two million dollars.'

There isn't a way for me to even describe how I reacted to that, Jack. I must have gone into shock. Not that it mattered because good old Doug was happy to keep talking, going on about how Dad had invented this special thing for computers in the eighties and how he'd sold it to some computer company and how he'd put the money into land at Ocean Grove and that land was now worth a fortune.

My head was spinning when he was telling me all this, mainly because none of it had ever been communicated to me before. Maybe some time in the eighties Dad had showed me an old computer with some tennis game called Pong on it and he'd said something like, 'This is going to be the next big thing, Snow.'

I knew that he had an old Atari computer, because he was one of the first to get one, not to use but to take apart in his shed. But he never said anything about inventing anything that anyone had given him money for, and even now I don't know how much he got paid, although I take it that it was enough to buy three blocks of land, beachfront at Ocean Grove, which wouldn't have been cheap even back then.

I told Doug, 'That makes no sense. Dad never had any money. He's been living in that old house in Deer Park forever, or else in the bungalow he rented when Mum threw him out. Why wouldn't he have sold that land and lived a bit better?'

I was remembering how I couldn't even talk Dad into taking down the wallpaper in the old house, wallpaper that had turned yellow. I couldn't talk him into trading in the old Hills hoist for a nice dryer.

'Why would I pay money to dry my clothes?' he'd say, 'when the sun's out there, 365 days a year, and completely free?'

I'd say, 'Because you're old, Dad, and it's hard for you to throw a sheet over the clothesline.' But he was one of those blokes who didn't believe in paying for things he could get for free, and maybe, looking back, if people had said, 'He's so cheap, he's probably hoarding a fortune somewhere,' they would have been right.

SISTERS OF MERCY

Anyway, I said to Doug, 'Why didn't you tell me any of this before? For that matter, why didn't *Dad* tell me any of this before?'

Doug said, 'You mean about the land? He didn't trust that partner of yours, Snow.'

I said, 'That's offensive, Doug. Do you know what me and Mark do in Bondi? We run a home for disabled children.'

Doug said, 'I know about that but your dad didn't trust him.'

I said, 'That's a bit of bad luck,' because really, the idea that I would be handing any of my dad's estate, let alone half of it, to a woman I'd never met before was ridiculous.

Doug said, 'It's not that easy. Once we've nailed down exactly what's in the estate and what it's worth, we'll need to make sure that your sister is offered half.'

I said, 'Are you sure you're being straight with me, Doug? Because how can it be that a so-called sister pops up just when Dad dies, and then gets half of his estate? That can't be legal.'

And think of it from my side, Jack, it didn't sound legal. I was trying to deal with the fact that firstly Dad had money, and secondly he had a past I didn't know anything about, and thirdly he didn't like Mark . . . Well, I knew that last bit because yes, he was always at me, saying, 'Why doesn't he work?' And, 'He doesn't seem to make you happy.' But this was all a bit much.

Doug said, 'Let's face it, Snow, there's going to be a lot of money – far more than you knew about – so it's not actually a blow to you. It leaves you with roughly what you thought you'd get and maybe more!'

I don't mind telling you, Jack, I was thinking to myself, 'Is this bloke an idiot?' I didn't care that it was more money, or less money, or whatever amount of money. The point is it was *my* money. I was an only child. That was just a fact, and no way was some stranger going to waltz into my life and walk off with half of my father's estate. So I said, 'You better tell me where this woman, this so-called sister, fits into the picture.'

Doug said, 'Well, she's older than you, Snow, a good deal older. She was born in London in 1940.'

Do you know what I thought when I heard that? I thought, 'Bingo! She's a fraud.' Because my parents weren't even married until 1947. But Doug said no, that was right, apparently she'd been born before my parents got married. He said, 'Your mum was sixteen when your sister was born, Snow. Jim – your dad – had already gone away to fight. The hospital where your sister was born got bombed. This was during the Blitz. The nuns told your mum, 'Leave the baby with us, and we'll send her into the countryside, out of harm's way. And according to Jim, they always intended to go back to get the little girl. But when they returned, she was gone.'

I said, 'Gone where?'

Doug said, 'Well, whoever was in charge by then said they didn't know! Your dad went with your mum to the hospital, and they spoke to the nuns, and they were told that all the war babies had been sent out of London to escape the Blitz and there was no record of what had happened to a lot of them. They told Jim and your mum, 'You need to put this behind you.'

Excuse my French, but I said, 'That all sounds like bullshit to me. Don't think I won't be asking for a DNA test,' and Doug nodded and said, 'Your father was pretty sure you'd say that but he told me to tell you that the story's true, and we have a birth certificate and so on to prove it.'

I said, 'I take it from what you're saying that this woman is definitely alive?'

Doug said, 'Oh, yes, she's alive!'

I said, 'And where exactly is she?'

Doug said, 'She lives in a little village called Bucklebury, just outside London. She's a widow, but she has two children and five grandchildren.'

And I thought, 'Oh great, I have a sister who's a grandma. Even more reason for her to come running for my money.'

I said, 'Have you spoken to this woman?'

And Doug said, 'I have. I've explained to her who her father was but she doesn't know about the clause in the will. I was waiting to tell you about it, before I told her.'

I said, 'How long ago did you speak to her, Doug?'

And he said, 'Not very long ago. Your father was dying, Snow, and he gave me clear instructions that this was something he wanted me to do. He wanted me to try to find out, once and for all, what had happened to this little girl. I think he thought I'd fail at it but so many of the old records have opened up. It wasn't even difficult. I went straight back to Jim the minute I found her, but he was so close to death there was no way for them to meet or even speak. But he said, "I want Snow to meet her."'

I said, 'He was obviously delirious. If he was so stuck on finding this woman why didn't he try to do it before?'

Doug said, 'I think he did, Snow. He made a number of enquiries on the internet over the years, with sites like Ancestry.com, but it had all come to nought. A lot of the old records have only recently become available. Maybe your mum didn't want him to do it, or maybe he thought this girl might be living with a different family and wouldn't want to know him . . . Maybe he was frightened of finding out she was dead . . . There could be a million reasons.'

I said, 'You had an obligation to tell me this while my father was still alive, Doug.' He gave me some waffle, but all I was thinking was, 'If any of this actually happens – if a stranger waltzes into my life and walks away with half that fortune – I'm going to sue Doug Grenfell for malpractice, for *not* telling me when Dad was still alive so I could get him to delete that ridiculous clause in his will.'

I said, 'Alright, thank you for all this, Doug, and I want you to know that you are no longer my lawyer, and I'm instructing you to take no further action on this matter and I will handle it.' But Doug just looked confused and said, 'But I was never your lawyer, Snow. I'm *Jim's* lawyer.'

I said, 'But my dad's dead,' and he said, 'I'm the executor of your father's estate. I work for him, or at the very least I'm working on his behalf. I'm instructed to put you in touch with Agnes Moore, and your dad made sure I put a clause in his will that requires the two of you to meet, so that you can offer her a portion of her father's estate, up to half its value.'

I said, 'Who is Agnes Moore?' And that's when it dawned on me that I hadn't even asked what her name was, that's how much in denial I was. Doug said, 'That's your sister's name. Well, it's her married name. She was Agnes Joan Bell when she was born – Bell was your mum's maiden name, wasn't it? – and now she's Agnes Moore.'

I said, 'You do know I'm going to challenge this, don't you, Doug?' But he just sighed like that was the most predictable reaction in the world and said, 'Your father thought you would, and he asked me to tell you not to bother. He had me draft a letter to you that I'd at least like you to read before you walk that path.'

He pushed this letter across the desk, and what can I tell you, it was like reading the last mad ravings of a dying man. I don't remember every word, mainly because I was feeling such total shock, but it was basically:

Dear Snow,
I realise this will have come as a great shock to you . . . this baby, Agnes, was something we kept a secret from everyone . . . your mum had no choice but to let her be sent away because I was away fighting the war . . . we went back to get her, nobody could tell us where she'd gone . . . we were told to forget the past, and get on with our lives . . . we never forgot her . . . when I got sick, I asked Doug to help me . . . it would mean a great deal to me to know that you two could meet . . .

And so on and so forth, a load of guilt spewed up on the page, most of it too stupid to even talk about.

Doug said, 'As I understand it, the point for your dad was really for the two of you to meet. He was concerned about you being alone in the world.'

I said, 'If that was the point, Doug, why didn't he simply say, "If this woman can be found, it would be great if they could meet?"'

Doug said, 'I suppose without the clause in there, there's nothing to make you do it.'

I said, 'Why didn't he leave it so that I could decide whether this woman gets anything? Or that I not get what is rightfully mine until

I've met her? That would be fair enough. This is ridiculous! She could walk away with half!'

Doug said, 'She could, but bear in mind she might not. You only have to offer. She doesn't have to accept.'

I said, 'Why wouldn't she accept? What kind of lunatic would turn down a million dollars, bang, just like that, out of the blue?'

Doug said, 'I'm fairly sure your father had in mind the two of you meeting to work it out.'

I looked at Doug and said, 'She better say no thanks. That's what I'd do if somebody I never met left me something that rightfully belonged to somebody else. I'd say no thanks!' Which probably isn't actually true but anyway that's what I said, and then I got up and pretty much stormed out of Doug's office, furious with him but also with Dad. Maybe there are some people who think, 'Oh, but wasn't it wonderful to have a sister turn up, after being an only child and everything?' But no, it wasn't wonderful.

What *would* have been wonderful would have been me going into Doug's office, getting the sale of the Deer Park house organised, closing Delaney House and moving to the Gold Coast on the proceeds of the sale of the land at Ocean Grove, instead of having to think to myself, 'I'm going to be spending the next five years in court, fighting over my father's estate.'

I went back to the house in Deer Park. There used to be a portrait of my parents on the sideboard in the front room, and I picked it up that day and looked at Dad, there on the dock at Port Melbourne with his hat and his suitcase, standing next to Mum, both of them on their first day in Australia, and there was nothing about the picture that said, 'We've already had a baby that we left behind.'

I was talking to the picture, saying, 'How come neither of you ever mentioned any of this to me? And why have you left me to deal with all this when it's actually got nothing to do with me? Can you not see that this is a prime-sized pain in the neck?'

I tossed up whether to phone Mark and tell him but I decided against it. Things had a habit of being my fault and I didn't want him all riled up and shouting down the line at me. I slept badly that night but when I woke up I thought, 'Okay, Snow, you better get to work on this.'

I made contact with a lawyer in the city – a proper lawyer, not a two-bit solicitor from the suburbs – and told him I had an emergency, and he agreed to see me. I put the problem directly to him, saying, 'How can it be that I'm expected to cover the cost of my father's funeral and everything else besides, while that land is sitting there in Ocean Grove? How can it be that I'm not permitted to sell my own house in Deer Park until we've spoken to this woman? How can I not be allowed to access my own inheritance, because of this stupid clause?'

This new lawyer seemed sympathetic, but then I was paying him to be sympathetic, wasn't I? He said, 'Oh, it's not at all unusual. Very often people will leave clauses like this in their wills and the main thing for the executor is to make sure the instructions are carried out to the letter.'

I said, 'I just want to sell up and forget about this,' and he said, 'No court is going to grant probate on that will until you've done what it asks you to do, which is meet up with your sister and offer her some part of the estate, up to half.' So that was basically another $500 wasted on advice that told me nothing I didn't already know.

I left that lawyer's office and went home and got back on the phone to Doug and said, 'Here's what I want you to do. I want you to write to this woman this week and tell her that I'm supposed to offer her half but I don't *want* to offer her half, and see what she says. And if she says, "Oh, I'll take half, thank you very much," tell her I'll see her in court.'

Doug wouldn't have it. He was saying, 'Oh, I can't do that, Snow. I have my instructions and they are to put you two in touch with each other so you can discuss this clause in the will.'

I said, 'That's all very well, Doug. You may have your instructions but I have my *bills*.' And I said, 'This is just ridiculous. You know I'm going to contest this, don't you? And this sister, if she can even prove she is a sister, will not stand a chance. She never even met my father.'

Doug said, 'I know it's disappointing, Snow, but try to see the upside. Don't you want to meet Agnes? She's your sister, the only family you have in the world!'

I could hardly believe what I was hearing. 'Why on earth would I want to meet her?' I said. And I hung up without bothering to say goodbye.

I probably don't need to tell you that Mark was furious when I got home and told him all about it, saying, 'How can this person have any claim at all?' And, 'Let's sue her.' But all we could really do was wait for Doug to go through the motions – getting back in touch with Agnes, telling her all about the will, and telling her that Dad's intention was that we get together to discuss it and that she had a right to take half – all of which was pretty sickening, especially waiting to hear what she'd come back with. Every time the phone went I'd have to snatch it up because Doug had one of those stupid blocked numbers, but finally it was him and, to the silly woman's credit, at least Agnes did the right thing.

'She has absolutely no interest in making a claim on the estate,' Doug told me.

I was obviously suspicious because, like I said, what kind of idiot walks away from a million dollars? I said, 'Are you sure?'

Doug said, 'Oh, quite sure. She sounds like the loveliest woman and she has no real need for money. She was just thrilled to get the news that she has a sister.'

I said, 'I'm not really a sister. We've never met.'

Doug said, 'She's really keen to meet you.'

I said, 'Did you tell her I've got no interest in meeting her?'

Doug said, 'She's never met a member of her biological family before. She grew up in an orphanage, and they told her she'd been abandoned.'

I said, 'I really couldn't care less. All I know is that Dad can't have had much interest in this person because he never mentioned her to me or to anyone. Why don't you ask her to scrap that whole "let the sisters meet up" thing?'

That was the way I felt, Jack. I had no desire to meet Agnes, and had it been up to me I would *never* have met her. But Doug was saying, 'She wants to come to Australia and she wants to go to the house in Deer Park. She wants to talk to you about her parents. She was dying for even a photograph.'

I said, 'I don't care. Tell her to sign whatever needs to be signed, whatever documents there are saying she doesn't want Dad's money, and that can be the end of it.' But Doug said, 'No, no, she wants to see where her parents lived, and where they're buried. She wants to lay flowers on their graves.'

I said, 'That's a bit of bad luck since Dad's ashes are here, with me, at Delaney House.' That got Doug all upset, and he was saying, 'I thought you'd have buried Jim next to your mother, at the Altona Lawn Cemetery,' and I had to say, 'Well, you've got yourself to blame for that. They wanted $5000 for that plot and I don't have $500 because all my money is tied up in Dad's estate.'

Doug said, 'Well, in any case, Snow, your sister wants to meet you, and I don't like to remind you, but she has the right. I won't be putting your father's will up for probate until that condition is met. You can either go there to London, or your sister is going to have to come here to Australia, but either way it has to happen.'

I put the phone down and when I reported all this to Mark, he said, 'I don't get it either, why does she want to come? Tell her to sign her rights away and piss off.' That was very, very good advice, and don't I wish I had taken that advice? But I didn't, and here's why: I couldn't shake the feeling that if I wasn't nice to this woman she might turn nasty on me. I was thinking, 'Don't cut off your nose to spite your face, Snow. If this woman wants nothing from the estate, and all she wants is to visit, let her visit. Don't upset her, let her come over, be nice, make sure she signs whatever she has to sign, and then she'll be out of your hair.'

On a scale of one to ten, how do you rate that decision, Jack? It's got to be up there with the worst decisions I've ever made. However much of a pain it would have been, I should have gone to England! But honestly, what kind of idiot comes out here and then gets lost?

Snow

Chapter Sixteen

I have often wondered how Agnes reacted when she first heard that she had a sister. It must have been a shock, but as far as Ruby is concerned that soon gave way to joy. 'She was absolutely over the moon,' she told me back at our first meeting at the Sir Stanford. 'And, where my first reaction would have been that it was a prank, Mum never thought so. She said the lawyer – Doug Grenfell – knew the names Mum was given at birth and he knew the names of Mum's parents, and there weren't that many people who had access to that kind of information about Mum. For the first sixty years of her life, Mum didn't even have a birth certificate.'

The waiters were milling around, clearing breakfast plates and the like.

I said, 'How was that possible? How did she do things, like get a driver's licence and travel around, or a passport, without a birth certificate?'

Ruby said, 'She had what was called a Certificate of Identity. Here, I'll show you.'

She fished around in her 'Mum' folder for it, and passed it across the table. It wasn't a birth certificate like you and I might have; it was a handwritten document with the words 'Certificate of Identity' across the top.

'None of the kids at the Fairbridge Farm School were ever given a birth certificate – they all got one of these when they left,' Ruby said.

Agnes must have kept it folded up, maybe in the back part of her purse behind her credit cards, because the creases were imprinted on it. It had basic information, such as her full name at birth – Agnes Joan Bell – and her date of birth in 1940, but it didn't give away the names of her parents.

'Mum gave a copy of that to Stella when she was doing the Family Tree assignment,' Ruby explained. 'I remember her saying, "This is all I've got, Stella. I'll never know more about where I came from than this." But when Stella's class did the search of the Births, Deaths and Marriages website – they do all that in their classroom these days, teaching them how to use the internet – she found a link especially for people who only had these Certificates of Identity, and when Stella followed that link, the website made it plain that after years of secrecy, all the old records had been opened to the public and Mum would be allowed to get a birth certificate.'

I asked Ruby how her mum reacted to that news. She said, 'She basically didn't believe it but Stella was excited, and I suppose I was too, so we all trooped off to Births, Deaths and Marriages together and the lady behind the counter was quite cheery. She looked at Mum's Certificate of Identity and said, "Do you want me to fish out your birth certificate?"

'Mum said, "Oh, I'm not supposed to have a birth certificate," and the lady said, "Everyone has one, and you can have yours if you want it." And I suppose they're used to dealing with the trauma there because she also said, "You don't have to say yes straightaway. You can sit and think and tell me what you decide."'

Ruby remembers sitting with her mum in the waiting area while she made up her mind. 'I was trying to stop Rocco from saying, "Do it, Granny, do it!" I wanted her to decide in her own time.'

After about ten minutes of what Ruby called 'faffing around' her mum finally declared she'd 'have a look, and why not?'

The lady behind the counter smiled, made a few clicks on her keyboard, and went behind a partition, coming back with Agnes's birth certificate, a copy of which Ruby had in her file. It read:

Name of Infant: Agnes Joan Bell
Date of Birth: 19 September 1940
Place of Birth: London Hospital for Mothers and Babies, City Road, London
Mother's name: Roslyn Joan Bell, 16, factory hand, London

Father's name: James John Olarenshaw, 20, able seaman, London

Ruby waited for me to finish looking at her copy of the document.

'I can still see Mum's face when she was holding that, or should I say the original of that,' she said. 'She had no idea, not until that day, what her parents were called. She had tears streaming down her face, and because she was crying. *I* was crying.

'She kept saying, "Look at this. I had a mum and a dad," which was exactly what she'd always been led to believe in the orphanage.

'She kept reading her dad's name out loud – James John – and she said, "Look, he's an able seaman, so he *was* probably at war." And, "Roslyn. Ros. That's a pretty name, isn't it? And look, she had a job in a factory. Probably making things for the war effort." So she was standing there at Births, Deaths and Marriages, coming up with a whole history, a whole back story, with that piece of paper in her hands.'

I handed the paper back to Ruby, who folded it carefully along the creases.

'It was Stella who had the idea of searching through all the newspapers from 1940 to see if Mum's birth had been recorded anywhere,' she said. 'You can do all that on the internet these days. They were at it for hours, searching for words like "Agnes" and "Bell" and "Olarenshaw" in the old copies of the *London Times,* Mum with her glasses on her nose, scrolling through the pages. That's how we found out that the hospital Mum had been born in – the London Hospital for Mothers and Babies – was bombed during the war. It was a direct hit, right on the corner ward, where the infants were sleeping, and it happened on 21 September, so two days after Mum was born.

'I guess her mother would still have been in there with her. And Mum loved the idea of having survived such a dramatic event. She kept saying, "What must it have been like! It would have been pitch black! Somebody must have had to scoop me up! I would have been so tiny!"'

Ruby said Stella put all the newspaper clippings about the bombing into her assignment and nobody was surprised when she got an A. But I was interested to know whether Agnes did any research of her own, after Stella was done. Ruby nodded, saying, 'Back then, the big question in Mum's mind was, what happened to her own mother after she was born? Was she killed in the war or had she abandoned her?

'We asked a couple of the girls at the Red Cross to run the searches for us – because the Red Cross in England does a lot of the searches for people who were raised in orphanages – but they couldn't find a death certificate for a Roslyn Bell in the 1940s. We asked if they could search for a marriage certificate instead, and the girl came back and said, "You were asking about Roslyn Joan Bell? I've got a Roslyn Joan Bell, factory hand, getting married in July 1947 at St Matthews Church on Old Kent Road."

'We asked if we could see that certificate, and we knew straightaway that they'd found the right one because there was her name – Roslyn Bell – and who had she married? James John Olarenshaw, returned seaman, of Jarrow.'

The way Ruby tells the story, her mum wasn't in denial about what she'd discovered. Neither of her parents had been killed in the war. Her father had joined the navy, and when he came back, he married his old sweetheart.

'They'd found each other again,' Ruby said, 'but they hadn't come back for Mum, and that hurt because the marriage certificate showed they were married in July 1947, and Mum was still in the orphanage in July of 1947. She didn't ship out until October. So the question was, why didn't they come and get her?'

I've done a few stories on the Forgotten Generation in my time and I asked Ruby if she knew that it wasn't uncommon for poor English mothers, and single mothers in particular, to be told that their babies had died, or been adopted out, even though it wasn't true.

She nodded, saying, 'We know that now, because Doug told us. Mum's parents did go back to the hospital where Mum had been left, and they did try to find out what had happened to her but they were told that Mum couldn't be found. But I'm not sure we knew it then and it was very confusing and upsetting for Mum.

'In any case, we kept on with the search, looking for any other documents that related to Mum's parents – council rates or TV licence, that kind of thing. Anything that might show where they lived, or any new birth, but there was no other reference to them, not in any of the files we searched.

'A girl at Births, Deaths and Marriages asked us if we'd considered the possibility that they had migrated. She said that where there were no records, that was the most likely explanation. But never in a million years did it occur to us that they'd sailed to Australia.'

I said, 'Although plenty of Britons did.'

'Plenty did,' Ruby agreed.

I said, 'And after hitting that brick wall, did your mum give up the search?'

'Oh, it wouldn't be fair to describe it as a search,' Ruby said. 'Mum had never been completely consumed by it, she was *interested*. It wasn't like there was a gaping hole to fill, just an interest, a *curiosity* as to her origins. And then, of course, years later the phone call from the Australian lawyer came.'

I asked Ruby if she'd by chance been there when her mum took the call from Doug Grenfell.

'I wasn't there, no, and worse, I was in the car when she rang to tell me about it,' Ruby said.

'The phone flashed and I couldn't answer because I was driving and Mum isn't the type to get the hint, to be quick when I say, "I'm driving!" Mum loves to talk. And when I say she loves to talk, I mean talk and *talk* about the simplest things. She might call to say, "I was walking in the park this afternoon, and I swear I saw a man who looked just like old Mr Jenkins. Do you remember Mr Jenkins?" Of course

I won't be able to remember Mr Jenkins, so I'll mumble something like, "I'm not sure, Mum," and she'll say, "Oh, Ruby-Tubes, you must remember, you used to play in his front garden all the time!" And then she'll be off on a long discussion about how I loved to play in Mr Jenkins' garden, and where the garden was in relation to our own, and so on.

'I don't mind, don't get me wrong, but with two kids and working part-time, I'm busy, so I sometimes put Mum on the speaker phone and go about my business while she chats away. Other times, perhaps when I'm in the car with two kids in the back, with one of them saying, "He poked me, he hit me," and six errands to run, my iPhone will go *bring, bring,* and I'll look down and it will be Mum and I'll think, "Let it go to message bank," because if I pick up it will be Mum saying, "It's just me, Ruby-Tubes! Just called for a chat!"

'But on that particular day – the day Mum got the call from Doug Grenfell – Mum called and I was driving so I let it go to message bank and when I picked up the message, there was Mum, completely calm on her message. She simply said, "Call me when you can, Ruby, I have some news."

'There was something about her voice that was odd, so I called back quite quickly and I said, "Good or bad?"

'She said, "I think it's good news, Ruby-Tubes," and out it all came: a lawyer had called from *Australia* of all places, to tell her that he worked for her father, and that her father had died, and he had left instructions in his will that Mum be contacted.'

I asked Ruby how she – meaning Ruby, not her mum – reacted to this news, and she said, 'Oh, like I said, my first instinct was that it must be a prank, like a Nigerian email scam, saying, "You've inherited a great deal of money and we need you to sign some paperwork." But Mum said, "No, no, this lawyer knows everything about me, he's going to send me a letter."'

Ruby opened her 'Mum' folder again and found a manila envelope of the type used to send important documents. It was a bit tatty, having made the journey from Deer Park to London and back again, this time in Ruby's suitcase, and Ruby's daughter Stella had apparently soaked the Australian wildflower stamps off some time earlier, but the letter inside was still intact. It was from Doug Grenfell on his office letterhead, explaining what he had already discussed with Agnes on the telephone: she was a beneficiary of Jim Olarenshaw's estate, and quite a bit of money was at stake – around $1 million, depending on how much they could get for the land at Ocean Grove.

'My brother, Steven, is better at numbers than me, and he did a quick conversion back to pounds,' Ruby said. 'He told Mum: "It's around £650,000 they're talking about." And the strange thing about that was that Mum has always been absolutely sure that she'd win the lottery one day. I don't know why she thought that. She's just funny that way. Apparently a clairvoyant told her once that she would come into money, so she bought her Lotto tickets every week from the man on the corner and she kept them under one of those gold cats with the waving arm you get from Chinatown. If she had called one day to tell me she'd actually won, I wouldn't have been surprised, because she was utterly convinced that it would happen and her belief in that never waivered, no matter how many times she took those dud tickets down to Mr Kumar on the corner to run through the machine. He'd shake his head, and say, "No luck this week, I'm afraid, Mrs Moore," and she'd say, "Never mind, Kumar, it will happen one day. And when it does I'll buy you a ticket back to India to see that family of yours."'

I remember I asked Ruby, 'Getting the call from Doug – that felt like winning the lottery to your mum?'

She put her tea cup down so suddenly that it rattled the spoon in her saucer.

'Oh, no!' she said, 'absolutely not. It felt like that to us – to Steven and me – but not to Mum.'

'She wasn't interested in the money?'

'Not at all. She was overwhelmed by the idea that she had a sister, an actual biological relative, living in Australia. But as to the inheritance, no. Look, I won't deny that we tried to talk her around. It was an awful lot of money. It was all very well for Mum to be saying, "But what on earth would I do with it?" because I could have given her some ideas: take a cruise! Give some to me! But Mum wouldn't hear of it. She said, "No, no, it isn't really mine. It belongs to my sister."'

I wondered whether Agnes's reaction had anything to do with the fact that Snow had made it plain to Doug Grenfell that she would fight any claim on her dad's estate.

Ruby nodded and said, 'Mum knew that Snow didn't want to offer her any of the money. But she wasn't angry. She said, "Imagine if somebody turned up out of the blue, claiming half of your father's estate. It wouldn't be right, would it? You'd fight that too, wouldn't you?" It was as if she was keen to make sense of Snow's reaction.

'She wrote back to Doug Grenfell saying it was very generous of her father to include her in his will but she wasn't in need of any money. She wanted to know if it was possible to have a photograph of her parents, and she wanted to know more about Snow: how old was she, and did she have any children? And yes, she was willing to come to Australia to ensure that the will could go to probate and Snow could get her money.

'She told me, "I want to see the house where my parents lived and I want to go to their graves." But mostly, she wanted to meet Snow – she *desperately* wanted to meet her. The number of times she said to me, in the lead-up to the trip, "I thought I was alone in this world but no, I've got a sister."

'I talked it over with her. I said, "Are you sure you want to do this, Mum? It's such a long way." She said, "It's much closer than it used to be!"

'I said, "Do you want me to come with you?" But she was adamant that this was a trip she wanted to make on her own. She kept saying, "I've done it before, I can do it again."'

Ruby took half a day off work to see her mum off at the airport, and she gave Rocco and Stella half a day off school so they could go too.

'The police have asked me what her mood was like when she left England,' Ruby said. 'All I can say is, yes, she was a little quiet, but who wouldn't be?'

There isn't much about Agnes's first few days in Australia that police don't know. Her plane – Qantas Flight 009 from Heathrow to Melbourne via Bangkok – landed at Tullamarine Airport at 6 a.m. on 19 September. Agnes collected her luggage from the carousel and made her way by taxi to Melbourne's Crown Casino.

Her room was ready early so she had her bags taken up and had a bit of a poke around the expensive shops. Shortly after 1 p.m., she sent an email to Ruby and Steven from a computer in the hotel foyer, letting them know she'd arrived safely and that she was tired. She said that Australia hadn't changed since she'd last seen it in the 1950s because it was still hot and dusty.

'She told Rocco that the Crown had big balls of fire that shot into the sky and she promised to bring some Vegemite back so Rocco could try it,' Ruby said. 'She said she was going to try to get an early night to shake the jetlag.'

Shortly after 10 a.m. the following day – 20 September 2009 – Doug Grenfell met Agnes in the Crown foyer so he could drive her out to her dad's old house in Deer Park.

'She was an absolutely delightful woman,' he told me. 'So grateful that I was taking the time to show her around, and so pleased to meet somebody who had known her parents. She sat in the passenger seat beside me, chattering away, asking a million questions in her lovely accent.

'She had a hard, shiny handbag on her lap, and I could tell by the way she was clutching it that she was a bit nervous. She didn't know me from Adam, after all. But she struck me as plucky, having come all the way out on her own under such circumstances.

'She told me, "It's one of the things you want to do on your own, isn't it? It's probably not important to anyone but me." But she was laughing as she said that.'

Doug pulled his car into Jim's old driveway and put his key into Jim's door, standing back so Agnes could be the one to open it.

'She was certainly emotional, but not hysterical,' he said. 'She walked down the hall, looking in this room and that room, more interested than anything. She said something about the place having an "old person's smell".

'I pointed out a photograph of her parents taken seven years after she was born, fresh off the boat from England. I opened the back door for her and told her how her dad liked to stand in the backyard feeding the rosellas, and she laughed and maybe there was a bit of a tear there. And that was basically that. It was a small house, so there wasn't much to see.

'We got back into the car and drove up to the high street so she could see where Olarenshaw Electrics had stood, and we drove up into Altona Lawn Cemetery so she could see her mother's grave.'

Agnes bought flowers – chrysanthemums – at the cemetery florist and Doug hung back a bit while she went and paid her respects.

'After that I took her back to the Crown Casino. We went over the arrangements for Sydney – she was going to check in to the Sir Stanford, and meet up with Snow the following day, and once that was done and the sisters had seen each other I'd send her the paperwork she needed to sign.'

Agnes left the Crown at 9 a.m. the following day – 21 September – and caught the 11 a.m. Qantas 'City Flyer' to Sydney. She made her way by taxi to the Sir Stanford hotel, arriving shortly after lunch.

Ruby said, 'As far as we know, Mum took it easy that first afternoon in Sydney. She checked in to the Sir Stanford, then she went to the Opera House and took some photographs and sent them to us on email. She went to Darling Harbour, where there's a Wildlife Park, and took plenty of photographs of the big insects for Rocco.

'It wasn't until the next day – the 22nd – that she was due to go to Delaney House. And what has always struck me as strange is that, having flown twenty-seven hours to get to Sydney to meet her sister, she spent less than three hours with her that day.'

CCTV footage from the Sir Stanford shows Agnes leaving the hotel at 12.25 p.m., and Snow says she arrived at Delaney House at 1 p.m.

She returned to the hotel at 3.20 p.m. and one of the first things she did was send an email to Ruby from the computer in the foyer, which I've copied in its entirety here:

SISTERS OF MERCY

My dearest Ruby,
Well, it's done. I have met my sister and I don't know what to say. Snow put on quite a spread. She lives in a large house at Bondi. You can tell Rocco I went to Bondi!
I'm not sure how I feel.
Snow looks quite a bit like me – twenty years ago!
Not much of a sense of humour.
There was a man named Mark there. They have the same last name – Delaney – but they aren't married, apparently. It's very odd.
I wasn't too impressed with either of them to be honest.
They take care of little kiddies with disabilities. It was a strange set-up. You expect something wonderful but that was not what I found. I will tell you more when I see you, but for now I'm fairly certain that I've decided we probably do need to get a lawyer to look at my father's will. Not for me but for the children.
I'll explain in person.
I'm going to have a bite to eat now, then an early night and I will call you, probably from Bangkok. The flight is at 11 a.m. so don't worry if you don't hear from me in the morning.
Love you very much,
Mum

Ruby didn't pick the email up until twelve hours after it was sent, obviously because it landed in her inbox during the night in England. By the time she retrieved it, her Mum was supposed to be in the air, so she did not try to respond.

'After I saw the stories about the dust storm, I called British Airways and they confirmed that all flights out of Sydney had been delayed and they gave me a new estimated arrival time,' Ruby said, twisting the end of a paper napkin. 'I thought, well, let's see how things go, and I kept checking and checking, and finally BA sent out an SMS saying the plane would land at such-and-such a time.

'I took Rocco out to Heathrow, mainly because he had bought one of those silver Welcome Home balloons and he wanted to show it to Mum, and I remember that we were standing waiting in the arrivals hall at Heathrow for so long that the balloon started to slump on its string. At some point, it became obvious that all the passengers were off the flight, and I thought, "Oh no, Mum must have missed the plane!" But that made no sense because she hadn't sent a message and she *definitely* would have sent a message.

'I went over to the British Airways counter, but BA has a policy of not telling you who is supposed to be on which plane – understandable but in those circumstances frustrating – so I looked up the number for the Sir Stanford in Sydney on my iPhone and they said that Mum hadn't even checked out of the hotel, which was more confusing still.

'I checked my email on the iPhone – not for the first time, obviously – and there was nothing. Just nothing. And for my mother that was astounding. I called Steven and said, "Have you heard from Mum?" He said he hadn't and that maybe it had something to do with the time difference, but I knew in my bones that that had nothing to do with it.'

Ruby then called Doug Grenfell, who hasn't forgotten the conversation.

'Ruby was very, very concerned,' he told me when we spoke in his Deer Park office. 'I told her, you need to call the police immediately.'

Ruby confirmed that account, saying, 'Doug Grenfell gave me the number for New South Wales police and I called them. I don't like to complain, but from early on we couldn't seem to make them understand how worried we were. It was at least three or four days, I think, before they talked to anyone at the Sir Stanford and maybe six days before they spoke to Snow.'

I asked Ruby, 'And when you came out for the first press conference, what did they tell you? Did they have any ideas, any clues?'

'They told me they'd tracked Mum's movements back to the hotel from Snow's place. She was seen on the CCTV coming from the foyer, and the data from her key card showed that she went back to her room.'

'And then nothing until she left her hotel room again at 5 a.m. on the day of the dust storm?' I asked.

'Not quite nothing: the police told us that Mum made one call from her room on the evening before she disappeared.'

It was the first I'd heard of that, so I probed for more information. Ruby said Agnes made one call from her room the day before she disappeared. It was to 999. That's the number for police, fire and ambulance in the UK. In Australia, it gets you nothing but a long beep.

Not only that, Agnes had also received one call in her room on the morning before she disappeared. It came from a blocked number, through the hotel switchboard.

The receptionist who put the call through can't remember if it was a man or a woman, but I don't suppose that matters all that much. Only a handful of people in the world knew that Agnes Moore was staying at the Sir Stanton that day: her daughter, Ruby, and her son, Steven, in England knew; Doug Grenfell knew; and so did Snow Delaney.

Chapter Seventeen

Dear Jack,

People say that I don't seem to care that my sister went missing after coming all the way out to Australia to visit me, but think about it from my point of view. I didn't want her to come out in the first place. Plus there seems to be this big fascination about what happened between us while she was at Delaney House, when *nothing* of any interest happened – we basically had lunch.

I didn't even want to have the lunch, remember? I got talked into it by good old Doug, and pretty much as soon as I agreed I wished I hadn't. I wanted to get it over with, but Doug had apparently told Agnes that she'd be able to meet some of the kids we had staying with us. I was so annoyed by that, and then the bell on the gate went and I was hardly even ready.

Was I curious to see what Agnes looked like? The answer is no, not really. But after she pushed the intercom I watched her on the security camera we had on the gate. The first thing I noticed was that she had a straw hat on with a ridiculous floppy brim, and

I remember thinking, 'That's an old lady hat.' And she was dressed like an old lady – she had on a straight skirt, made of some kind of brown material – and she had an old lady face, and Mark, who was looking over my shoulder, said, 'Anyone who saw her would think she was going to church.'

He buzzed her in, and I watched her coming down the path, thinking, 'Let's get this over with.' She had two of those Harrods shopping bags – green ones – and you can guess what was in them. It was so typical: English shortbread in one of those tartan boxes for me, like you can't get them here or something! – and she had some Beefeater dolls in plastic tubes, which I suppose she thought we would give to the kids we were looking after.

Anyway, I opened the door and I was going to shake her hand, but she dropped the bags on the porch and said, 'Oh, Snow!' like we were actually family, and went to hug me. I'm not much of a hugger, so that was a bit awkward.

I invited her into the kitchen to put her bags down and I introduced her to Mark. She was raving about the house, going on about how she loved the trees in the front yard, the ones that Mark had cut into animal shapes. I'd already laid the table for lunch and I wasn't keen for things to drag on. I'd cooked a leg of lamb, since that's a sort of British thing. I did honeyed carrots and new potatoes, and gravy in a boat. She was at least nice about that, saying, 'I can't believe you've gone to so much trouble.'

Just before I was about to serve, Mark wheeled two of the children out to meet her – from memory it was Sonya and Nadia, both in electronic wheelchairs and maybe not looking very cute. I'd combed their hair and restrained their hands so they couldn't scratch their faces and make them bleed, but obviously it's still a shock to some people when they see kids like that.

Agnes was very good, saying, 'Oh, oh, I hadn't realised!' And then she was full of praise for what we were doing at Delaney House, and full of questions about how many kids we'd had over the years, and asking how we managed.

I showed her a few little tricks that we did to make life easier for us, and for the kids that came to us, and then Mark took the girls back to their room and I got on with serving the lunch.

The police have asked me a hundred times what we talked about, and I'll tell you what I told them: she basically bored me with tales of coming to Australia when she was a girl. She went on and on about her own family – that daughter Ruby, the one I call the troublemaker, and her brother, Steven, who sounded dull, and five grandchildren whose names I can't remember. And the big elephant in the room was my father's will because she never mentioned that.

She wanted to see some photographs of Mum and Dad, and of me when I was growing up. I had prepared for that and put an album on the table. She was going through all the pictures of my dad when he was a younger man, saying, 'Oh, isn't he handsome! Look at that pork-pie hat,' and so on, all boring.

At some point she got up and went to the loo, and she must have taken a wrong turn off the corridor because she was gone for ages. By the time I found her she was looking all confused, like old ladies look when they're lost.

I served chopped jelly for dessert – red and green cubes, in bowls – and I was trying to get her to have a cup of tea, so I could sort of bring the lunch to an end, but then she announced that Doug had told her I had Dad's ashes. That was true – I did – but there was no way I was going to get the little silk bag and put it out on the lunch table.

And then she was going on about Dad, saying, 'I wish I'd known him.' I couldn't help myself, I said, 'Well, too late for that, I suppose,' which was meant to be a bit light and funny, but she didn't seem to get that I was joking.

Pretty soon after that we called her a cab and off she went, and that was the last we saw of her. But then maybe two days later her daughter, that Ruby, rang me saying, 'Have you seen our mum?'

I told her, 'She left here two days ago!' She sounded like that didn't make sense and in the end I had to tell her that it wasn't my business what her mum was getting up to in Sydney, plus I was busy washing all the sheets and towels because of all the red dust that had come into the house.

Next thing I knew the cops had come knocking, which freaked Mark out because he didn't like police coming to the house and I always assumed it meant he'd done something wrong. I didn't let them past the front door. They said, 'We've been asked to have a look at this missing person's report.' I said, 'Don't tell me she's still missing?' Because I assumed she must have just taken a day trip or something.

The cops wanted to know what taxi company we'd called, and they said they were trying to track down the cab driver who took Agnes back to the hotel, but they also knew all about Dad's will and how Agnes had come out to Australia to talk to me about it and they seemed to find that very fascinating.

I said there was no problem about the will because Agnes didn't want any money, and if they didn't believe me they should ring

Doug and he'd set them straight. I said, 'He's drawn up the papers for her to sign, making sure I get the estate, which is mine after all, and she was happy to do that.'

Ten days later, or maybe two weeks later, I got another phone call from Ruby saying she was in Australia and could she come and see me because she was worried sick about her mum. I said there was no point coming to visit me because I didn't know anything, and I said, 'I'm sorry, Ruby, I realise you're worried, but I have children here, special-needs children, and I can't spend all this time on the phone speculating about this. I have my hands full, thank you very much.' And from memory I have never spoken to her since.

Snow

Chapter Eighteen

I can't say for certain when New South Wales police decided that Snow Delaney was the prime suspect in the disappearance of her sister, but it was obviously earlier than my contact at Rose Bay let on because according to evidence given at Snow's trial, police had surveillance on Delaney House from the second week of October.

By surveillance I don't mean blokes in vans. I mean they put bugs in the intercom in the front fence, and near the doorbell; and they had taps on Snow's mobile phone and on Mark's too. They got absolutely nothing of interest from any of the conversations they overheard, which pretty much told them everything they needed to know.

Think about it: if your sister, whom you'd only just met, had gone missing shortly after visiting you, wouldn't it be a topic of conversation in your house?

Wouldn't you say something like, 'I wonder if the police have had any word on Agnes?' Even in passing? Or maybe you'd say, 'I wish the police would stop bothering us about Agnes going missing.'

Nothing like that was said by either Snow or Mark in the three weeks that police had bugs in the house, which means they either couldn't care less, which stretches my credulity, or else they were passing notes, which is what people who are hiding something tend to do.

Of course the cops also visited the house, but as Snow said in her letter, she didn't let them get further than the lounge room. Contrary to popular belief, police can't charge into a private home and demand to search all the rooms, and it's not as easy as people think to get a search warrant. You need what's called a 'reasonable suspicion' that a crime has taken place. But what crime had taken place? Agnes Moore was missing but nobody was yet saying that she might be dead.

I don't like to second-guess cops, but to my mind the next press conference – the one they called two days before Christmas with both Ruby and Steven in attendance – was an exercise in what we journos call 'shaking the tree'.

To explain: when police aren't getting anywhere in a particular investigation, it sometimes pays to 'shake the tree' or make a bit of noise – that can mean holding a press conference or bumping up the reward for information leading to an arrest – to see if it triggers any kind of reaction.

Shaking the tree can put a bit of pressure on a culprit because it's a sign that neither the cops nor the family are going away. It can lead suspects to do something stupid. For example, they might head out to check on a body to make sure it's still covered up.

A press conference can shake a new witness out of the tree too. Somebody who maybe saw something suspicious but hadn't made the connection in their mind with the case at hand. And that is precisely what happened when Ruby and her brother put themselves before the cameras in the run-up to Christmas 2009.

My contact from Rose Bay tells me that he left the press conference, did some routine paperwork, went home for the day, and by morning there was a message from Crimestoppers saying somebody had called in about the missing Agnes Moore.

That person was Lenore Wallace. To be clear, I wasn't allowed to talk to Mrs Wallace during Snow's trial. She was a witness, and as such had been warned off speaking to the media until after the trial was over and the jury had made its decision, but pretty much as soon as the trial was over, I made it my business to try to catch up with her.

I remember the day we met. Mrs Wallace has a house in Tempe, in Sydney's south. She invited me over and offered me a seat in a floral armchair that had doilies over the armrests, and she brought out a tray with proper leaf tea and jam tarts, and I thought, 'I'm in the home of an old-fashioned Australian lady here!'

You'd trust her with your life, is what I mean.

I asked Mrs Wallace what exactly it was about Ruby and Steven's press conference that prompted her to call

Crimestoppers. She put her cup straight down into her saucer and said, 'It was a no-brainer! The minute I saw the footage of Snow Delaney's house . . . well, I nearly fell off my chair. I turned to my husband, and I said, "That's where I took Polly that time!"'

Polly is Mrs Wallace's foster daughter. She's been in care since she was born, mainly because she has a range of physical and intellectual disabilities. Polly would be coming up to her 19th birthday now, but her IQ is probably that of an eight-year-old. She has lived with Mrs Wallace and her husband, Brad, since 1994.

'A lot of foster carers like to say, oh, our foster child came to us sort of by accident! But it wasn't that way with Polly,' Mrs Wallace told me. 'Brad and I, we had three children of our own and once they were up and on their feet and out of home, we decided – or *I* decided, I suppose you'd say – that I wasn't ready to have an empty nest.

'Like most people, I'd heard that there are plenty of children who need good homes, and with our kids gone we had room. So we put our names down to become foster parents. Not that it's ever as simple as that. There are all these hoops you have to jump through, a mountain of paperwork to fill out, and from memory we were on a waiting list for about a year. Then, on 1 October 1994, and I remember the day exactly, the Catholic Welfare Bureau called to tell us that a little baby had been born, and she was looking for a home.'

The Catholic Welfare Bureau told Mrs Wallace that the newborn's mother (she can't be named for legal reasons) was a heroin addict and a prostitute whose last known address was the back room behind the Pink Pussycat in Kings Cross.

'Staff at the hospital told us upfront that Polly was probably brain-damaged,' Mrs Wallace said. 'There's no use beating about the bush as to why: her mother had tried to abort the pregnancy in the back room of the strip club but she was too far gone. A Maori bouncer had carried her down the street to St Vincent's emergency and that's where Polly was born, three months premature.'

'The staff did their best to try to keep her mum in so she could bond with her baby and maybe even breastfeed, but she wanted nothing to do with Polly,' Mrs Wallace said. 'She wanted to get back on the streets and back on drugs, so the Department had to step in and make Polly a ward of the state.

'That's when the Catholic Welfare Bureau called us, saying, "This little girl needs a home but she's going to have significant problems."'

Mrs Wallace and her husband went to St Vincent's to meet baby Polly when she was just six weeks old. Mrs Wallace isn't the type to hide how she felt.

'The moment I laid eyes on her I was gone, just completely gone,' she told me. 'She was so tiny and so needy – all swaddled up in a hospital blanket with a crocheted bonnet on her little head. I couldn't believe that anyone would abandon so precious a child, but the doctor said, "Look, just so you know, she's going to have real problems, so be aware of what you're taking on." But it was too late, she was already mine.'

Polly's mother had given the baby a name – Nhung, which in Vietnamese means Velvet – but over time Mrs Wallace started to call her Polly. 'I think because she was so small, when I was up at night and rocking her, I would say, "Look at you, you're so small you could fit into my pocket,"' she said, 'and so I suppose somehow she became Pocket, and then Polly Pocket, and then just Polly.'

'It's all lovely now, but the first few weeks...' Mrs Wallace said, shaking her head at the memory, 'I had to get up twice a night to give her methadone from a syringe, orally. She was tiny so she wouldn't take much food. I wouldn't like to count the number of appointments she's had over her life: speech therapy, occupational therapy, everything. And she still struggles.'

Mrs Wallace soldiered on, enrolling Polly in different classes for special-needs children until she turned eight, when her biological mother suddenly turned up again, determined to get her daughter back.

'We'd heard that could happen,' Mrs Wallace said, 'and we were terrified, having to go to court to fight for Polly. I can only thank God that the magistrate wasn't born yesterday. He was sympathetic to the mum, sitting there in her borrowed suit, but I think he could see that she was mainly in it for the money. She'd get a pension if she was a single mum, you see. He said it was probably best for Polly to stay with us, and to visit her mother on a regular basis.'

That decision was welcome but it still put Mrs Wallace into a kind of legal limbo: technically she was now Polly's legal guardian, but that did not give her the same rights as a parent.

'There are things I can't do with Polly,' she explained to me during our meeting in her home. 'I can't authorise any serious medical procedures for her, and we also can't travel with her interstate.'

If that last condition seems odd, it shouldn't: child welfare is a State concern, and children who are State wards are routinely prevented from travelling across State lines.

'If you have a State ward in your care, you simply can't leave the State with them – not without the Department's permission – and that's often difficult to get,' Mrs Wallace said. 'So we've always understood that if we wanted a holiday it would have to be in New South Wales, to Bega on the south coast, for example. But on two occasions in the past ten years, I've had to ask the Department for respite care for Polly, meaning she had to go and stay somewhere else.'

On the first occasion, when Mrs Wallace underwent day surgery for what she called 'women's problems' and her husband was unexpectedly called away to a family emergency, Polly went to Emu Cottage.

'That's where I first met Snow Delaney,' she said. 'She was one of three or four assistants on that day. She seemed pleasant enough, maybe a little cold. But Polly was only there for the day.'

The second time Mrs Wallace needed respite was when her father died in Noosa in 2006.

'I had to go up for the funeral,' she said. 'Brad and the kids had to come with me – he was their Pop, after all, but what would we do with Polly?

'I called the Department and explained the situation, hoping they'd say, "Well, we'll get permission for you to take Polly with you," but what they said was, "Not to worry, there's this couple we've been using for overnight care, and they're fine." I very clearly remember that. They didn't say, "Oh, they're brilliant, or marvellous, or wonderful." They said, "They're *fine*."'

Having never left Polly alone overnight before, Mrs Wallace was anxious. The Department tried to put her mind at rest by sending her a brochure for Delaney House.

'I'll never forget that either,' Mrs Wallace said. 'Folded up inside it was a list of rules that parents had to accept. Under the heading "No Comfort Toys" somebody had written, "Please don't bring dummies, blankets, or other comfort toys to Delaney House when dropping a child for respite. These items carry germs. Delaney House staff will confiscate all comfort toys and ARE NOT responsible for their return."

'I thought, "They don't sound like nice people," but what choice did I have, other than to drop Polly off there? I had to go to Noosa for my father's funeral. I would have loved to have taken her with me but I just didn't have permission. So on the day I drove Polly across town from our home in Tempe, to the address on the Delaney House brochure. It was a big house with a fence all around that you couldn't see through because of all the weeds and you had to buzz to get in. The front garden was enormous, and there were these wonderful manicured trees: one cut to look like a kangaroo, from memory; and another one like an emu.

'I thought, "Well, that's nice. That's a sign of somebody taking some care at least." But I also remember that the front windows were covered over with foil of some kind, so they reflected back and you couldn't see in.'

Mrs Wallace pressed the buzzer. The door opened, and there stood Snow Delaney.

'I immediately got the feeling that I knew her from somewhere, and then it clicked: Emu Cottage!' Mrs Wallace said. 'I immediately felt relieved. Here was somebody who had met Polly previously. But then I waited for her to invite me in and she just didn't. She stuck her hand out for Polly's bag, like I might just walk off without even seeing inside, and I can tell you now that was not going to happen.

'There was no way I was leaving Polly without having a good look at where she was going to be sleeping. So I said, "I'll just come in and help Polly settle," and basically let myself inside.

'Brad says I only feel this in hindsight, but something about the place was making me uneasy. I was trying to chat to Snow and make my way further into the house, and she kept standing half in front of me, like I'd gone far enough or something.

'I did my best to just ignore the feeling that I wasn't welcome. I said, "How many children will you have here this week? Will there be children for Polly to play with?"'

The way Mrs Wallace remembers it, Snow hesitated for a second and said, 'There will be three other children here this weekend.'

Mrs Wallace said, 'I'd love to meet them. Polly's probably dying to meet them too, aren't you, Polly?'

Snow said, 'I think they're asleep.'

'Now, you can call me pushy,' Mrs Wallace told me, 'but I said, "Oh, I'd love to have a little peek! Children are so cute when they're sleeping."

'So, finally Snow set off down a long hallway, toward a heavy door, and I followed her. She pushed the door open and stood back to let me see inside, and I hope it didn't show, but I was shocked. Just absolutely shocked.'

I asked Mrs Wallace to describe precisely what she saw.

'It wasn't dirty or filthy or anything like that,' she said, shaking her head. 'It was in fact exactly the opposite. It was an enormous white space – two or more rooms, made into one – and it was essentially empty except for three hospital beds with heavy rubber wheels – the ones with the steel sides that come up?

'Above each bed was a canvas sling on a hook and chain, like you see in nursing homes, to lift patients in and out of bed. Across the ceiling, there were thick plastic light tubes flashing red, white and blue. And in the beds there were children.'

'How many were there?' I asked, and Mrs Wallace said, 'Three.'

'How old would you say they were?' I asked.

'They were between twelve and fifteen years of age,' Mrs Wallace said. 'And each of them was lying in their own bed, under the flashing lights. They were naked except for towels around their waists – towels that somebody had folded and pinned into place, so they'd look like nappies. And right at each child's waist there was a tube – a thick plastic tube, a bit like the tubes that were carrying coloured lights across the ceiling – and those tubes were stuck in the children's stomachs at one end, and hooked up to a plastic bottle of pink liquid at the other end.

'And above each child was a sign, "nil by mouth".

'Now, I don't like to stare but I *was* staring. The children were . . . well, they were absolutely enormous for one thing, just huge, and they looked to me more like seals than children, with their big, vacant eyes and their huge, pale stomachs exposed. They were staring blindly at the ceiling and their mouths were open and their tongues were lolling out. Their hair seemed to be wet, or slicked with sweat, and their feet had curled up on themselves.

'Their hands were hooked up toward their chests.'

I asked what Snow was doing as Mrs Wallace took in the scene.

'She was standing by the door, looking pleased as punch.' She said, "This is Sonya, and her sister Nadia, and that one, that's Bruno, their brother."

'I said, "But what on earth happened to them?" And Snow said, "They have a genetic condition. They started out normal – I remember she used that word, *normal* – but they've been degenerating, losing the ability to talk, and then to go to the toilet, and then to walk. Now they can't do anything."

'Snow said, and I remember it shocked me, "They end up like this: vegetables, and pretty soon they'll die."'

I asked about Snow's tone of voice as she said these things, and Mrs Wallace said, 'It wasn't cruel. She wasn't mocking. She was entirely matter-of-fact.'

Mrs Wallace, by contrast, was overcome with sorrow.

'I was saying, "The poor things!" But Snow was saying, "Oh, they don't know anything. I put those lights up" – she meant the coloured light tubes winding across the ceiling – "because the Department thought it might be good for stimulation. But in my view they haven't got a clue what's going on and that's a blessing."'

Mrs Wallace struggled with what she called 'competing emotions' at the situation: sadness for these children, and I suppose a kind of grudging respect for Snow Delaney for taking in all three long after their parents had given up. 'I certainly wasn't judging her by her demeanour. I know that some people – surgeons and undertakers and aged-care workers – sometimes have a blunt manner of speaking, even a kind of gallows humour, just to help them cope.

'And it wasn't as if I was bearing witness to any abuse. The room was clean – there was nothing in there to get cluttered – and the children seemed to be as comfortable as they could possibly be in the circumstances.

'So, to be honest with you, Mr Fawcett, my main concern at that moment wasn't for them, it was for how Polly might fit into a home like Delaney House. I remember saying to Snow as we walked back down the hall, "Polly's obviously much less . . ." And Snow said, "Yes, your Polly's probably Category One."

'I'd never heard a phrase like that before and I must have looked a bit confused, because Snow said, "Most of the children we take here are Category Two. We're getting $600 a week for each of these. For your Polly, we'll obviously get less than that."'

'How did you react when she mentioned money?' I asked.

'I was concerned! It didn't seem right. But then again, who was I to judge? She was doing respite work for money. No shame in that. I'd been told that Snow was a registered nurse, so why shouldn't she be paid? And as I say, there was nothing there I could actually fault: the room was clean, and the children weren't in pain or anything like that.'

Mrs Wallace says it took some time to detach Polly's fingers from around her neck as she tried to leave. 'That bothered me, but again, it was the first time I'd ever left Polly overnight so why wouldn't we both be upset? But at the same time, if it were not for the fact that I was flying to Queensland to bury my father that afternoon, I'm not sure I would have left Polly there, and I can tell you now, the minute I got home from burying Dad – I rushed through all the paperwork and I organised an earlier flight home by the way – I went straight there to pick her up.

'Brad warned me against it. He said, "But we're not supposed to go until tomorrow morning." I said, "I'm sorry, but I won't wait."

'I must have broken some land-speed records getting around to Delaney House that afternoon, and Snow was definitely startled to see me. I said, "I'm sorry, I know I'm not supposed to be here until tomorrow but I've been missing her so much. I hope you don't mind!"'

I asked Mrs Wallace how Snow reacted to her early arrival.

'Oh, she was put out! She was definitely put out,' she said. 'But I didn't care. I stood my ground at the door, waiting for Polly to come running, and that was another strange thing: Polly didn't come running! I thought, "Okay, it's a large house, and perhaps she hasn't heard me." I said, "Goodness, is she having a nap? Or she's down in the garden, I bet!"

'Snow said, "Wait here and I'll get her." Just like that: "Wait here, and I'll get her." She went down the hall, and I heard a series of doors open and close. She was gone something like five minutes and I didn't hear any of the usual sounds, like Snow saying: "Come along, Polly, let's get your things," or "Your mum's here, run and say hi!"

'Eventually, she came back down the hall with Polly, and this is not my imagination, Polly was walking quite strangely, as if she were dazed. She still didn't run toward me, as I would have expected. I held out my arms and said, "Polly!" She didn't react. I moved toward her and when I took her into my embrace, she was stiff like a board.

'It was so obvious to me that something was wrong. I looked up at Snow and I said, "Has she not been well?" Because her reaction was odd, like she was completely out of sorts, but Snow said, no, she'd been sleeping. *Sleeping!* I don't care if she was sleeping, she still would have been so pleased to see me.'

I asked Mrs Wallace how long Polly seemed to be, as she said, 'out of sorts'.

'She was subdued in the car, and coughed up phlegm,' she said. 'I kept trying to make eye contact with her in the rear-vision mirror but she was looking out the window, with the edges of her mouth drawn down. I thought she might snap out of whatever it was quite quickly but for a long time afterwards she was clingy. I was tempted to take her to the doctor, I was that worried about it, but I suppose I put it down to her being distressed at my having to leave her.'

It was at about that point in our conversation that Polly wandered into the lounge room. I got to my feet but Mrs Wallace smiled and said, 'No, sit down,' and drew her daughter to her. Polly was a slightly built girl with waist-length dark hair. She was immaculately dressed in clothes that seemed to me to be of her own choosing – pink trainers with glitter, and that kind of thing.

Mrs Wallace said, 'Say hi to Mr Fawcett,' but saying hi obviously wasn't Polly's bag. She burrowed her hip deep into her foster mum's lap, not for one second taking her eyes off the jam tarts.

Mrs Wallace said, 'Go on then, just take one,' and quick as a bird Polly snatched one up and bolted from the room.

'So that's about the opposite of the way she was after she got out of Delaney House,' Mrs Wallace said, watching her skip off. 'And I should tell you this, a month or so after we left there, I ran into Snow Delaney at Coles in Bondi Junction. Now, if I'd known that I was going to run into her I'd have gone the other way, but you know how it happens: you turn, and there she is. I said, "Oh, hello, Mrs Delaney." She looked a bit confused. I suppose because I was out of context there at Coles, and she couldn't place my face.

'I said, "You had my little girl, Polly, for respite some months back." And that's when I noticed how strange Polly was behaving! She had gone absolutely stock still and she drew herself to me like a magnet.

'She was holding my leg, saying no, no. I said, "What's wrong, Polly?" but there was no getting sense out of her. She was shaking her head hard. I was a bit embarrassed, and I said, "Must be the stress of Christmas. You know how frantic they get. Santa's coming, isn't he, Polly? Santa's coming?"

'Snow leaned toward her and said, "Will he come down the chimney or through the window, Polly?" And it was the first time I'd ever seen Polly do anything like it, but she pushed Snow back – I mean, really shoved her – and arched her back away from her. I thought at that moment, "No, there's something wrong with this woman;

something wrong with what she's doing; something wrong with Delaney House."'

'Did you communicate that concern to anyone?' I asked. 'The people at the Department who recommended Delaney House to you, maybe?'

Mrs Wallace said, 'Yes, I did, when I got home I tried, twice, to call the welfare hotline – they have a special telephone line for people with concerns about the welfare of children – but I was fobbed off when I couldn't properly articulate my anxieties. I mean, what was I supposed to say? Polly looked funny when I picked her up. She reacted strangely when she saw Snow Delaney again at the supermarket. It doesn't add up to much. But then when I saw those poor people on the TV pleading for information about their mum, and police saying she'd been in Sydney visiting her sister, and I saw the footage of Delaney House in the background, it was like a shot of electricity up my spine.

'I thought, "Don't tell me some poor lady has just gone missing from there and that Snow Delaney doesn't know anything about it. That woman is strange and that place is *warped*." And I got straight on the telephone to Crimestoppers and I told them, "I put my daughter, Polly, in Delaney House for respite once, and I would never, *ever* do it again. The place is strange. Those people are strange." And straightaway, the police said, "Do you mind if we come over? We'd like to interview you."'

According to my contact at Rose Bay, the call from Mrs Wallace was like manna from heaven to detectives.

'They told me they were dying for an excuse to get inside and have a look around Delaney House,' Mrs Wallace continued. 'The trouble was, they had no grounds to ask for a search warrant so they kept saying to me, do you believe your daughter – they meant Polly – do you believe your daughter was badly treated, or neglected at Delaney House?

'I could tell they really wanted the answer to be *yes*, because then they could raid the place – they'd have suspicions of child abuse, you see. I said, "Well, the truth is, I don't know what went on but Polly was very, very strange after she went to Delaney House."

'That obviously wasn't *quite* enough for them because they said, "So, you *suspect* that she may have been badly treated while she was there?" And one of the police actually admitted to me, "Because if you do think that, we'd really have to search that place." So I thought, to hell with it, and I said, "Yes! Yes, I do think that something might have happened to Polly while she was there. Yes, I do."'

A matter of seconds after Mrs Wallace said those words, two of the plain-clothed police who had been standing with their backs to the wall, watching the interview, strode from her lounge room, phones to their ears. And not forty-eight hours later, a special team of New South Wales police and child protection workers raided Delaney House.

Chapter Nineteen

No journalist likes to admit that they missed the big break in a story but I have to confess that I missed the raid on Delaney House. In my defence I was out of town when it happened, in Victoria, covering an inquest into a different case altogether – so I was left to watch reports of it on the news, feeling gutted that I couldn't be there.

As soon as I got back to Sydney, I went down to Bat Street in Bondi to see if I could find a neighbour who witnessed the whole thing. I was in luck, because the bloke I'd seen painting his fence, back when I'd first gone out to Delaney House with Ruby to see if we could get Snow to talk to us, had seen the whole thing.

Bill Carson had moved to Bondi forty-two years ago, when Bondi was 'the kind of place real estate agents were embarrassed to show you around'. His wife, Shirl, grew up in Bondi, 'back when you couldn't swim because there were floaters in the water'.

Bill is now retired but Shirl – despite being sixty-three – still works part-time at the BP on Bondi Road.

'Wouldn't give up work if they paid me,' she told me, with her lipstick-coated durry between her lips. 'First thing that happens when you stop work is you drop dead.'

'Didn't happen to me,' said Bill.

The Carsons live directly opposite Delaney House, on the high side of the street, and they have a deck on the front that looks down into the Delaneys' front yard.

'You're not the first to figure out that I would have had the best view of that raid,' Bill Carson said, when I explained that the purpose of my visit was to try to piece together how the raid unfolded.

'The Channel Nine guys, when they arrived, were right onto it. They'd got a tip-off, they told me, that a raid was going to happen, and they'd scoped out the street and decided that the best place to watch matters unfold was from my deck.'

He led me through his house, past 1950s furniture that your modern Bondi hipster would pay a fortune for, and past at least eleven overflowing ashtrays, studded with Shirl's stained butts.

'I put this deck on myself twenty years ago. Didn't get a permit, so don't tell the council,' Bill said, swinging the flywire door open. 'Shirl wasn't keen on the idea. She was always, who's going to want to sit out there with the stink from the sea? But now she's out here all the time.'

The deck that Bill Carson built is about two metres wide, made of timber and concrete, with a steel balustrade and, I hope he doesn't mind me saying, not exactly stable. It clings to the side of his house with bolts, and the front end sags a little toward the ground. It's perhaps not big enough for a table, but there were two worn cane chairs with seat cushions with a faded palm-tree pattern. There's also an old white birdcage with Shirl's budgerigar in it. She calls him Tony Abbott.

'You can see the ocean over there, and whales from May to September, if you get the binoculars out,' Shirl said, but what I wanted to see was directly below me: the front garden of Delaney House.

'So, there she is,' Bill Carson said, seeing me looking down. 'You get a good view of the place, don't you?'

He'd taken a seat in one of the cane chairs, and had his slippered feet up on the balustrade. 'So, pull up a pew.'

It was clear to me that the raid on Delaney House was a bit of a thrill for people like Bill, a retiree who says himself that he mostly fills his days 'walking back and forward to the post office or running a lawn mower across the nature strip'.

'I'd actually been out in the car that morning, getting petrol and a bag of ice, and when I came back I couldn't get into my own street,' he said. 'The cops had blocked both ends off with those chunky orange barricades you see at the City2Surf. I pulled up beside one of them – the one at the Bondi Road end of the street – and said, "What's going on?

I live down there." But they were busy getting lids off their coffee cups, and not in a mood to discuss things with me. I said, "At least tell me it's not my house you're interested in," and they said, "This has got nothing to do with you, mate, unless you live at Delaney House."'

I asked Bill if he knew immediately which of the houses in Bat Street was Delaney House and he looked at me like I might be simple.

'Of course I did!' he said. 'I've lived here for forty-two years, haven't I? Give me some credit for knowing what goes on. I knew straightaway it was the place across the road from mine, the old boarding house. I said to the cops, "What's gone on there?" The cop said, "Look, we can't say much." And I said, "Well, how am I supposed to get home if I can't get by you?" And they said I'd have to park and walk.'

I imagined old Bill, in stubbies like he had on the day I interviewed him, weighed down on both sides with bags of ice, trundling down Bat Street toward his house, eyes and ears at the ready.

'Sure, I had a big stickybeak as I went by,' he said. 'There wasn't much to see, though, not at that point.'

'That's because you missed it all,' said Shirl. 'The SWAT team had already broken the door down before you even got home.'

Bill let that go, saying, 'I wouldn't have been home two minutes when the blokes from Channel Nine turned up. They'd been smart. They'd parked in the street behind, and come down the dunny lane.

'They said, "We got a tip there's going to be a raid on a property in your street." I said, "You're too late, the cops are already in there." They said, "Mind if we set up on your balcony?" I said, "Do what you like. Shirl will make you a cup of tea."

'The young bloke – what was his name, Shirl? – said he'd be happy to sling us fifty bucks for the privilege of the view, but I said, "You're right. I can see you've got a job to do." And Shirl brought them tea, didn't you, Shirl?'

Shirl nodded.

'It was that lovely Ben Kentor, he's on the *Today Show* now, and he's got that afternoon show on the radio,' she said. 'Lovely young man – so polite.'

'I felt a bit sorry for him,' Bill said, 'in that nothing was actually happening. He and the camera guy – they were all set up but there was nothing to see – just the two cop cars, which weren't that interesting.'

I've seen the Nine footage from the day of the raid and it seems to me that they were doing a live cross every half an hour or so, and Bill was right, Ben didn't have that much to report. So it was mostly shots of him, earpiece in, holding the mike, saying, 'Well, we're coming to you live from a major police operation here at Bondi,' and shots of the two cars outside Delaney House and the trees, shaped like kangaroos and emus.

I mentioned the trees to Bill Carson. They looked a bit shabby to my eye but then I'm no horticulturalist.

Shirl said, 'It was Mark Delaney who cut those trees. He used to do it in his underpants.'

Bill said, 'Shirl.'

Shirl said, 'Well, it's true, Bill. He'd come out in his old underpants – leg elastic gone, the type I wouldn't hang on the line – and he'd clip away all afternoon, with a cigarette hanging out of his mouth.'

I said, 'Did he ever talk to you?'

Shirl said, 'Not a word. Wouldn't even look up and wave. I'd be up here, feeding Tony Abbott –' she meant the budgie '– and I might catch his eye and I'd wave, but no, nothing. I'd get nothing back.'

I said, 'What about when you were on the street, maybe getting the mail?'

Shirl took a good drag on her ciggie and shook her head, 'Nothing. He was a rude man, in my opinion, and the woman – Snow – she was a bitter one. Never laughed. Never smiled. No, they kept to themselves.'

I said, 'How long do you think the police were in there?'

'Oh, they were there right through lunch. I know that,' Bill said, 'because around noon Shirl said, "I better put on some sandwiches," and she was getting the ham out of the fridge when I said, "Uh oh, better come out, Shirl, there's movement at the station."'

Shirl said, 'It was the ambulances. The ambulances came first.'

'That's right. There were ambulances. Count 'em! Six. They came in a convoy. No lights. No sirens. Nice and quiet and orderly, but in a convoy, being waved through by the cops.'

'That must have created a scene!' I said.

'Too right. Every man and his dog was out in the street, or out on their balconies to see it. The poor Nine cameraman – he was lucky not to knock Shirl's cuppa over, the way he jumped up to get a shot of it all.'

I said, 'And what did the ambulances do, just pull up outside, or . . .?'

'That's right. They just pulled up outside, and the doors swung open and the ambos got out – they had on those white jumpsuits they wear and they were carrying those red plastic boxes – and they went in the gate.'

'Were they running, Bill?'

'No, they were walking pretty calmly down the path, past those funny trees. And then we noticed a few more cars coming into the street. White cars, like the old Telecom cars. Same deal, nice and quiet and orderly, but instead of cops getting out, people in suits were getting out – people with clipboards, like government people – and they were going down the path too.'

'And all these people, they disappeared inside Delaney House?'

'That's right, they went inside, and the front door was shut behind them. Then it was just the cops outside again, the uniformed cops, and all these empty ambulances and empty government cars parked out the front. Of course, every stickybeak in the neighbourhood was out, speculating, wondering, us included. You know how it is.'

'And did you see the children?'

'Oh yes,' said Shirl. 'I couldn't help but see them, standing up here. I mean, down at street level the police were doing their best to shield them from the stickybeaks. They'd put up those white sheets, like white tents really, but from up here we could see it all.'

'How did they look?'

Shirl said, 'The first ones, they weren't too bad.'

Bill said, 'They were pretty bad.'

'It was more a shock than anything,' Shirl continued. 'They came out barefoot, wrapped in those silver blankets they give people at the end of a marathon. They were bald, and maybe a bit too thin.'

Bill shook his head. 'Have you gone mad, Shirl? What are you on about? Not too bad? They looked bloody terrible! Don't you remember I said to you, "Good God, would you look at them?" They looked like skeletons. They had crooked legs and they were blue. They looked the same as those kids they carried out of Belsen after the war.'

Shirl said, 'No, Bill's right, it was pretty bad. And I mean, I was absolutely bug-eyed, thinking, "How many will there be?" Because they were coming out of the house, and they just kept coming, all with that strange look about them, like they hadn't been outside in years.'

'And that was just the walking wounded,' Bill added. 'Once they were out, they started on the wheelchair kids. They were next, weren't they, Shirl?'

Shirl nodded, saying, 'That's right, the wheelchair ones were next. Not wheelchairs like normal wheelchairs – I'm talking now about those padded chairs with the padding all around the headrest. And some of them had those helmets on. So these were pretty severely disabled children. They didn't look good at all. They had their mouths hanging open and their heads were rocking around.'

Bill said, 'Their hands were all clenched up, and their tongues were hanging out. They were making these moaning noises. How many of them would you say there were, Shirl?'

'I'd say at least seven.'

'Oh, there were definitely seven. Seven, minimum.'

'And that wasn't even the worst of it,' Shirl said. 'Bringing up the rear, they had the kids in the hospital beds. You know the kind of beds I mean? The hospital beds with the wheels and the IV drips overhead? They were coming out and they had children on board, and I've got to admit, when I first saw them, I thought, "Heaven help us, they're dead." Because that's what it looked like: they were flat out on these hospital beds and they had big, round, bloated bodies, but they weren't dead, they were very much alive. I could see that after a while. They were alive because their stomachs were going up and down, so they were breathing. The ambos had them attached to tubes. I don't want to say the wrong thing here, but they were that pink, and that swollen, it really didn't look right.'

Bill said, 'They were trying to get them into the ambulances, without too many people seeing. But the camera guy we had up here, he was filming everything, and Ben was going nuts, saying, shoot this and shoot that. And when

I saw what he'd put together, later on the news that night, he'd captured it perfectly. He said, "It was like after a bomb has gone off, with the walking wounded, then the wheelchairs, and then stretchers, into the ambulances."'

'How long would you say that whole process took, Shirl?' I asked.

She made a face like she was thinking about it and said, 'I reckon it took a good hour. I'm talking from the time the first of the walking ones came out in the silver blankets to when the ambulances took off from the street. And I thought, "Well, that's the drama over then." But the camera guy knew better. He said, "They've still got to bring the culprits out."'

'The Delaneys?'

Bill said, 'The Delaneys, that's right. There was a bit of a break between the children being carried out and the Delaneys being marched out, but everyone in the street knew by then what was going on, and there was jeering. First came the bloke with the scruffy goatee and the tatts – Mark, the one who cut the trees – and then came his missus, the one they call Snow.'

I asked, 'Were they handcuffed, Bill?'

Bill nodded, saying, 'They were. They were handcuffed, and they were walked straight to the police cars and they were put in. Not together. One in each car. They weren't saying anything, or not anything that I could see. She – the woman, Snow – had her mouth shut in a tight line. A female police officer had her hand on top of her head and was pushing her down so her knees bent and she had to get in the car. A male police officer was doing the same thing to the bloke, pushing him into the car, and you could see he didn't want to go.'

'And then both cars took off?'

Bill said, 'Right. Both cars took off. But that wasn't the end of the circus either. Because when the barriers at the end of the street came down, the media swarmed in, and Ben took a call on his mobile and he said, "There's going to be a press conference, I better get down there," and he and the cameraman packed up – didn't leave a mess, nothing, came and went like they'd never been here – and took off, and next thing, we saw them in a big pack around this poor police officer who was trying to explain what had gone on.'

'They did the press conference here on the street?'

'They did, and it was like you've seen on TV, with the fluffy mikes waving around and the blokes with cameras on their shoulders.'

Like I said earlier, I didn't make it to Bondi on the day of the raid, so it goes without saying that I also missed the press conference, but I've watched the tape of it, one that Ben gave me, and I've seen the transcript. New South Wales police media liaison officer Brett Masonwells took the questions. You'd know Masonwells if you saw him. He's the guy who always speaks for the police and he looks exactly like you'd expect: grey hair, perfectly cut, under a shiny police hat. Fifty-eight or maybe fifty-nine years old, career officer, upright bearing, badges across the chest.

Ben opened up the questions. He said, 'The house you raided today – Delaney House – is it the same house that the British tourist, Agnes Moore, went missing from?'

It seems like Masonwells hadn't expected this, at least not as the first question. I imagine he'd expected it would be about all the kids in various states of undress that had just been carted out of an old house in Bondi. He said, 'Not exactly right, Ben. Agnes Moore visited this house – the house we raided today – before she disappeared last September.'

Ben said, 'She was here the day she disappeared, wasn't she?'

Masonwells said, 'No, the day before, I believe.'

'And it's her sister, isn't it, who runs this place?'

'That's right.'

I could see some of the other reporters, recorders and mikes up to Masonwells's mouth, getting a bit frustrated with Ben's line of questioning. Clearly they wanted to get on to the topic of the kids who had just been carted out of the house, and couldn't get where Ben was going.

But Ben, who's like a dog with a bone, said, 'Right, so what's the link between today's raid and the disappearance of Agnes Moore?'

Masonwells sighed and said, 'Look, Ben, I can see where you're going but we're not commenting on that at this stage. I'm here today to talk about the raid on Delaney House if that's okay with you.'

A second reporter – he's out of frame so I'm not sure who it was – said, 'Why did you raid Delaney House today? And whose children are they that you've taken out of there?'

'Look, this is a complicated investigation,' Masonwells replied. 'It's going to take some time for the details to unravel. Delaney House is obviously a facility for disabled children. It's a residential facility. The children who live here, they are placed here by the welfare department, and all I can really say is that the police raided Delaney House today on the basis of information we received from a third party.'

A reporter can be heard saying, 'What third party?'

Masonwells said, 'No, I'm not going to name the third party. It was a tip-off from the public. What I will say is that in response to various concerns, we have removed a number of children from the house.'

Obviously that person was Lenore Wallace but her name was then being kept out of it.

A fourth reporter piped up: 'But why have you removed them? Is it a case of child neglect, or child abuse? And how many children are we talking about?'

'In total, we removed twenty children from the house.'

From this point the questions started coming thick and fast from several directions, and it seems to me that Masonwells was having difficulty making out what was being asked of him. But one question he did answer was: 'What kind of state were the children in when your officers found them?'

Masonwells said, 'Well, obviously we expected the children to be disabled, or to have illnesses of some kind. But they . . .' He paused for a moment, before adding: 'Actually, I don't think I want to say more than that at this stage.'

A reporter can be heard shouting, 'But why, why have you taken them out of there if that's where they live? What kind of report did you get to trigger the raid?'

Masonwells said, 'I'm not going to go into that.'

This went on for a bit longer, with reporters yelling questions, and Masonwells not giving much away, and then a reporter from News Limited, Joe Potter, a bloke with better contacts that most reporters, who had been standing back waiting for his moment said, 'According to my sources, the Department only placed nineteen children in the care of Delaney House, but you removed twenty from that property today, didn't you?'

Where he got that little tidbit from, I can't tell you, but it was certainly an interesting angle and the rest of the reporters could do nothing but hold their little tape decks and microphones up a bit higher, to make sure they got whatever answer Masonwells was going to give.

Watching the TV tapes, you can see Masonwells swallowing, and pausing, and then he said, 'Your information is correct, in that we have removed twenty children from Delaney House today, yes.'

Potter continued, 'But the Department only placed *nineteen* children in that house.'

Masonwells said, 'I'm not sure what your question is, but it's probably one for the Department.'

Potter wouldn't give up. 'Well, my sources have told me

that the Department placed nineteen children in the house, so where did the twentieth child come from?'

But clearly Masonwells had reached his limit. 'Joe, I'm sorry, mate, that's as far as I'll go. We might be in a position to reveal more information as it comes to hand but I think we're probably done for today. It's an ongoing investigation . . . I thank you all for your interest and your patience today. Appreciated.'

There would have been journos who walked away from that media conference reasonably satisfied, story-wise, with what they had: twenty kids removed from a carer after some kind of tip-off from a member of the public, but there was more to come, most of it revealed by Joe Potter in a report that had a big EXCLUSIVE tag across the top in *The Daily Telegraph* the very next day:

New South Wales police uncovered a medieval House of Horrors during yesterday's raid on Delaney House in Bondi.

Seven children were found so malnourished they were barely able to walk to waiting ambulances.

At least another dozen children were found tethered by medical tubes to their beds.

All wore heavy collars, tagged not with their names but with numbers.

Police sources have told the Telegraph *that all of the children were subjected to bizarre medical practices, designed to keep their behaviour under control.*

SISTERS OF MERCY

Maybe you can see what he's getting at. In case you can't, the headline gave it away. 'UNSPEAKABLE,' it said, and under that, the words that nobody could quite get their heads around:

'THEY CUT OUT THEIR TONGUES.'

Chapter Twenty

Dear Jack,

I've been thinking about this for a while now and I've decided that I'm going to sue somebody for how Delaney House got raided, because it was absolutely shocking, just completely outrageous, what the police did to us. I don't know how much you know about it since you said in one of your letters that you weren't there, but what happened was I was walking past the front door on my way into the kitchen and next thing I knew, the door came flying in. I mean that literally – the door flew right off the hinges. Why the police thought they needed a battering ram to bring it down, I cannot tell you. The door was a hundred years old, Jack – it would have come down with a good shove. But it was like you see in the movies. Cops with a battering ram in full riot gear, boots, vests, the lot. Talk about an over-reaction!

I mean, for goodness sake, I'm . . . what . . . all of five foot tall, and I was standing in the kitchen with a cup of tea in my hand, so it wasn't like I was a threatening presence. Mark was sitting in his old armchair, with the laptop in front of him, probably on the punt. Couldn't they just have knocked? Of course they couldn't because they wanted the scene to be dramatic. They wanted the spectacle, the media circus. I put my tea down on the kitchen bench. I said, 'Excuse me, but what on earth's going on?'

A detective stepped forward. I assume he was a detective since he was one of the few not dressed in a black bodysuit like he was on the hunt for Osama bin Laden. He wore civilian clothes but he flashed his badge at me, so he was definitely a cop. He also used my full name, which is something only a cop might do. He said, 'Are you Sally Narelle Delaney?'

I said, 'I am.'

He said, 'I have a warrant. We're authorised to search these premises. Where are the children?'

Mark said, 'Don't say anything, Snow.' And then, like an idiot – I mean, God love him, but what an idiot – he made for the back door. Of course they ran after him, and of course they caught him. Before he'd taken even three steps they had him on his knees, hands cuffed behind his back, telling him, shut up, shut up, don't say anything. I was saying, 'Get off him, he's done nothing wrong!' But again, they just weren't listening.

The detective said, 'Where are the children, Ms Delaney?'

I said, 'They're in their room, of course.'

The detective said, 'Which room?' And I said, 'In their room off the end of the hall, and if everyone would calm down I'd be quite happy to show it to you.'

That seemed to surprise him. Really, the detective was quite stunned by that. He motioned to his SWAT team to set off down the hall. Like maybe I was going to hide the fact that I had children in the house. Why would I hide it? They were there perfectly legitimately. But then when the SWAT team started off down the hall I saw the women – women who looked suspiciously like they were from the welfare department.

Oh, don't ask me how I knew that's where they were from, Jack, it's just that they all have a certain look – the social-worker look – with big coloured earrings and short cropped hair and cheap shoes and kaftan dresses that might have come from Nepal or somewhere. I said to them, 'Are you police? If you're not police what are you doing here? How can I help you?' But they wouldn't talk to me, wouldn't even look me in the eye.

The detective – the one who had addressed me as Sally Narelle – said, 'How many children are we looking for?' And whoever those Departmental women were, they either couldn't bring themselves to say the number or they basically didn't know, because instead of answering they started burrowing into their clipboards, which is another favourite thing for social workers to do.

I got so sick of waiting for them to answer, I said, 'We have nineteen children in our care – nineteen State wards. What's the problem here? I've been a registered carer in this house for years.'

But nobody was listening to me, Jack. They were all off down the hall, where the SWAT team had already broken another door down – this time the door to the children's room, the big one we created by knocking out a few walls, not that they had any idea what they wanted to do once they'd knocked the door down. I don't know what they expected to find. There were only children in there, most of them on their beds.

'They're naked,' one of the SWAT people said.

'They've got collars,' said one of the others, as if everyone couldn't see that.

'They're attached to the beds.'

'Call the lady.'

I guessed they meant me, so I came down the hall and I stood there in the broken doorway with my hands on my hips, looking at the damage they'd done to my door, and I said, 'What's going on here?'

'What are these collars?' the detective said. 'What are these numbers?'

I said, 'What do you mean, what are those numbers? They're my numbers.'

The detective said, 'Why are they in collars? Why are there numbers on the collars?'

I didn't try to hide *anything*, Jack. I said, 'The numbers are for identification purposes. The children who come to me, they come with a case file number. I need that number in order to get a payment for each child.'

The detective said, 'You get paid to have these kids here?'

I said, 'Of course I do. It's not something you'd do for nothing! I'm not a free hospital! Of course I get paid. I get an allowance. All foster carers get an allowance. But you wouldn't believe how often the Department screws up the payments. Every week, there's some kind of mistake. So I make sure I keep the numbers and the children together, so I can keep track of the payments.'

The detective said, 'But why do you put the numbers on collars? Why couldn't you put the numbers on the wall behind the bed, or on a wristband? Why these heavy neck collars?'

Which had me thinking, 'Honestly, do these people know nothing?'

I tried to be patient. I said, 'Because the children we have here would chew straight through a wristband and probably swallow it, and how much trouble would there be then?'

What I meant was, I had no choice other than to put on neck collars, same as people have to with a dog or a cat. You have to put their identification tag where they can't get at it and chew on it. And most of the children we had, they were so oblivious to the world around them, they wouldn't have known the collars were there!

But why let the facts get in the way of a good story? The detective was appalled. He spoke into his little chest walkie-talkie thing, something about needing a doctor, and probably two, I suppose for the children. To me he said, 'We're going to be removing these children from your care today, Ms Delaney.'

Call me an idiot, Jack, but I was quite shocked to hear that. I said, 'You can't do that, I'm their registered carer.' But they were a step ahead of me: one of the clipboard ladies came forward saying, 'I'm from the Department and we are revoking your carer's licence.'

So, just like that, after years of caring for children that nobody else wanted. I was out, gone. No excuse, no reason given, they threw me on the junk heap. I said, 'On what grounds?' The clipboard lady said, 'The Department doesn't need grounds. The Department can revoke your accreditation at any time.'

I said, 'What am I supposed to have done?' But they couldn't answer me because I hadn't done anything, had I? But of course I knew what was going on. I'd been taking kids for the Department for years, no complaints, and no questions asked. Of course I knew there was supposed to be a six-kid limit, like you couldn't take more than six at a time, and everyone knew that the Department just ignored that and shoved kids wherever they could find places, and tried to make sure the Minister and the media never found out. And they were supposed to come and check on the kids all the time, and basically never did. And so our numbers had built up and built up, and I don't believe anyone in the Department knew for certain how many kids we had in the end. They get staff moving through there like crazy, the turnover is massive, you've got different people ringing you all the time, nobody knows whether they're Arthur or Martha, and so the numbers just went up and up, and since we never complained, what was the problem?

But then suddenly somebody had made a complaint about us – I didn't find out until later that it was that crazy lady, Polly's mum – and since the cops were looking for any excuse to stickybeak around my house because of Agnes going missing, they jumped on it. And so all the files got pulled and suddenly it's whoa! She's got nineteen in there! And that's way out of bounds! And there's been an allegation of some kind of abuse or I don't know what. So let's raid the place!

I went back into the kitchen where Mark was now sitting at the bench, and slumped down next to him. I could see where the whole thing was heading. Somebody had to be hauled over the coals, and the Department has a way of making sure nothing is ever their fault.

At some point a bunch of paramedics arrived – people in white coats with first-aid boxes – and they charged down the hall and into the children's room like they were suddenly the big experts on how to take care of disabled kids.

I followed them back down there – nobody stopped me – and saw them putting their big plastic medical boxes down and getting on their knees, close to the kids, taking their blood pressure, taking their temperature, that kind of thing. I was saying, 'What are you expecting to find, exactly? You certainly won't find anything wrong with them. Not with the care I've been giving them. You can see they're perfectly content here, they're in good health. What are you looking for?'

Nobody would answer me. It was like I didn't exist. One of the female ambos, a young Indian girl, was examining the face of one of the Yugoslav children – Sonya, or maybe it was Nadia – like she was trying to get her – Sonya or Nadia, whichever one it was – to open her mouth and say 'Ah', but that wasn't going to work with a vegetable child. So finally she prised her mouth open, and then she – the Indian girl, I mean – she fell right back onto her bottom, like what she had seen in Sonya–Nadia's mouth had really shocked her. She said, 'Oh God!' really loud, so everybody heard, and everybody was standing looking at her, on her bum on the ground, saying, 'Oh God!'

I said, 'For goodness sake, pull yourself together!'

She looked at me like I was a witch or something – just horror on her face – and she said, 'What's in her mouth? Are they *ants* in her mouth? What have you done?'

I said, 'Ants? Are you mad? What makes you think they're ants?' But some other doctor had rushed over and was holding Sonja–Nadia by the face and was looking in her mouth and saying, 'Jesus.'

I was quite offended. I said, 'It's not ants! It's only fishing line.' And the Indian girl, still on her bum, still with her mouth open, still acting all horrified, said, 'You've got fishing line in her *mouth*?' as if she'd never heard of such a thing.

I said, 'Of course I have, it's for her tongue.' But it was like nobody could understand what I was saying. The Indian girl scrambled up, racing around to all the kids, opening their mouths and looking in, and saying, 'They all have it! They all have it!' And people were demanding to know, 'Why have they all got fishing line in their mouths? What are you doing to them? What's going on?'

I tried to explain it. Very slowly and very patiently, as simply as I could, since these people were obviously idiots, I said, 'These children aren't normal. They have problems with their tongues – their tongues protrude, and if they're left like that, they get problems.'

The Indian girl was saying, 'What problems? What problems?'

I said, 'Clearly you know nothing about children with poor motor function. If you have children who can't keep their tongues in their mouth, they get chin rashes. They are also at risk of swallowing their tongue. It is very dangerous. The fishing line, it's what I put in there to help them.'

But they didn't seem to get it, Jack. It was like they couldn't understand. The Indian girl kept saying, 'But what's it for? What's it for? How is it supposed to help?'

I had to start all over again, saying, 'When a child has a tongue that causes them all kind of problems – like swallowing it or biting it or letting it lie on their chin so they get a rash – you've got to do something about it. You have to try to bring the size of the tongue down.'

I told them, 'Plastic surgeons do it all the time with the Down syndrome kids. They trim their tongues, so the tongues don't hang out so much. But I can't afford that and I can't get permission to do it, not for every child I have in my care, so I came up with this.'

They said, 'You cut their tongues with *fishing* line?'

I said, 'I don't *cut* them.' Because that was complete and total rubbish. You can't go cutting somebody's tongue out, because if you try they're going to bleed to death. There's a lot of gristle in the tongue but there's a lot of blood too, and it's going to be painful. How are you going to stop the blood from flowing out? So no, I never cut anybody's tongue out. It was such an exaggeration.

What I did was very humane. I'm quite happy to explain it: I *trimmed* their tongues – only those who needed it – and not with a knife. I did it with the fishing line! It was actually ingenious, the idea behind it. I don't say that because it was my idea – it wasn't. I actually got the idea from the Wentworth Courier. They had a story about one of those young guys at the tattoo parlour on Campbell Parade – Beach Skin Art, I think the place was called – and he was doing tongue forking on people as a kind of fashion statement. Some politician was up in arms about whether tongue forking was Satanic, or whether it should be banned for people under the age of eighteen, or some such thing. Anyway, the Wentworth Courier did a story on it, and it got me interested.

The tattoo artist – he was one of those strange-looking people with the large metal circles in his ears – was interviewed, saying tongue forking is perfectly safe, provided you know what you're doing, and why shouldn't people be able to fork their own tongues? I thought, how interesting, and not long after that I went to his studio. The tattooist was actually working when I got there – he had his little tattoo gun in his hands and he had his silicon gloves on – and he said, 'May I help you?'

I thought he'd be a bit snickery because I suppose a person like me – a nurse, and so on – wasn't his normal clientele, but he was fine. I told him, 'It's not a tattoo I'm interested in, I'm interested in the tongue forking.'

He said, 'Oh, well, you're going to have to come back for that.'

And I said, 'No, it isn't for me. I don't want it done. I'm interested in how you do it.'

He said, 'Well, I'm in the middle of something here.' But his client – there was a man face down on the chair getting tattooed – said, 'I'm happy to take a break.' So the tattooist put his gun down and went over to the cabinet where he kept all his wands for navel piercings and the eyebrow studs, and he said, 'You can basically use any of these for the tongue.'

I said, 'It's not the jewellery I'm interested in. I'm interested to know how you do it. I saw the article where you said it's easy. Do you have a special tool, and what do you do about the blood?'

The tattooist said, 'There isn't much blood, not the way we do it.' He ran through the method with me: he was basically taking his own tongue by the tip, and he grabbed that band of flesh that sits under there – the bit that holds the tongue to the floor of your mouth – and he said, 'That flap there, that's about the halfway mark of the tongue.'

Well, I could see that. We all can. Grab your tongue and feel for yourself – the bit where the band of skin holds it down, that's about the middle of your tongue.

The tattooist said, 'We drive a piercing gun through the tongue at that point. Then, once you've got the hole in, we take a piece of fishing line and thread it over the tongue, and we thread it vertical so it's right down the middle of the tongue. And we tie the fishing line at the tip – tight as you can.'

He was holding his own tongue as he said this. 'Then what you do is basically pull the line a bit tighter every day, so it's cutting a vertical line into the tongue. You pull it and pull it, and after six weeks or so, the tongue just splits, and there's no blood.'

The bloke on the leather chair had been watching and listening, and he said, 'I saw somewhere that when you've got a forked tongue, each half can do its own thing.' The tattoo guy said, 'It takes some practice,' and he shot his own tongue out again, and it was forked. He could make each of the two sides jerk about, or he could hold them together, whatever he liked, and it was foul in my opinion but I had the information I needed, so I said, 'Thank you.'

And here's something funny, Jack. The tattooist said, 'Is it for you or are you thinking for your girlfriend?'

I said, 'Sorry?' And he said, 'A lot of the ladies with lady partners are interested.'

I said, 'Oh, it's not for me!' I didn't tell him who it was for because I knew what kind of reaction I'd get, like: oh, how cruel!

That wasn't how Mark reacted. When I went home and explained the concept to him, he got it straightaway. He said, 'Oh yeah, I heard you can amputate a finger like that,' though he was absolutely useless in terms of helping me. So squeamish! But I had no problems. I mean, a couple of the kids resisted it. They didn't like their tongues being messed around with, same as anyone, but that's what you learn when you're a nurse, you've just got to get on with what's got to be done, whether it's giving somebody a needle or taking out stitches, you can't afford to have them pulling and pushing away from you and screaming, you've got to get it done.

The ones in the beds, the ones who didn't have much motor control, they were pretty easy. I eventually got fishing line into their tongues and tied it around, horizontal, not vertical, and over time the tips just came off.

Just the tips, that's all.

People have gone off their heads about it – people like you, the media I mean – but to this day I'll argue that those kids were better off for having it done. The only problem was, their tongues would keep growing, and sometimes we'd have to do it a second or a third time. It was just our bad luck that we were in the middle of one of those sessions when the raid happened. And when I tried to explain to the woman who was freaking out what it actually was that I was doing – 'The fishing line helps bring the tip off . . . it's gradual, it's not too painful' – she looked at me like I was doing something evil, and it would be against her ethics. I wouldn't be surprised if she was behind all the stories that leaked out.

I mean, 'They Cut Out Their Tongues!' It was ridiculous. And that wasn't even the worst of it because the stories kept coming. One day the *Telegraph,* or whatever that tabloid rag is called, would say, 'They cut out their tongues!' and the next day it would be: 'And they crippled them!' Or it would be: 'Nil by mouth! Children force-fed by tube in House of Horrors!'

Honestly, reading some of that, I thought, 'Are you people serious?' They made it sound like we were picking the kids up and breaking their legs or something. I've tried a hundred times to explain what we were doing: some of those kids had spastic hands. Anyone who has ever worked with disabled kids will know about spastic hands. It's when the fingers curl up into the palms, and the fingernails cut into the palms and you have to try to wrench them open, but when they're seriously spastic, it's hard to break the lock on the hand. You have to sit for hours and massage the hands to try to get them open. But how were we supposed to manage that with the number of kids we had?

So, okay, from time to time I'd make a small cut – just a tiny little cut – into the nerve that holds the hand closed, and bang, it would spring open, and that became: 'They crippled them!'

The media was going on about it – once the nerve is cut, you can't use the hand any more – but those kids weren't using their hands before I cut the nerve! They weren't feeding themselves, or sitting reading. They were vegetables, unless you count the way they'd try to scratch their own eyes out.

The other thing people forget is that I was trained at all these things – I'm a nurse! – so it was no problem to me to modify the hand, or make the tongue a bit shorter or to do whatever else had to be done with the stomach tubes. And yes, we did use stomach tubes to feed them, or most of them, because how many hours do people think there are in a day? Was I supposed to sit there and spoon-feed nineteen children three times a day? Clean up after nineteen children after they've dropped food all down their chin?

People said, 'Some of them were so skinny! You can't have been feeding them properly because of how skinny some of them were!' That's rubbish too. The skinny ones were skinny because they pulled their stomach tubes out. That was their choice to do that, not my choice, and they couldn't expect to get another meal because there were no other meals, so the ones who pulled their tubes out got skinny, and the tube kids got nice and fat.

People say that's cruel, and they can say what they like, but the fact of the matter is Delaney House was as quiet as any other house on the street, which is another way of saying I ran that place like clockwork, and the only person who had a problem with it was that silly sister of mine, Agnes Bloody Moore.

Snow

Chapter Twenty-one

Those of you who have been following Snow's letters closely will know that last letter was the first time that Snow admitted her sister did have a problem with what she was doing at Delaney House. She didn't say what it was, but that is still more than she has ever told police.

I know that because I got hold of the transcript of the first conversation Snow had with police – technically, I suppose it was an interview – after her trial, using the Freedom of Information laws.

I'm going to run through a few of the important points here, but the first thing you should know is that there is a special squad of officers within the New South Wales police force whose identities are always kept secret. It's called JERT, which stands for the Juvenile Emergency Response Team, and its members deal only with crimes against children.

When Snow Delaney was taken in after the raid on Delaney House it was JERT officers who led the questioning. Two officers – by law, one of them had to be female – sat down in chairs on one side of an old police desk, facing her, with a video recorder mounted in the corner of the room.

Mark Delaney was in another room, with different detectives from the same unit, and his interview was also filmed.

It probably goes without saying that Snow and Mark weren't allowed to talk to each other, mainly because the cops would have wanted to stop them from colluding, and because there's always the chance that if you suggest to one of them that the other one is coughing up details, they might decide to talk.

Each was allowed to have a lawyer, but Mark Delaney didn't seem interested in that. He wanted only to exercise his right to silence. As a result, the transcript of the interview between Mark Delaney and the two JERT detectives makes for pretty dull reading. They take turns asking questions, and he basically says nothing other than, 'I ain't got nothing to say.'

The transcript of the interview between Snow and her detectives is much more interesting. She clearly was not bothered about maintaining her right to silence at that point.

Bear in mind that while these detectives were talking to Snow, there was a team of doctors and social workers from the welfare department working behind the scenes, frantically trying to identify each of the kids who had been removed from Delaney House; whether (and how) any of them had been harmed; how many of them had parents that needed to be contacted (most of the children found in Delaney House had been formally relinquished to the care of the State); and they were also trying to match the numbers on Snow's collars to data from their own files.

One of the first things to become clear as that process got underway was that there were way more children in the house than there ever should have been. According to the Department's own guidelines, there should have been a maximum of six. But Snow was quite happy to explain to the police how she ended up with three times as many, saying, 'They kept bringing them, so we kept taking them.'

One of the detectives – the one playing 'good cop' in the 'good cop/bad cop' thing (although, if you study the transcript, it does seem like both of them were playing 'good cop' for a while there) – said, 'The Department must have been so grateful. I imagine it's difficult to get people to take children with such severe disabilities. You must be a saint to take so many in.'

Snow responds, 'From my point of view, it's the more disabled the better.'

The detective said, 'And why's that? Because you feel with your qualifications that they're better off with you than perhaps with somebody who isn't a nurse, or doesn't have the same training?'

Snow said, 'No, it's not that. I only take Category Two. If it's just a matter of them lying there in bed and having the tube, I can take as many as they want. It's not like it's difficult.'

To their credit, neither detective responded to that, although it must have been tempting.

Next came the matter that had already been raised by Joe Potter at the press conference outside Delaney House: how twenty children came to be removed from the house, despite the Department having placed only nineteen children in Snow's care.

One of the two detectives said, 'We're a bit confused, how is it that there were twenty children in Delaney House?'

Snow said, 'I already told police at the house. Why do I have to keep explaining everything? One of them is Mark's. I'm not going to deny that. One of the little boys, he comes from Mark.'

The first detective says, 'And that little boy, what's his name?'

Snow said, 'Mark calls him Angus.'

The detective said, 'I take it you're not the mum?'

'No way.'

'Would you mind telling us who the mother is? We're going to want to contact her, obviously.'

Snow said, 'You're not going to have to look far. You'll have the mum in your custody already.'

Of course I've got the benefit of hindsight, but reading the transcript it took me about a second to work out what she meant: Mark had fathered the child with one of the children she was supposed to be taking care of, in Delaney House. But the detective who was asking the questions didn't seem to be able to get his head around it.

He said, 'Your husband had a child with one of the children?'

Snow said, 'He's not my husband, and it wasn't his fault. He was raped.'

The detective said, 'Excuse me?'

Snow said, 'He was raped by one of those girls. Most of them are nymphomaniacs. Talk to anyone who works with them, the ones with mental problems in particular, they can't stop themselves. You have to pull them off each other, they go at it like rabbits.'

I know enough about policing to know a few of the old techniques, one of which is to maintain one's cool, to try to make the person in the hot seat feel what they're saying is totally reasonable when it's actually reprehensible.

The detective said, 'That must have been hard for Mark, having girls around, flirting all the time.'

You can't pick up tone from an interview transcript, but my guess would be that Snow answered pretty enthusiastically. She said, 'I'm not blind to Mark's faults. He has a problem with the pokies. I wish he'd give the smokes way. But the idea that he was interested in any of the children we got from the Department, I can tell you now, no way. He was raped! This girl, she's an absolute monster, always taking her underpants off in public, always waving her tail around, and she threw herself at him. I saw it happen. He pulled away as soon as he heard me, ran out of the room with his pants around his ankles, stumbling and falling toward the hall. I thought, how could he? And I followed him down to the bedroom, saying, 'What are you playing at, Mark?' But he explained to me, she was basically leading him on. Because they were like that. It's part of the reason I stopped taking ones that could walk and talk.

'I said to Mark, "Don't you let them do it. Don't let them corner you." But it was too late because next thing, nine months on or whatever, I found the same girl crouched over the toilet complaining of a "sore tummy". I looked in the bowl, and there was a pool of blood in it. I pulled her off the toilet, into the hall, and it was clear to me that this was more than a miscarriage or what-have-you. She was having the baby, there in the toilet.'

The detective, still trying to play cool, says, 'How is it that you didn't notice that, Ms Delaney? Before she actually began having the baby, I mean?'

Snow said, 'She was so fat! All the mentally retarded ones are so fat! They don't do any exercise. They've got no control over their appetite. They'd eat sweets all day if you let them, and sugar right out of the bowl, spoons of Milo, everything. That's part of why I went on to tube-feeding.'

The second detective said, 'What did you do, Ms Delaney, when the baby started coming?'

Snow said, 'I did what I could. I lay the mother down, and helped pull the thing out – not easy with her moaning and groaning and howling and thrashing and saying, "It hurts, it hurts" – and I was saying, "Well, of course it hurts, you stupid little girl. What have you done to yourself?" And I was pretty angry with Mark, too, but he kept saying, "It wasn't my fault, she jumped me." And that made sense, because that's what the mother was like, so I went back to where she was lying on the floor, and there was this infant, and I said to Mark, "What are we going to do?" And what could we do? We would simply have to accommodate one more.'

The detective said, 'And so Angus became one of the family?'

Snow said, 'I wouldn't put it like that. I took him in. What choice did I have?'

The detective said, 'And the mother is one of the girls that's still with you?'

Snow said, 'Of course! But she doesn't know she's got a baby. She thinks Angus is a doll.'

The whole transcript is like that, strange and cold, but despite all that she was admitting to, in terms of cutting the tongues and clipping the limbs of the children, Snow seemed to think, right until the last hurdle, that she'd be walking out of that interview room that day, when actually what happened was that she was marched out to the divvy van, taken to court and charged with child abuse.

Chapter Twenty-two

Dear Jack,

You asked me what it was like going into remand at Silverwater, and I don't mind admitting that I was in a panic about it, but it's amazing what you can cope with.

    Silverwater is the same prison where they've got Kath Knight, and if you don't know her, she's the lady who stabbed and stripped and skinned her boyfriend, boiled his head in a pot with leeks and potatoes, carved up his flesh for his children to eat, and served it on plates in the dining room.

    When they told me I was going to Silverwater I thought, 'Are they really going to put me in with people like that?' And I thought, 'Are they really going to strip me and force me into the showers in front of everyone? Are they going to want to search me for drugs in all my private places?'

    Just so you know, they did do all of that. They tested me for diseases and gave me some supplies, like a T-shirt and a tracksuit and socks, and they checked me for drugs but they've got it down to a fine art, so it's pretty quick.

They asked me what I'd brought with me and that was something I didn't get, that you're actually allowed to bring things in when you're on remand, even a TV if you want one. Then they took me down a corridor, with the doors beeping and clicking, because I was supposed to see a psychologist so they could find out if I was going to kill myself.

The psychologist told me I'd be going into solitary confinement for seven days and I said, 'Why? I haven't done anything wrong,' and she said, 'It's the rules.' And let me tell you now, if I've heard that phrase once since I've been in here, I've heard it nine million times . . . it's the rules . . . it's the rules!

Solitary confinement wasn't too bad: just another beige room, like every other beige room in this place, with a steel toilet and a bed.

If you want to know what I was thinking, I wasn't thinking about me, I was worried about Mark because he might act all tough when he's drunk but it's only when he's drunk that he's got any courage. Most of the time, he's a pussycat, still a little boy like the little boy who was abandoned by his mum and punched up by his step-dad, and I knew he wouldn't cope in prison.

I was asking and asking to talk to him, but they said it wasn't allowed, and when I got out of solitary and got the right to have a phone call I said I wanted to make my call to Mark, and they said, you can't call another prisoner. So I took it that Mark hadn't got bail either.

After solitary, I went into the main part of the remand section, and because of the newspapers everybody knew who I was and a couple came over to make friends, but I wasn't interested in making friends because I was thinking that I wouldn't be in there very long.

They would be slumping down in the plastic chairs in the TV room, saying, 'What's on?' and I'd ignore them.

I suppose I'd been on remand about three weeks when one of the corrective services officers – that's what we're supposed to call the guards here – told me I'd be getting a visit from the lawyer I got through Legal Aid. You'll know who I got – it was John Barrett SC.

The SC apparently means something special but I don't see what was so special about this bloke. He came to visit me at the remand centre, all excited about representing the lady from the Horror House, but the only thing I wanted to know was, 'When can you get me out of here?'

Do you know what he said? He said, 'Don't worry, I'm planning to get as many women off the jury as I can.' Honestly, that's what he said!

I said, 'What's that supposed to mean?' He said, 'Women tend to be much tougher on other women than men are, especially when it's crimes against children.'

I said, 'I haven't committed any crimes, and I definitely haven't committed any crimes against children.'

He seemed to think that was hilarious, saying, 'That's what I want to hear! You're off to a good start!'

He also told me, 'The reason they have you on remand is that they hope you'll talk to somebody in here about what you've done, so trust nobody and say nothing.'

I said, 'As if I'd talk to anyone in here.'

He sat back in his chair with his hands behind his head, kind of smiling, and said, 'You know there's a Facebook page in your honour?' He looked pretty pleased, but then he sat bolt upright and said, 'But that's the kind of publicity we don't want!'

Of course I also asked him about Mark, saying, 'Who's he got representing him? He's not going to be able to cope in here. He's got addiction problems.' But Barrett would only tell me that Mark was in 'good hands', whatever that meant.

He asked me if there was anything he could do on the outside for me, like organise to get any cats fed, and I said I had no cats. He said, 'Do you want me to organise to get Delaney House rented out? Mark has told his lawyer that it's up to you,' and I said, 'Why would we want to rent it out? We're going to move back in there when we get bail.'

Barrett said, 'Bail! You need to understand that they're going to hold you here until the trial and that could be next year, Snow. The wheels of justice move pretty slowly in New South Wales.'

I said, 'Hang on a minute, isn't it your job to get me out of here?'

He said, 'The problem is, you've already been tried in the court of public opinion, and what do you think would happen if the judge let you out on bail? The newspapers would go nuts; the Premier would carry on; the Opposition would do the whole "soft on crime" drama.'

I said, 'Alright, rent it out, but only for six months until we get out,' and I was thinking, 'I wonder how much we will get for it?' And, 'We might actually make money while I'm here on remand, and wouldn't that be funny?' But that dream didn't last long because the next time Barrett came back he said he couldn't rent Delaney House out after all.

I said, 'And why is that?' And he said, 'Police are digging the place up.'

I'm not going to deny that I was stunned. I said, 'What are you talking about, they're digging the place up?'

He said, 'It's in all the papers: police moved into the back yard about a week ago. They've got earth-moving equipment, and cadaver dogs.'

At first I didn't get what he was talking about: cadaver dogs? But then he said, 'They're the dogs that sniff out bones. They're looking for your sister, Agnes Moore. There's been a story about it in the paper, pretty much every day.'

I said, 'That's outrageous. How is it they're allowed to just march onto our property and start digging it up?'

Barrett seemed to think that was an idiotic question. He said, 'It's a crime scene, Snow. They've got a warrant. Of course they can dig it up.'

I said, 'Well, whatever. Tell them from me to make sure they put everything back like they found it, and I don't know what they think they're going to find.'

He said, 'Agnes, obviously.'

I told him, 'That's just ridiculous,' but then a week later he was back saying, 'They've found a skeleton.'

Snow

Chapter Twenty-three

Pretty much the instant I heard that police had moved cadaver dogs into Delaney House, I went down to Bat Street in Bondi and knocked on Bill Carson's door.

'I thought you'd be back,' he said as he led me through the house. 'I hope they don't find anything. Shirl's having nightmares and she keeps saying we won't be able to live here any more if that poor lady turns up under a rose bush.'

I couldn't help feeling bad for her when the *Telegraph* scooped the rest of us with the headline:

'SKELETON FOUND AT BONDI'S HOUSE OF HORRORS.'

As is normal practice, the cops didn't say who it was, but I suppose, like pretty much everyone else, I thought, 'Well, we hardly need to wait for forensics to know that it's going to be Agnes Moore.'

But Snow wasn't wrong when she told her lawyer that

her sister wouldn't be found on her property, because the skeleton wasn't Agnes Moore.

It was Beth Bannerman.

Dear Jack,

Do you ever have those days where you suddenly think, 'I could really do with a bit of good news for a change?' Because that's exactly what I thought when Barrett came to tell me that police had found a skeleton at Delaney House.

I said, 'A skeleton? What next, a ghost?'

It sounded ridiculous. I said, 'First they try to pin child-abuse charges on me when all I've done my whole life is try to help children, and now they say I've got a skeleton buried in the back yard? Don't tell me it's supposed to be Agnes?'

Barrett said, 'No, it's not Agnes. The police are waiting on forensics to come back but to us they're saying the bones are much older.'

I said, 'Well, that's fine. Delaney House is ancient. The skeleton is probably ancient. It's certainly got nothing to do with me.'

Barrett said, 'They're doing DNA tests. Like everyone, we're going to have to wait.'

I said, fine, whatever, and to be honest I was more curious than anything, and maybe a bit creeped out by the idea that there'd been a body in the back yard all the time I'd been living at Delaney House, and for who knows how long. But then three weeks or something went by, and the forensics or whatever they call it came back, and Barrett said, oh, it's Beth Bannerman.

I was that stunned, Jack, I just said, 'How can it be Beth Bannerman?' Because as far as I knew, Beth Bannerman had gone to visit her niece one weekend while I was visiting Mum in Melbourne and I hadn't seen her since.

'How could her corpse have been found in the back yard?' I said to Barrett. 'Where was she exactly?'

He said, 'She was under the deck.'

I said, 'What are you talking about, she was under the deck?'

He said, 'Under the concrete deck. Police are talking about laying some kind of charge.'

I said, 'How can they charge me with anything? I didn't even know that Mrs Bannerman was dead, let alone that she was buried at Delaney House. Has nobody even considered that she might have had an accident? That she was so old, maybe she had a heart attack?'

But Barrett kept saying, 'She was buried under concrete, Snow . . . under the deck that Mark put down,' like he was trying to get me to put two and two together and get five.

I said, 'You're not trying to tell me that Mark did anything to Mrs Bannerman. He loved his Aunt Beth.'

Barrett said, 'The police are going to want to interview you.' So the cops came out to the remand centre and introduced themselves and said, 'We'd like to ask you some questions about the death of Mrs Bannerman.'

I said, 'What do you want to know? She was a very old, very crazy lady, and something like eight years ago, she told my Mark that she was going to visit some niece of hers who had showed up at the house. He never seemed worried about it and it wasn't my business to be worried about it either. Now my lawyer tells me you've found a skeleton under the deck and it's hers, and all I can think is, she must have had a heart attack and fallen in the old pit we had there.'

The police said, 'Okay, well, when was the last time you saw Mrs Bannerman?'

I said, 'It was in September 2001, just before I went to Melbourne. It was when my mother was dying.'

The detectives said, 'And Mrs Bannerman was gone when you got back?'

I said, 'That's right.'

They said, 'Did Mark tell you where she'd gone?'

I said, 'He told me that some woman had come to the house, claiming to be Beth's niece. It didn't take much to figure out what she was after, which was obviously Aunt Beth's money.

'But Mark wasn't born yesterday and when I asked him, "Did you let her in?" he said, "No way." I said, "Did you tell Aunt Beth she was here?" He said, "I didn't tell her straightaway," but then he decided he would tell her, and she decided she would go and visit this niece, and she put on her hat, and she left.'

They said, 'And you weren't at home when this happened?'

I said, 'No, I was in Melbourne because Mum had cancer and she was dying. When I got back I noticed that Mrs Bannerman wasn't around and I asked Mark about it, and he said, 'She put on her sunhat, and said she was going to visit her niece.'

One of the cops said, 'She did all this, despite having dementia?'

I said, 'People with dementia can have good days and bad days.'

The cop said, 'And it was after this that Mark started putting a deck on the back of the house, was it?'

I could see what they were getting at – you'd have to be an idiot not to see it – but I said, 'Don't you try to frame Mark for this, just because he built that deck. He built that deck because he wanted to do something nice for me because my mum was dying. If you're saying he did that to cover up old Mrs Bannerman, that's ridiculous.'

SISTERS OF MERCY

The detective said, 'You don't think he'd notice that he was covering over a human body?'

I said, 'The spot where he built that deck – there was a huge crater there, a big hole from a Japanese sub. That pit was filled with old car parts and machinery and weeds. There could have been anything in there, and who would know?'

The homicide detective said, 'And you're trying to suggest that Mrs Bannerman might have fallen into that pit, got tangled up somehow, and Mark didn't know that he was covering her over?'

I said, 'You can speculate all you like but I'm telling you now: I was always on at Mark to do something about that pit. You couldn't open the back door without thinking you might fall into it. He went to a lot of trouble to make that area nice. He sank the pylons, he poured the concrete, he hired the nail gun.'

It all made perfect sense to me, but the cops kept asking leading questions.

The detective said, 'Mrs Bannerman wasn't really Mark's aunt, was she?'

I said, 'She was as good as an aunt. She had always been his Aunt Beth.'

The police said, 'But you said that Mrs Bannerman had gone to visit a real niece?'

I said, 'That's what Mark told me. The way he explained it, she had a brother but they hadn't talked to each other for years, and this woman was his daughter. Maybe Beth didn't want to die without putting things right. Maybe that's why she wandered off to see her. Old people do strange things like that.'

The detective said, 'But she didn't wander off, did she? Because she was found in the back yard.'

I said, 'But I didn't know that until now.'

'Did you consider reporting Mrs Bannerman missing at that point?' asked the other detective.

I said, 'Why would I report her missing?'

'Because she never returned to her house?'

I said, 'I wasn't in the business of keeping tabs on Mrs Bannerman. She basically lived in the garden. She slept in a bungalow out the back. She was a grown woman, and a demented one.'

The detective said, 'So, do you mean to tell us that you were not concerned about the fact that Mrs Bannerman has never, in all these years, returned to her home?'

Again I said, 'I'm not her keeper. I thought she must be enjoying herself, spending time with her niece.'

They said, 'For eight years?'

I said, 'It was actually after seven years that I did report her missing.'

The detective said, 'Right, because for some reason, last year, you decided to apply to the Coroner for a death certificate for Mrs Bannerman?'

I said, 'You're making it sound like I was up to something. I couldn't have reported Beth missing any earlier than that. You have to wait seven years before you can apply for that certificate.'

The detective said, 'So, after seven years you suddenly decided she must be dead?'

I said, 'I didn't know what had happened to her, but she obviously wasn't around. And after seven years, you can apply to have somebody declared dead. Everyone knows that.'

They said, 'But why would you do that, if you didn't know whether she was dead or not?'

I said, 'Because you can do it after seven years.'

They said, 'And of course, you and Mark are the beneficiaries of Beth's will, aren't you? So if she's dead, the two of you inherit Delaney House.'

I said, 'That's right, but that had nothing to do with it. I've been living at Delaney House forever. It's been as good as mine forever. I'm running my business there.'

They said, 'When did you become a beneficiary of Mrs Bannerman's will?'

I said, 'It's funny because it was just before Beth went missing.'

They said, 'What an amazing coincidence!' or something like that, and I said, 'Not really. After that niece turned up at the house, Beth just decided that she didn't want her to inherit the house. She wanted me and Mark to inherit it. And I suppose she thought she better get that sorted out so she got Mark to send a new will off to her solicitor, all signed.'

They said, 'But you said she was demented.'

I said, 'Well, maybe she was but not demented enough not to know what she wanted done with her house.'

They said, 'And then she went missing?'

And I said, 'Right.'

They said, 'And when the Coroner contacted Mrs Bannerman's family to ask if they had any objection to him issuing a death certificate, they said they didn't even know that their Aunt Beth was missing.'

I said, 'Right, and doesn't that tell you what kind of family they are? She's been missing seven years and they don't even know?'

The detectives said, 'Why would you say nothing for seven years, and then as soon as the seven years was up, report Mrs Bannerman missing?'

I said, 'I suppose I was thinking, "She's just a crazy old coot. She'll turn up."'

And then, when she did turn up, it was under the deck that Mark built. I felt so sorry for him, Jack. I mean, think about it: it must have broken his heart to know what he'd done, covering her over, and having barbecues on the deck, right on top of her. I was really badly worried about how he'd take it. And I wasn't wrong because how long did he last in prison after he heard that? And after he heard that cops were thinking of ways to charge him with manslaughter, or maybe even murder, and of charging me with something too? He lasted barely a week, that's how long he lasted.

It was Barrett who came and told me what he'd done. He said, 'I have to tell you, Mark's gone,' and at first I thought, 'They've let him out!' But Barrett said, 'No, no, he's committed suicide,' and I just didn't believe it, I just flat out didn't believe it. I was saying, no, no, no, and he had to show me the story from the newspaper before I would believe it.

Mark Delaney of the now infamous House of Horrors at Bondi was found dead in his cell last night.

That's what they wrote, like it was good news. And it wasn't true. He was not 'found dead' in his cell at all. He was still alive when they cut him down, and the police, being malicious, rushed him to hospital so they could get him on a life-support system.

'They were after the deathbed confession,' was how Barrett put it to me. 'They kept him alive for a full day and they had a warrant so they could keep questioning him.'

It made me sick, hearing that. The idea of him lying there, full of tubes, with those cops probing him, saying, 'If Snow's got anything to do with this – with Beth, or with Agnes going missing – tell us now, and give the families some closure while you've still got a chance.'

I asked Barrett, 'Is that even legal, keeping somebody alive like that? And whatever they said, you couldn't use that in court, could you?' Not that I was worried what Mark said but because cops shouldn't be allowed to use stuff they get from people they've been torturing. Mark never wanted to be put on life support. He hated the idea of being kept alive, a vegetable like the children we'd had at Delaney House, with all that indignity. But they kept him alive – in a coma, but alive – trying to get some sort of confession from him. And what did they get?

Nothing, and here's why: he had nothing to tell them. They were prodding him and saying, 'Dob in Snow! Dob in Snow!' But by this stage, even my own lawyer, Barrett, was on my case about it, and especially after what happened to Mark he kept saying, 'Why not talk to the police, Snow? Make things easier on yourself. How much of what happened was really his fault?'

I could see what he was doing, trying to make me turn on Mark because Mark was dead, but there was nothing to turn on Mark about because we didn't do anything. So I said, 'No, I'm done talking to the cops. The stuff they want to pin on me is ridiculous. They can go to hell.'

I told Barrett, 'I'm not saying another word, not about Aunt Beth, not about Agnes, not about anything.' And I've kept my word on that. I said not one more word to police since then and the only thing I said in court when they brought me up on those stupid child-abuse charges was a big 'NOT GUILTY'.

Barrett said, 'You understand that the judge will go harder on you if you don't plead guilty and you refuse to show remorse?'

I said, 'You're talking like I'm guilty of something!'

Then as soon as I got into court on the first day of my trail I could see what he'd been getting at, which was that I was gone. There was a mob up on the steps, hysterical people jeering and carrying on, mums from all these disabled groups who had brought their kids along to chant about rights for the handicapped, like I hadn't been working for handicapped kids all my life.

Kids all propped up in wheelchairs, howling at me, while the police and Barrett were trying to get me from the prison van into the court.

As soon as I saw that mob I knew they'd find me guilty. There would be no point speaking up because people see kids like that and they think it's not fair for them to have to live like that and somebody has to pay, so why not me?

Anyway we got inside, and that's where Barrett started off on his plan to object to having any women on the jury. 'No, I'm sorry, I must object, Your Honour,' he'd say, 'that juror is not acceptable to us.' The prosecution isn't silly. At one point, their senior counsel stood and said, 'What is the basis of your objection, Barrett? Is it because the juror is wearing a skirt?'

So the game was up, and as you probably know, Jack, being an award-winning journalist and all, you only get to make so many objections without actually having a valid reason. So we ended up with four women on the jury, all of them completely biased against me from the start. Not that the men weren't biased against me too. One man who turned up to court on the first day, for example, hadn't trimmed his beard for at least twenty years, and was wearing a brown knitted jumper and wash 'n' wear slacks, and he glared at me like I was dirt. And that was before even a day's worth of evidence had been taken.

As for the foreman – actually a forewoman– she had a face like a twisted lemon. She had decided, I'm absolutely sure of this, that I was guilty before she'd finished taking the oath. She was scowling at me.

I probably don't need to go through all the ins and outs of the trial. You were there. You saw it. That stupid police officer who kept going on about finding a 'hidden room', like you can hide a room with nineteen kids in it. It wasn't hidden, it was behind a door that Mark made, to keep the noise down. Then the Lenore Wallace woman, who had dropped that Polly off with us, appeared on the stand. I must admit, I couldn't even remember who she was when she first stepped up, but then when she spoke, I thought, 'Oh yes, I remembered that child. Polly. She was an absolute pest of a kid.'

This lady, I remembered, had come to us with a whole list of instructions of how I was supposed to look after her. How she had asthma; she had a congenital heart defect; she had seizures; she had problems with her weight, and needed to be on a special diet; she had hearing aides in each ear; she could be stubborn and uncooperative; she needed to be reminded to brush her teeth; we had to be patient when she had something to say because she would stammer and stutter and pause between words; she found it difficult to get up from a sitting position; she couldn't see without her glasses; she had patches of eczema; she needed to have her comfort toys, although we had a quite clear rule – no comfort toys because they'd get lost and the parents would have to go hunting around, trying to find them.

She was going on about how she 'inspected Delaney House', which was a lie, and saw three children on the bed 'like seals, not making a sound'. I felt like yelling out, 'Because they couldn't talk!'

Then that ear, nose and throat specialist all the journos loved so much got up and talked about how she'd examined our kids, and all had short tongues so they couldn't make a lot of noise and wouldn't have been able to eat properly. Again I felt like yelling out, 'They didn't eat! They had stomach tubes.' She went on for quite a while, saying that all the tongues were cut in the same way, with the fishing line, so that the front section of the tongue – the bit in front of the webbing – was gone, and that would have made speech difficult. I was thinking, 'Like they talked before?'

They dragged up the mothers of some of the children we'd taken in, including some drug addict junkie deadbeat single mother who had abandoned her disabled child to Delaney House. She actually stood there in the court room giving evidence against me.

I thought, 'The cheek! The hide!'

Her head was bowed forward and her shoulders were hunched, and she was wiping her nose and her eyes, and saying, 'I was told that my child had been sent to a lovely place called Delaney House, and they told me she would be safe!'

I felt like standing up and saying, 'Oh, look, this is ridiculous, are you seriously trying to suggest that the child would have been better off with this junkie? She *abandoned* the infant. Wanted nothing to do with her! Now she stands there, presuming to judge *me?*'

But on it went, a parade of people pointing the finger at me for doing my best.

There was all the rubbish about the money we supposedly earned. A forensic accountant, whatever that's supposed to be, said we had nineteen kids, $600 a week each, so that's $11,400 a week, and $220,000 for such and such financial year, which had all the journos up and running for the corridors to get on their phones so they could write their big stories:

'House of Horrors Foster Mum Was Making a Fortune!'

Not that there was any secret about where it went, not with Mark putting at least that much into the Star City pokies every year.

But anyway, no way was I going to survive testimony like that, obviously, which isn't to say that I didn't enjoy some of the trial. Like when the Department got a grilling from the prosecutor. Dalrymple, that was the prosecutor's name, wasn't it? In my own mind, I was calling him Rumple because of his suit, which always looked like he'd slept in it. Did you see him when he said to the deputy director of foster care, 'How did nineteen children end up in Delaney House, when the Department's own limit is six?' Which all the newspapers had already been asking anyway. And this woman, she had to say, 'It was an oversight,' like you could just overlook what happened to nineteen kids! And Rumple was saying, 'To your knowledge, did any of the children placed in Delaney House by your department attend speech therapy?' And she had to say no. He said, 'Did any of the children placed in Delaney House by your department attend occupational therapy?' And she had to say no again. 'Did any of the children placed in Delaney House by your department attend swimming lessons, for the purpose of rehabilitation or exercise?' She had to say no. 'And did any of the children placed in Delaney House by your department go to school?' And yet again she had to say no.

You could see the jurors sitting there, shaking their heads, like, how hopeless is this mob? And that's the point of all this, isn't it? That all I was doing was what they asked me to do, which was put a roof over the children's heads and keep them safe and fed, and it was the Department that was supposed to tell me if I was doing things wrong.

But they'd dropped the ball, which you could see when Rumple asked this lady, 'When was the last time an officer from your department paid a home visit to Snow Delaney?' She had to say in 2004, and he said, 'So nobody from your department had visited Delaney House for seven years?' And she had to admit that was true.

I've already told you that I basically didn't speak. I saw what you said about that: 'Snow didn't take the stand lest she incriminate herself.' What rubbish, Jack. The way you wrote that, you made it sound like if I opened my mouth, everyone would immediately see that I was guilty. But the reason I didn't speak was I could see it was a farce. They were going to find me guilty whatever I said. And so I just let them do whatever, until that Friday in April when I was asked to stand, and the foreman, or in my case the forewoman, Miss Sucked-on-a-Lemon, also stood up.

The judge said, 'Have you reached a verdict?'

Ms Pinched-Face said, 'We have, Your Honour.' And the way she said it, I knew that they'd found me guilty.

The judge said, 'And what is your verdict?'

Ms Pinched-Face said, 'We find the defendant *guilty*, Your Honour' – and again, it was in that smarmy voice, with all the emphasis on 'guilty', like Little Miss Sucked-on-a-Lemon was suddenly so important.

I couldn't help it, I snorted. The newspapers the next day reported that snort as my 'contempt' of the court. 'Snow Delaney let out a snort of derision when the verdict was delivered,' was how the *Sydney Morning Herald* put it. Was it derision? Maybe it was, but maybe I was snorting at how smug they all looked, passing judgement on me. And what was I supposed to do when the verdict came down? Start crying? What good would that do? Look shocked? But wouldn't that have been a bit *fake*, to be shocked at a verdict I'd expected all along?

And it's what everyone expected. It's what newspapers like yours pretty much *demanded.* Don't try to deny it. Why do you think that old juror in his moth-eaten brown jumper had it in for me before a skerrick of evidence was offered? Why do you think Miss Face-like-a-Slapped-Arse was staring so filthily at me, before I'd even been asked to say whether I wanted to plead guilty or not? It's because they'd already determined that I was guilty. And why did they think so? Because they'd read all about the case in newspapers like yours, and because they'd seen all the ridiculous headlines, and they had watched footage on *News Tonight* and they'd made up their minds before they got there. And because they were hearing reporters like you going on about how my sister was missing, and about how Beth had been found in the yard and that was such a coincidence, wasn't it! Snow must have something to do with it! Let's not worry that there's no evidence that Agnes is even dead! That I've not been charged with anything to do with her going missing! That's why they found me guilty. Trial by media, that's what it was.

The judge thanked Miss-Lemon-Face for her verdict, and she shot me the most satisfied, cat-that-got-the-cream look I've ever seen as she sat down. But I had to stay standing while the judge lectured me.

He said, 'You've been found guilty of the charges against you. I'll adjourn the sentencing hearing for three weeks. You'll be held on remand, Ms Delaney, while I consider the appropriate sentence. You can take that as an indication of the way I'm leaning.'

I asked Barrett, 'What's that supposed to mean?'

He said, 'It means that the judge has decided that a custodial sentence is the way to go.'

I said, 'I'm going back to prison?'

And Barrett said, 'Yes.'

I have to tell you, Jack, I was surprised to hear it. I thought probation was what I'd get – probation and maybe a fine. People can laugh but I couldn't see what anyone would gain from putting me in prison. Like I said at the outset, I'd never been in trouble with the police before they came to arrest me, and I obviously was never going to care for any children again. They could find some other bunny to do it.

It would cost the State a fortune to hold me in prison, and what would be the point of it? But that's not the way things work. People wanted me punished – and punished hard – for what I was supposed to have done, and prison is how we punish people in the State of New South Wales. In that respect, it hasn't changed much since the convict days.

People will tell you, maybe even with a straight face, that prison's about rehabilitation, but, like I said when I first wrote to you, there's no rehabilitation in prison. There are English lessons, but I speak English. They'll help you sit the HSC, but I have my HSC. You get to use computers so you might one day be able to get a job, but I've never had any problem getting a job, so how was I going to be rehabilitated exactly?

What they wanted was to punish me. That's what putting me in prison was all about.

So there I was, coming out of court with my hands in cuffs in front of my body, being led like a prize sow into a show ring, toward the police van, and I could hear people clapping, and one of the mothers of one of the children I'd been caring for shouted out, 'I hope you rot in hell, Snow Delaney!'

I have to tell you, that made my blood boil. And people wonder why I fired Barrett ahead of the sentencing. It should be obvious!

Snow

Chapter Twenty-four

It's against the law to take a camera or any other kind of recording device into court in New South Wales. You can take a pen and paper in, but that's it, and I guess that's one of the things that makes court-reporting feel so old-fashioned – that and the fact that you've got to bow to the judge if you want to leave the room, and everyone's got to stand when he comes in to take his seat with that horse-hair wig on his head.

The ban on recording devices means that court staff have got used to setting some seats aside for the media. They're a bit different from normal seats in that they've got a little wooden desk that folds up when you want to get up, and folds down when you want to scribble in your notebook.

Most of them were already taken by the time I arrived to see Snow Delaney get sent to prison in May 2011, but I managed to squeeze into the last one in the row. This was before I'd heard from Snow, remember. The story that prompted her to write to me – 'Secrets of Snow' – wouldn't be published until a week after she was sent away.

The sentencing judge was Samuel Hulme. I could summarise his address for you, but I think it's better that people read it for themselves. He said:

Snow Delaney, please stand.

You have been found guilty of acts which together add up to an unspeakable cruelty.

You volunteered to care for the community's most vulnerable children and you betrayed the trust that was placed in you.

You cut through the nerves in their hands to avoid having to massage them.

You used a barbaric, near-medieval method to sever the tips of their tongues.

You denied them access to basic health services. You restrained them on beds for hours, indeed weeks, on end. You kept the door to their bedroom locked at all times. You restricted them to diets delivered only by feeding tube. You forced them to wear heavy collars with not names but numbers attached to them.

Your level of actual care for them extended to turning their bodies to ensure they did not develop pressure sores. Occasionally, you sponged them down.

There is no evidence you showed them any compassion or human kindness. Your motive, it seems, in taking them in was not to make a contribution to society, to ease their suffering, but to make money.

Questions must be asked about the Department's failure to detect your abuse of the children they placed in your care. How is it that you were able to take in so many children? How can it be that no inspections of any kind were ever done?

The only answer I can fathom is that, as a community, we are failing to take proper care of the children who need us most.

And here now is the worst of it: you, Snow Delaney, are a registered nurse, and nursing is a magnificent profession. Men and woman with your skills and training have for hundreds of years placed great pride in their ability to relieve the suffering of those most in need. It is not for nothing that nurses were once known as the Sisters of Mercy.

How badly you have betrayed those who share your calling, Ms Delaney. How badly you have betrayed us all.'

I was sitting and listening and taking it all down in my lousy shorthand, waiting for the bit that everyone wanted to know: how much would she get? It's no big secret any more. Justice Hulme gave her twelve years, with an eight-year minimum.

People have asked me how Snow reacted, and the answer is, she didn't, by which I mean she didn't fall down screaming like Keli Lane did, when the same court sent her to prison for the murder of her baby Tegan; she didn't get all red and swollen in the face and make like she was going to pop, like Robert Farquharson did, when they sentenced him to life for drowning his three boys in the dam in Melbourne; she didn't turn to the public gallery, trying to get her shouting family to be quiet, like Schapelle Corby did.

She just kept standing, head tipped slightly to the side, the big floppy bow on her collar hanging soft and loose against her blouse. The only sign that she'd even heard what the judge had said was the faintest twitch in the fingertips of her right hand. I wondered what she was thinking. It wasn't long before I found out.

Chapter Twenty-five

Dear Jack,

You were in court on the day I got sentenced, weren't you? You saw the judge, with that ridiculous wig on his head, going on and on about what an evil person I was.

I was thinking, 'Okay, I get it, you're not happy with me, and obviously you think you could have done better, but Mr Chief Justice Whatever-Your-Name-Is, how exactly did you expect me to take care of nineteen children, if I wasn't supposed to keep them in their beds all day? Some of them had nothing but a brain stem in their head! Was I supposed to make a small train to pull them all along? Was I supposed to stay up all night, every night, turning this one, and then that one, and then this one, and then that one, putting this one back in its bed, chasing that one down the hall?'

I could see how marvellous everybody else thought the verdict was. The *Herald* was saying, 'Oh, Snow showed no remorse as she was led from the court to the van that would take her back to

Silverwater.' What was I supposed to do? Stand up and say, 'Sorry, everyone!' I don't believe I've got anything to be sorry about.

So, here I am at Silverwater, planning my appeal like everyone else. You probably know I've got a new lawyer? He seems to think I'm in with a good chance, so maybe I'll be out before you even get this letter!

People are probably thinking, 'I wonder what she'll do when she gets out.' I can tell you, Jack. My plan for when I get out of here is to go straight back to Delaney House.

I won't be taking any sick kids in. They can be somebody else's problem. I'm just going to kick back there and relax.

You're probably thinking, but how can she do that? How can she go back to Delaney House? Simple: because it's my house!

Mrs Bannerman is dead, remember, and who is the beneficiary of her will? Me!

Maybe you're thinking, 'But how can they let Snow take the house, when Mrs Bannerman was found under it?' But answer me this: who's going to stop me? It's not like I'm charged with anything to do with Mrs Bannerman going missing, and if they had something on me, they would have charged me by now.

Same goes for Agnes, by the way. Don't think they wouldn't charge me if they had something on me. Big problem for them, then, that they don't.

Snow

Chapter Twenty-six

It isn't always easy as a journo to get people to talk to you, and I'll admit that I've been pretty lucky this past year, in that most of the people I've wanted to interview about Snow have been willing to sit down with me.

Beth Bannerman's niece, Rebecca Bannerman, was no exception. I called her one Sunday afternoon about six months ago, and explained where I was at: Snow had been writing to me from prison, and I'd been writing back. Snow was trying to convince me that she had nothing to do with her sister going missing.

Rebecca said she'd be more than happy to help in any way she could, and when I pulled into the street opposite her house she was already standing at the door. She's forty-eight, a mother of three, and slim as a twig. She had black leggings on; flat, black shoes that were more like slippers, and a black polo-neck jumper. And there was a black labradoodle with curls all over its forehead standing beside her at the front door. Her fingers were working the curls on his forehead. She didn't look nervous about a reporter coming to visit. She looked as keen as I was to get something done.

'I suppose you already know this, but my Aunt Beth was always a little strange,' she said, pretty much as soon as we'd settled down into the chairs on her back porch. 'I wouldn't have met her more than once or twice, because she was at war with my father, her brother, over something.'

I asked Rebecca if she knew what the feud was about. She said, 'No, but it was long-standing, and it was all on Beth's side. I always thought it was a shame because Dad would basically say, she doesn't want a bar of me, and I can't figure out why. I quizzed him a few times, and that was the only answer I got, although of course I'd also heard around the traps that Aunt Beth was an "eccentric", which I took to mean she was a bit mad.'

Rebecca's home is on Sydney's north shore and she doesn't often visit Bondi, so years went by without her seeing her aunt's house.

'Some time in the 1970s, Dad became aware that a young man – it was Mark Delaney, although we didn't know his name at the time – had been living with Beth for some years, and that was a bit of a concern.

'Dad made some enquiries with people he knew from when he and Beth were still on speaking terms, people who lived around her in Bondi. They said, "There doesn't appear to be anything to it. There's a bloke there, but he's mostly helping her around the property."

'I think on some level, at least at the beginning, Dad was pretty pleased about it – the idea of having a bloke on the property, I mean. But over time I suppose we grew suspicious. We heard on the grapevine that Aunt Beth was telling neighbours that Mark was her boyfriend. We heard that he was "massaging her legs" – whatever that meant – and helping her into the bath.

'My father said, "Don't tell me he's giving her one?" I thought to myself, "More likely if she's demented she probably doesn't know what she's saying." I'm not sure that we ever heard that a young woman had also moved in, but in any case, at some point Dad heard that the house had been fixed up a bit, at least around the front, and that the trees were being clipped into these strange animal shapes, and that was a little odd. So, at Dad's request, I did agree to go with my husband one afternoon while we were in Bondi to have a bit of a look around.'

I asked Rebecca when this was, and she said, 'It was September 2001, and I remember that because I guess it was a time when we were all on a bit of high alert, because of what had happened in New York.'

Rebecca doesn't deny that she was also interested in seeing her aunt's house. 'Because Beth was widowed, and she had no children, Dad often told me, "I don't expect to get a cent, but with some luck she'll leave that house to you, Bec." And then, after we heard that a man had moved in, we were a bit concerned. What if he tried to run off with the house?

'So yes, I was looking after my inheritance. But Beth was my aunt, and she was getting on. I was keen to know if there was any possibility of her patching things up with Dad, of perhaps getting to know her a little better, maybe taking the kids around to meet her.'

Rebecca drove out with her husband. 'There was a security buzzer on the fence but it appeared to be out of action, so I pushed the gate and walked down to the front porch, past those manicured trees that everyone talks about and I knocked on the door.

'A man answered. He was short, with a sandy goatee. It could only have been Mark Delaney.

'I said, "Hello," and he said, "Hello." I said, "My name is Rebecca Bannerman. I'm looking for my Aunt Beth." And that seemed to leave him absolutely stunned. He said, "Who did you say you were?" I explained that I was Beth's niece, and although I hadn't seen her since I was a little girl, I was in the area and thought I might pop in.

'The man told me he had "no idea" where Beth was.

'I said, "Well, do you know when she's coming back?"

'The man said, "No, I don't."

'It seemed to me that he was being deliberately vague, perhaps even cagey. I had a feeling – call it women's instinct – that there was something not right. I thought, 'Maybe she's gone into a nursing home and he doesn't want to tell us,' because if she had gone into a home he'd have no right to stay in her house.

'I said, "Well, perhaps I could come back tomorrow?" He said, "Beth won't be here tomorrow either," which seemed a very strange response. And then, coming from somewhere in the house behind him, there was a noise, like somebody shifting pots and pans around in the kitchen.

'There was this long silence between us – between me and this Mark person, I mean – but then he said, "That's not Aunt Beth." I remember he said it like that, "That's not Aunt Beth," like he meant *his* Aunt Beth not *your* Aunt Beth. He said, "That's my missus."

'A woman came down the hall – she was only there for an instant, but long enough for me to see that she had been the one making the noise, because she was holding a saucepan with a pink lid – and it was Snow Delaney.'

I sat there like a stunned mullet. I said, 'Are you sure about that?'

Rebecca said, 'I'm absolutely sure. I didn't know it back then, of course – I wouldn't have known Snow Delaney from Adam – but of course I know who she is now, and it was Snow Delaney.'

Again, I said, 'You're absolutely, one hundred per cent sure?'

She said, 'I'm one hundred per cent sure. She came down the hall, and she was holding an old aluminum pot, like one of those pots with a pink-coloured lid, a cheapish lid, and it was definitely her.'

Obviously that doesn't tally with what Snow told me, which was that she was in Melbourne with her mum when

Beth's niece dropped by – and that Beth was already gone by the time she got back.

I asked Rebecca, 'Do you know if your Aunt Beth was still there?'

Rebecca said, 'I can't say for certain. I can only say I didn't see her there.'

I said, 'She had a bungalow out by the passionfruit vine where she lived, but that was out the back.'

Rebecca said, 'Right. And I didn't get further than the front door. But Snow was definitely there.'

I asked Rebecca if she'd swear to that in a court of law and she said of course she would, and she told me about going back to the car where her husband was waiting and calling her dad from the car. I said to him, "Well, no luck. I knocked on the door, and that man you spoke about, Mark, he was there, but there was no sign of Aunt Beth."

'Dad said, "Well, did you ask where she was?" I said yes, and Mark had fobbed me off, and that was that. And then, the first we heard about my aunt being missing, let alone missing for *seven years*, was when we received a telephone call from the State Coroner saying that Snow Delaney had applied to have her declared dead.

'This was in 2008, I think. My first reaction, when Dad told me, was "What happened to her?" He said he had no idea, all he knew was that Snow was claiming that she had been missing for seven years – she had not been seen at all in that time – and Snow wanted her declared dead because she had a will that left everything to her and Mark.'

I asked Rebecca if the Coroner had said when it was, exactly, that Beth was supposed to have gone missing.

She said, 'Yes, it was shortly after I visited. Mark had given a statement to the Coroner, in which he said that he'd told her I'd dropped by and she'd expressed an interest in seeing me, and a day or so later she'd put on a hat and gone out the door, saying she'd catch the bus up to my place.

'Which is a total nonsense. She would have had no idea where I lived. I hadn't seen her since I was a child. She wouldn't have known how to find me, other than to call Dad, and she didn't call Dad.

'Besides which, everyone who saw Beth at any time in the past fifteen years was convinced that she had dementia. She never spoke any sense, not for years. And yet that very same weekend, she was supposed to have signed a new will, giving everything to Mark and Snow.'

'I take it they wouldn't inherit, unless your aunt was dead?' I asked.

'Right. Which was why we were in a difficult spot. If the Coroner said that Beth was dead, Snow and Mark would inherit the house,' Rebecca said, 'unless we could prove that they'd done something to make her disappear, which to me was fairly obvious.'

The Bannermans were in the process of petitioning the Coroner for an inquest when Mrs Bannerman's remains turned up, as part of the search for Agnes Moore.

'That must have been horrible,' I said.

'Oh, appalling. But to me it was pretty clear what happened,' Rebecca said. 'The Delaneys got the shock of their lives when I knocked on the door. Maybe they hadn't known there was any family, or else they'd assumed that whatever family my aunt had were gone from her life.

'It was just one day later that they had that will drawn up. I know that, because I've seen the date on it. I'm supposed to believe that's a coincidence? It's no coincidence. I strongly believe that Snow and Mark Delaney had something to do with Aunt Beth's disappearance, and nothing will ever convince me otherwise.

'The idea that Aunt Beth fell into the pit and Mark Delaney built a deck over her quite by chance at the time she disappeared, it's fanciful. It's ridiculous! I'm sorry that Mark Delaney killed himself. Sorry because I wanted to see him face a trial. If there is any justice in the world, Snow Delaney will stand trial for my aunt's murder.'

I left Rebecca's house and got straight on the phone to my contact at Rose Bay. I told him what Rebecca had told me — that Snow wasn't in Melbourne when Beth disappeared; she was at Delaney House — but I've got to say, the reception I got was pretty underwhelming.

I said, 'Maybe your team could go and interview Snow again?'

He said, 'Interview her, how? She's got this new counsel who is like your worst nightmare as far as lawyers go. He basically tells her, you don't have to say anything, so she doesn't.'

I said, 'But you should be able to prove that she didn't catch a flight to Melbourne that weekend before the will was signed?'

He said, 'Sure. But she did fly to Melbourne some time in September 2001, and we know that because we know when her Mum died. So all she's going to say is she got her dates wrong.'

I said, 'But she was at Delaney House when Beth Bannerman's niece turned up, even though she said she wasn't!'

He said, 'Which proves what, Tap?'

I put down the phone, feeling pretty frustrated. I can't say what was driving me but I felt like I needed to take a walk, and next thing I know I was standing outside Delaney House.

Not much has changed since the raid. It's sitting where it's sat for a hundred years, high on the cliff, with the weathervane all rusted on the roof.

The Paterson's curse that covered the old fence when Snow first moved in has pretty much taken over the front yard. The trees that Mark Delaney cut into animal shapes have all grown out, and look a bit shaggy.

The cobwebs the size of bed sheets are still there, with big, fat spiders, and there's a cast-iron bath with fancy legs in the front yard.

The security on the front gate hadn't been fixed since the raid so I pushed through and went and knocked on the front door, and I've got to admit I was surprised when somebody answered. There's two young backpackers living there – one

Irish guy, who's a carpenter, and one Brazilian girl, who is learning English and doing some part-time work as a barista. She answered the door, all coffee-coloured from her holidays, barefoot, and wearing those loose Bali pants.

She told me she and her boyfriend – the Irish guy – had working visas but they were basically squatting in the house.

'For us, it is good,' she said. 'Some people would say, no, it looks to be falling down. But for a traveller it is good. We can have some parties.'

I asked if she knew who owned the house or what had gone on there. When she said no I told her a bit about Delaney House, and about Beth Bannerman being found under the deck, and she shuddered and said, 'That's not nice! In my country we have a belief in ghosts.'

I probably shouldn't have done it, but I told her that another lady – the owner's sister – had also gone missing and hadn't been found.

She said, 'Oh no! Maybe the police will come and look for her?'

I told her I didn't think so. Cops practically lifted Delaney House off its foundations after they found Beth Bannerman's body, and they moved thirty-two trailers worth of soil.

Mrs Moore isn't there.

It seems to me that the investigation has basically stalled. That's as frustrating for me as it is for anyone. I'd love to be able to wrap it all up in a bow for you, and say, yes, they found her! And Ruby's got some peace of mind. But this is real life, not a TV crime drama, and some disappearances just go unsolved, and all the gut feeling in the world won't make the police charge Snow Delaney with the murder of either of the women who went missing from that house.

At most, what they have is circumstantial evidence.

They've got the fact that Beth Bannerman's body was found at Delaney House, but that doesn't tell anyone anything about how she ended up dead.

They've got the email Mrs Moore wrote to Ruby after the lunch, where she mentioned wanting to do something 'for the children'.

To my mind, that should qualify as evidence that Mrs Moore *had* changed her mind about not making a claim on her father's estate, particularly when you add the fact that Snow told me in one of her letters that 'Agnes Bloody Moore' had some kind of problem with what she saw at Delaney House.

There's also the fact that Mrs Moore tried to call 999 from her room at the Sir Stanford the night before she went missing. Obviously she was trying to reach police. She wasn't in a panic. She didn't call immediately upon returning to the hotel. She dialled only once so maybe, like Lenore Wallace, she couldn't quite put her finger on what it was about Delaney House that bugged her.

Then there's the call she received, just before she went out. Who knew she was at the hotel, if not Snow Delaney?

I've pretty much given up arguing about the case with my mate from Rose Bay, but I remember one particular night, we pulled up bar stools at the Bondi Hotel, and he basically said, 'I'd love to be able to place a call to Mrs Moore's family in London, saying, "We've charged Snow Delaney with murder." But it's not going to happen. We've got no body. We've got no forensics. We've got no nothing.'

I said, 'You've got Snow's letter to me, saying that "Agnes Bloody Moore" did have a problem with how she was treating those kids.'

He said, 'Which proves what? That Snow killed her? Show me the body, Tap.'

I said, 'You've got a body – under the deck.'

He said, 'But that's the wrong body, Tap! That's the wrong body.'

I told him I was going to write to the Police Minister, telling him what I'd been able to extract from Snow since she'd started writing to me. He warned me against it, and I wish I'd listened to him because next thing I know I'm sending my regular letters to Snow, and they're coming back 'Return to Sender'. It made no sense, so I called the prison, and a bloke there who declined to give his name told me that I wasn't on Snow's list of 'approved contacts' any more.

I asked why not, and he wouldn't say, so I made a few more calls, such as to a senior staffer in the office of the Minister for Corrective Services, who told me in an off-the-record way that since it's against the law for journos to be in contact with prisoners in the first place, I should let the matter drop.

'They're ropeable that all these letters have changed hands,' he told me. 'Whoever is supposed to be in charge of screening those things at Silverwater really dropped the ball.'

I said, 'What about the fact that Snow's been dropping clues here and there – that she wasn't where she says she was when Beth Bannerman disappeared, for example?'

He said, 'Leave it to the cops, Tap.'

So, okay, I'll leave it to the cops. What choice have I really got? Snow's stopped writing to me, and I've been warned off writing to her. Whatever window I managed to open, to get her to talk, has obviously been slammed shut.

That said, there isn't a law that can stop me from making public the letters I've already received from Snow. They're my property, after all.

So that's what I'm doing here – putting Snow's letters out there, along with my own thoughts and Ruby's.

Call it an exercise in shaking the tree to see what falls out.

Ruby has signed off on the project. Ask anyone who's lost their mum: the pain doesn't go away, and when they're missing and you don't know why, it's unbearable.

She told me recently, 'I pick up the phone sometimes because I want to call Mum to say, "Rocco got an A on something" or "Stella's got boyfriend trouble," and then I remember that I can't do it. The iPhone flashes, and it's never Mum.'

After reading what I've put together here, including all of Snow's letters, Ruby wrote back to me, saying, 'Well, it's a sad state of affairs, isn't it? She has no intention of telling us what happened, does she? She intends to deny what she's done for the rest of her life.'

As hard as it is for Ruby to say so, she's not in denial about the fact that her mum is probably dead. She told me in an email recently, 'Rocco is always saying, "We don't know for sure, Mum. You hear of people turning up after years and years! Granny could turn up at any time!" But there came a point – I can't say when it was exactly – when I had to accept that my mother was gone and that she would not be coming back.'

Like me, Ruby believes that Snow got rid of Beth Bannerman so she could inherit the big house at Bondi; and she got rid of her sister for the same reason: money.

Both of us would like to see that theory put before a jury, but since Snow isn't even charged in relation to either crime, I guess that's not going to happen.

In the meantime, what Ruby wants is to be able to bury her mum with dignity.

'I want Mum to be somewhere where I can visit her,' she told me just last week.

She also told me a story that I'll tell you, because to my mind it sums up how much Agnes loved the life she built for herself, after having such a rough start.

The story is basically about a time when one of Ruby's pets died and Agnes had to sit her up on her knee and explain the concept of death to her.

No parent likes having that chat.

She said, everything dies and everyone dies, and death is forever. That is a very hard lesson for children to learn. And Ruby said, 'I was only about seven or eight, and I've never forgotten the way my mother eased the blow for me. I remember saying, "Will I die, Mum?" And she said, "Well, not for a long time."

'I said, "And will you die, Mum?" Because that was just too much to cope with.'

'Mum said, "Oh, yes, but not for a very long time." And then she said, and I've never forgotten, "But do you know what, Ruby? When it happens, I don't want you to worry, because I have had such a happy life. I've been so lucky." And over the years, she honed that message. She'd say, "I was *so lucky* to survive that blast in the London hospital where I was born. I was *so lucky* to be allowed to sail to Australia, *so lucky* to meet your dad, so lucky to have two such beautiful children, and five such gorgeous grandchildren.

'"So I don't ever want any of you to worry about me. When I go, you just bury my ashes under some lovely old tree and don't cry, because remember I was so lucky to have the life I had."

'And that's what I want,' Ruby said, 'To be able to bury Mum under a lovely old tree. She deserves that, not to be dumped, or discarded, or whatever has happened to her.'

I asked Ruby if there was anything she wanted to say directly to Snow.

She said, 'Yes, Jack, there is,' and since I'm not allowed to write to Snow any more, I suppose I've got to publish Ruby's letter to her aunt right here:

SISTERS OF MERCY

Dear Snow,
I am writing to you to say that I'm so sorry for what has happened to you in your life.

It must have been very difficult, watching your parents separate, and having your home broken up when you were still a little girl.

Jack Fawcett has been kind enough to share many of the letters you've written to him, and I know how diligently you trained as a nurse, and how dismayed you were when all your efforts to improve the lives of people at Caloola came to nothing.

I know that you feel that you did good works with the children at Delaney House, and that you do not deserve to be in prison.

I'm asking you, as your niece, to consider the prison that we are in.

I know that you didn't know my mum – your sister – all that well, but I hope that you can understand that while she wasn't important to you, she was everything to us.

I know that you've told Jack Fawcett that you don't have a clue as to where she might be, but I know in my heart that my mother would never, ever willingly leave us, and so I guess I've had to face the fact that something must have happened to her, and that nothing can now change that.

And that is why I'm writing to you, Snow.

I believe that all of us are born with a conscience, and I'm asking you, please, Snow, ease your conscience by telling us what you know.

CAROLINE OVERINGTON

Tell us where our mother is, Snow.
Tell us so that we might bury her.
We will never stop asking you.

Reading Group Questions

1. *Sisters of Mercy* starts with Jack saying he was surprised to get a letter from Snow Delaney in Silverwater Prison. What does she hope to achieve in writing to a journalist?

2. What was Jack trying to achieve in writing back to Snow?

3. Would you, as a reader, like to have seen more of Jack's letters to Snow? Why do you think the author – who is herself a journalist – chose to leave them out?

4. Jack kept all of Snow's letters and published them in a book without her consent. Is that a fair thing for him to have done? Should he have sought Snow's permission to publish the letters or is she fair game?

5. Jack seems to be of the view that the police investigation into Agnes Moore's disappearance was slow and perhaps even flawed from the start. Do you agree?

6. Agnes was left in an orphanage during the war. Do you think her mother thought she would be safer there or is Snow right when she says that her mother never wanted any children?

7. Snow goes into her first real job at Caloola full of hope as to what she might be able to achieve. As a reader do you have any experience of social programs like 'normalisation?' What do you think of the decision to close all the old institutions? Is there enough support for parents of disabled children today?

8. In *Sisters of Mercy* no checks were done on Delaney House for many years, and Snow was able to do what she wanted to the children in her care essentially. Can you easily believe that such a thing is possible?

9. Jack seems to think there is enough evidence to charge Snow in relation to the disappearance of her sister. Do you agree? What would the charge be? How well does the evidence against her stack up?

10. Imagine that you were a juror at Snow's trial. Would you be satisfied beyond reasonable doubt that Snow is guilty of murder?

Ghost Child

The past is always close behind

CAROLINE OVERINGTON

FIVE-STAR RATING
★★★★★
a stellar read
money-back guarantee*
*go to www.randomhouse.com.au/stellarread
RANDOM HOUSE AUSTRALIA

Also by the Author

GHOST CHILD

In 1982 Victorian police were called to a home on a housing estate an hour west of Melbourne. There, they found a five-year-old boy lying still and silent on the carpet. There were no obvious signs of trauma, but the child, Jacob, died the next day. The story made the headlines and hundreds attended the funeral. Few people were surprised when the boy's mother and her boyfriend went to prison for the crime. Police declared themselves satisfied with the result, saying there was no doubt that justice had been done. And yet, for years rumours swept the estate, clinging like cobwebs to the long-vacant house: there had been a cover-up. The real perpetrator, at least according to local gossip, was the boy's six-year-old sister, Lauren . . .

Twenty years on, Lauren has created a new life for herself, but details of Jacob's death begin to resurface and the story again makes the newspapers. As Lauren struggles with the ghosts of her childhood, it seems only a matter of time before the past catches up with her.

Read on for an extract . . .

Prologue

On 11 November 1982, Victorian police were called to a home on the Barrett housing estate, an hour west of Melbourne. In the lounge room of an otherwise ordinary brick-veneer home, they found a five-year-old boy lying still and silent on the carpet. His arms were by his sides, his palms flat.

There were no obvious signs of trauma. The boy was neither bruised nor bleeding, but when paramedics turned him gently onto his side they found an almost imperceptible indentation in his skull, as broad as a man's hand and as shallow as a soap dish.

The boy's mother told police her son had been walking through the schoolyard with one of his younger brothers when they were approached by a man who wanted the change in their pockets. The brothers refused to hand over the money so the man knocked the older boy to the ground and began to kick and punch him.

The younger boy ran home to raise the alarm. Their mother carried the injured boy home in her arms. She called an ambulance, but nothing could be done.

The story made the front page of *The Sun* newspaper in Melbourne and the TV news.

Police made a public appeal for witnesses but, in truth, nobody really believed the mother's version of events. The Barrett Estate was poor but no one was bashing children for loose change – not then. Ultimately, the mother and her boyfriend were called in for questioning. Police believed that one of them – possibly both – was involved in the boy's death.

There was a great deal of interest in the case, but when it finally came to court, the Chief Justice closed the hearing. The verdict would be released; so, too, would any sentence that was handed down. But the events leading up to the little boy's death would remain a mystery.

Few people were surprised to hear that the boy's mother and her boyfriend went to prison for the crime. Police declared themselves satisfied with the result, saying there was no doubt justice had been done. And yet for years rumours swept the Barrett Estate, passing from neighbour to neighbour and clinging like cobwebs to the long-vacant house: there had been a cover-up. The real perpetrator, at least according to local gossip, was the boy's six-year-old sister, Lauren.

Lauren Cameron

When a young woman lives by herself, it's assumed she must be lonely. I'd say the opposite is true. In fact, if anybody had asked me what it was like when I first started living on my own, I would have said, 'It was perfect.' I was completely alone – I had no close friends, and nobody I called family – and that was precisely what I wanted.

The place I moved into was basically a shed, and it was built on a battle-axe block behind somebody else's house. The property itself was on Sydney's northern beaches. There was a family living in the main house, the one that fronted the beach. They owned the block and, like many Sydneysiders who had beachside property in the 1980s, they decided to make the most of it by carving a driveway down the side, building a granny flat

GHOST CHILD

After the first meeting, when they gave me the keys and we talked about the rent, I had nothing whatsoever to do with them. They were a family – a mum, a dad and two teenage kids – living in the main house, and I was the boarder. I could get to my place without bothering them. I just walked down the driveway, opened my door and I was home. I had my own toilet, shower and enough of a kitchen, so there was no reason to go knocking.

Before I moved in, I bought four things. The most expensive was a queen-size sheet set in a leopard-skin print, with two pillowcases. I bought a box of black crockery, with dinner plates shaped like hexagons. I had this idea, then, that I might one day have close friends who could come over for dinner. I also bought a new steam iron and ironing-board, these last things because it was a condition of my employment that my uniform be straight and clean.

I still remember the first morning I woke in my own place. I was seventeen years old. I padded into the kitchen in my moccasins, put the kettle on the stove top, and pressed the red button to make the flame ignite. I took the plastic cover off the new ironing-board and scrunched it into a ball. I was fiddling underneath the board, trying to find the lever that makes the legs stick out, when the kettle began to whistle itself into hysterics. I put the ironing-board down and took a cup from the crockery set, removing some of the cardboard that had been packed around it, and made a cup of tea – hot and sugary, with the bag taken out, not left in – and I thought to myself, 'This is just like playing house! I'm okay here. Things are going to be fine.'

When the family told the neighbours they'd rented out the granny flat, they probably wanted to know whether I was going to cause trouble – whether I was going to bring boys home and make a racket. But the answer was no, I was not. I amused myself in the granny flat by learning new and humble domestic tasks: sweeping the floor with a straw broom; bending to collect the mess in a dustpan and brush; buying garbage bags with two handles that tied at the top. My idea of a good night was to eat Tim Tams in bed and to smoke cigarettes on the porch, although only after I saw the lights in the main house go out.

The owners would have said, 'Oh, she's the perfect tenant, like a mouse, so quiet, you never even know she's there.'

From time to time, I'd bump into the mum – not my mum, but the mum who lived in the main house. I'd be heading out to work and she'd be on the nature strip, getting shopping bags out of the boot of her car or something, and she'd smile at me – probably because everybody approves of hospital staff – and I'd smile back at her.

I didn't see much of the dad. Perhaps he'd decided that there was nothing to be gained from getting too close to the girl who lived in his shed. I had nothing much to do with the children, either. I was closer in age to them than to their parents, but really, what did we have in common? They came out from time to time, to jump on the trampoline and to sit under the pirate flag in the old tree house, but we rarely spoke.

I'd taken a job as a nurse's aide in a city hospital, and I'm sure my co-workers at first understood why I lived alone. I was new to Sydney so it made sense, at least in the beginning, that I wouldn't have many friends. After I'd settled, though, they must have wondered why I continued to live in a granny flat when I could easily have shared a city apartment with one of the other aides. The noticeboard at work often had handwritten signs tacked up, advertising rooms for rent. 'Outgoing girl wanted to share FUN FLAT!' one of the ads said. The truth is, the things the other girls wanted to do – going to nightclubs, drinking Fluffy Ducks and Orgasms and Harvey Wallbangers – didn't sound like fun to me.

Of course, I wasn't famous then, far from it. I was just the quiet girl, the churchy girl that lived alone, prayed in the hospital chapel, and never socialised. I'm sure they all got a shock when photographs of me started appearing in newspapers, just as I'm sure the family I boarded with got a shock when journalists swarmed the granny flat, waving microphones on sticks.

I got a bit of a shock myself. I took refuge in my bed, hiding under the leopard-skin sheets, trying to fight the urge to *run*. Because, really, run where? There was nowhere to go.

I don't know how long I would have stayed under the covers if Harley hadn't turned up. He walked down the side drive, past the windows of the main house. I heard the mum rap on the glass. 'Hey, you,' she said. 'Off our property!'

Harley said, 'I'm not with the media. I'm Harley Cashman. Lauren's my sister.'

She would have been startled. For one thing, the mum knew me not as Lauren Cashman but as Lauren *Cameron,* which was the name I'd given her when I moved in. She didn't know I had a brother, either. I'd told them what I used to tell everyone: 'I have no family.'

Harley knocked at my door and when I didn't answer, I heard him push it open. I didn't stir but I could feel warm sunshine pour across my bed.

Harley said, 'Mate, what *are* you doing? Everyone's looking for you.'

I didn't respond so he pulled back the doona and said, 'Lauren, seriously, this is ridiculous. Get up.'

I felt so frightened and overwhelmed that I wasn't sure that I could. I said to Harley, 'I can't.'

He said, 'Sure you can.'

We went on like that for a while, him saying, 'Come on, Lauren,' and me saying, 'Just go away, Harley,' until he said, 'Okay, look, I'm not going to hang around here forever. If you want me gone, I'm gone.'

It was then that I realised I didn't want him to go, not without me, not ever again. I rose from the bed, untangling myself from the sheets, and said, 'Okay, all right.'

'That's right,' he said. 'Get up, and let's get you out of here.'

I was wearing only a T-shirt and a pair of knickers.

'You're going to need to get dressed,' he said, and started picking up some clothes I'd flung onto the floor. Compared with him – with anyone – I was tiny. He held up a pair of my pants and said, 'How do you even get one leg in here?'

I snatched them away and went into the bathroom to dress myself.

'Good on you,' he said when I emerged. 'Now, let's go.'

He ushered me to the door and we left the granny flat together, me with a jumper over my head in case there was a photographer still lurking, trying to get a picture. He'd parked his car on the nature strip. I couldn't see anything because the jumper was over my face so he guided me into the passenger seat. It was only once we'd started moving, once I was sure we were clear of the suburban streets and onto a freeway, that I took the jumper off, and said, 'Where are we going?'

Harley said, 'I've decided that you should meet the folks.'

I said, '*Whose* folks?'

He said, 'Mum is gonna love you.'

I thought, '*Your* mum. Not mine.'

I rolled the jumper into a ball and put it on the floor near my feet. I said, 'She doesn't even *know* me, Harley.'

He said, 'Mate, you're my *sister*. What more is there to know?'

I didn't answer. What more was there to know? What do any of us know? We think we know the basic facts about our lives: those are my parents and these are my siblings and this is my story, at least as I've come to tell it. But, really, how much of it is true?

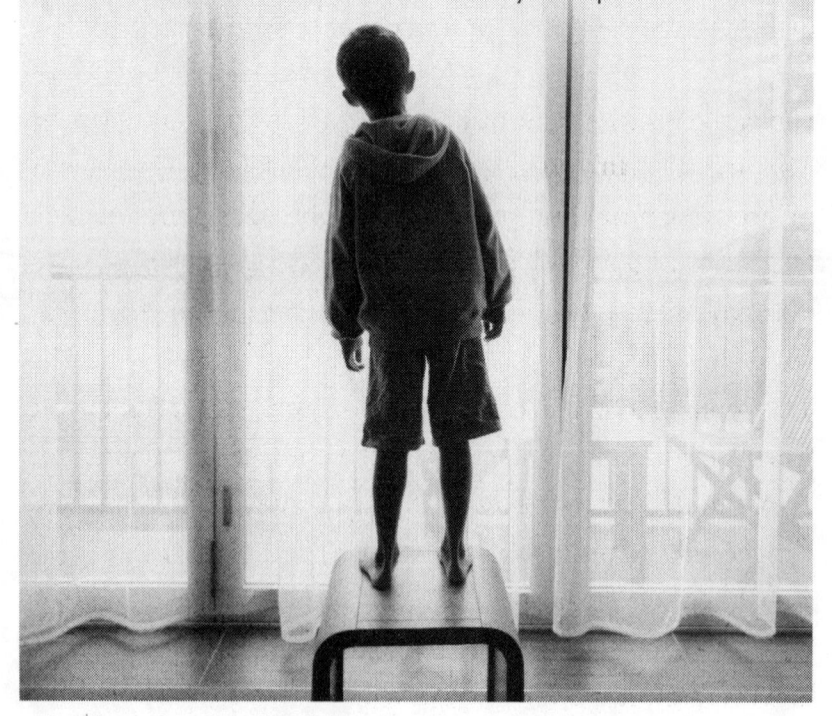

'Amazing' **Mia Freedman**

CAROLINE OVERINGTON

I Came to Say Goodbye

Who is left behind when a family falls apart?

I CAME TO SAY GOODBYE

It was four o'clock in the morning. A young woman pushed through the front doors. Staff would later say they thought the woman was a new mother, returning to her child – and in a way, she was.

She walked into the nursery, where a baby girl lay sleeping. The infant didn't wake when the woman placed her gently in the shopping bag she had brought with her. There is CCTV footage of what happened next, and most Australians would have seen it, either on the internet or the news.

The woman walked out to the car park, towards an old Corolla. For a moment, she held the child gently against her breast and, with her eyes closed, she smelled her. She then clipped the infant into the car, got in and drove off.

That is where the footage ends. It isn't where the story ends, however. It's not even where the story starts.

In the struggle between
warring parents, who will
protect the child?

Matilda is Missing
CAROLINE OVERINGTON

'A gripping and emotional tale of love and marriage'
Australian Women's Weekly

MATILDA IS MISSING

Softie was sophisticated, a career woman, who owned a nice apartment overlooking St Kilda Beach. Garry had a few rough edges, plus one failed marriage and an assortment of jobs under his belt.

But Softie's body clock was ticking, and Garry wanted children . . .

So they got married, and produced the only thing they ever had in common. Matilda.

Now, two years later, their golden-haired child is at the centre of a bitter custody battle. Both parents insist that her well-being is the only thing they care about.

Yet, in truth, Matilda was always the one most likely to become lost.

You've finished the book but there's much more waiting for you at

www.randomhouse.com.au

- ▶ Author interviews
- ▶ Videos
- ▶ Competitions
- ▶ Free chapters
- ▶ Games

- ▶ Newsletters with exclusive previews, breaking news and inside author information.
- ▶ Reading group notes and tips.
- ▶ VIP event updates and much more.

ENHANCE YOUR READING EXPERIENCE

www.randomhouse.com.au